Taramae
Return of the Ghost Girl

WHEN COURAGE MUST OVERCOME DEATH

HALENE PETERSEN DAHLSTROM

AN AUTHOR OF HOPE, HEALING, AND MYSTERY

PUBLICATION
CONSULTANTS

We Believe In The Power Of Authors

8370 Eleusis Drive, Anchorage, Alaska 99502-4630
books@publicationconsultants.com—www.publicationconsultants.com

ISBN Number: 978-1-63747-144-9
eBook ISBN Number: 978-1-63747-145-6

Library of Congress Number: 2025919851

Manufactured in the United States of America

DEDICATION

It felt so real, this vivid dream from 2014. I walked through the village, knew where everyone lived, and the parts they would play. Yet writing such a story seemed an impossible task—too big an undertaking by my usual standards. Doubts of others fed into mine. A family crisis and several health problems caused a ten-year delay. Still, the village called.

Finally, hope and arduous work triumphed with the help of Heaven, as well as family and friends who believed and encouraged along the way, especially editor Marthy Johnson, and Evan Swensen.

Thank you all *very* much. Happy reading!

CONTENTS

Chapter 1: The Watcher

A shrill whistle pierced the peace of the village each morning. It meant that the gatekeeper was preparing to open the gates for the day, and it was time for Smote to get up. He was the Watcher in the Tower from the time the Crim fortress opened at first light until it was closed at dusk.

Smote grumbled as he carefully rolled upright, reached for a roughly woven tunic, and groaning, pulled it on over his ever-aching head. His leather breeches had been worn to bed. It was easier than fighting to get them off every night when his back spasmed and his twisted left foot rarely cooperated. Each day of his existence began the same. Half-stumbling, he walked to the three-legged stool by the large, shuttered window.

He was supposed to alert of looming danger by blowing the long, twisted horn that leaned against the corner within arm's reach of the window. However, during the months he had been at his station, nothing threatening had ever happened and rarely anything exciting.

By now, Smote could tell the morning routine step by step. "Here comes the gatekeeper," he mumbled. "He looks over the gate from top to bottom. Why does he do that? How could its appearance have changed overnight? The gatekeeper checks to see if the latch is secure. Why? It is right where he left it. He pauses as if to gather strength and forcefully slides the latch. He flinches, then shakes his hand. It pinches him every time, so why does he keep doing it the same way? He whistles again to warn anyone on the other side and pushes the heavy gate open one side at a time, placing a hefty rock near the end of each to keep it in place throughout the day.

Then the gatekeeper rubs his back and goes home. Once again, nothing new there, Owl," he said aloud as if the small, hand-carved wooden bird in his tunic pocket could hear him.

Of course, Owl did not answer. It would have been markedly disturbing if it did. But it was a good listener. Where it came from, Smote had no idea and speculating about it caused more head pain. To remedy that, he simply quit wondering about it.

Being the Watcher was better than staying abed all day, marking the intensity of each pain that awakened in his decrepit body. It was the least he could do to repay the kindness of those who had taken him in, a broken stranger, and healed him as much as possible.

Crim was a tranquil hamlet. Occasionally there were angry outbursts outside the Groggery. However, nothing had ever warranted the blowing of the horn to alert the village, so it remained in the corner, gathering dust. Smote felt much the same way about himself.

Having the highest vantage point from the old sentry tower, Smote could see all activity within the village. Vertical wooden slats made airflow possible and allowed him to covertly watch without those below becoming concerned about who was observing them. The sight of him would likely cause others distress. Indeed, he himself found the scars and facial distortion shocking when he saw his reflection in the washbowl. He had come to a humorous acceptance of sorts, and one day simply looked at himself and proclaimed, "You have been smote!" From that point on it seemed as good a name as any.

Memory was foreign to him. He did not remember where his home was nor even his age. His body was battered, his face misshapen, but his hands, though they had been used for work, were not wrinkled as an elderly man's might be. An occasional fragment of recollection flashed across Smote's consciousness, but whenever he tried to grasp it, the head pain worsened.

Smote's mind, but whenever he tried to grasp it, the pain worsened. After sitting about an hour, his stomach grumbled loudly, and since no one had entered through the gate, Smote took time to look for something to eat. His room had the barest of amenities. There was a padded cot to sleep on, a table just big enough for a plate and cup on one side and a washbowl on the other. He had a three-legged stool, and a squat pot. Passing the table, Smote shook an ant off the crust of bread he had left from the day before. "Sorry, Owl. There is nothing to share. You may have the ant."

He glanced around the tiny space he called home. He knew the dimensions well—three paces wide by five paces long. Many days, with little to do, he had verified them, though dragging the left foot made for less than perfect measurements. Not surprisingly, each time the room was still three paces wide by five paces long. The walls were nine stone blocks high, and when the peaked roof above whistled in the wind, tiny dust particles or water droplets descended upon him.

As he sat back down, he noticed Wise Woman Kess coming out from the passageway on First Side on her way to take potions or healing broths to ailing people. Her dwelling was in a row behind the inn and Groggery, therefore not visible to Smote, but he was familiar with her comings and goings and looked forward to her afternoon visits.

An older, kind-hearted woman, Kess brought village news—of which there was little and gossip—of which there was plenty—to cheer his day. It was his only entertainment. Her ointments provided temporary relief to his still-healing wounds. When the Wise Woman entered a dwelling across the way, Smote's shoulders sagged. "Sorry, Owl," he consoled. "I know you were hoping that she would come early. She said something about a festival today. Perhaps the girl with the food has forgotten us."

Smote fidgeted on the stool. Hunger made sitting still difficult. He shuffled his feet and stretched his neck forward and backward, instead of the usual side to side. At least he could do that. The motion was different. The crackling pain was the same. Thus the hours of his watching dripped by. How he wished that something—anything— different would happen!

Chapter 2: The Something

A new sound suddenly caught Smote's attention. It grew louder and louder as an overloaded merchant wagon entered through the fortress gate. Squee-eek, plod, snap! Squee-eek, plod, snap! The wheels whined and lurched forward each time the feet of the two heavy oxen hit the ground. A grungy-looking man impatiently lashed the air with a long whip, cursing at the beasts. His character seemed to match that of the angry serpent engraved upon the wagon's side.

Smote became uneasy. Instead of a twinge of excitement, a foreboding feeling twisted his gut. "You are imagining things, Owl!" he scolded, but his watching intensified.

The profane merchant stopped at the dwelling of Leader Adris and went inside. All merchants met first with the village leader before proceeding to the storehouse or selling from carts near the Pavilion. This was not unusual. What *was* unusual was what Smote saw next.

A rustling began inside the merchant's wagon, a slow, deliberate wave of furs and other goods. Suddenly from underneath, a head appeared. Was it a boy or a girl? Smote could not tell until the slight shoulders emerged. It was a girl! She looked in all directions. When the shifting contents made a noise, she stopped, listened, and then continued until she was fully free.

Her clothes were rumpled and ill-fitting. Her hair, disheveled and oddly cut, looked nothing like the neatly-arranged braids of other women of Crim. She shakily climbed out of the wagon and moved quickly, yet awkwardly to the village well nearby. She pressed against the shadowed side of the cracked outer wall, seeming to catch her breath.

Smote's adrenaline rose. He almost reached for the horn. "Who *is* this, Owl? If she is a guest for the festival, why would she present herself like that? And why would she hide?"

Smote looked away for an instant as the grungy merchant returned to his wagon. The man immediately noticed that things were in disarray, eyed the area suspiciously, cursed again, and drove to the storehouse. When Smote turned again to the mysterious girl's hiding place—she was gone! Panic welled in his chest. "You should have sounded the horn!" he reproached himself, and a mental tug-of-war began. She did not appear to be dangerous. Still, it was his duty to keep everyone safe. But if he blew the horn and she was harmless or someone's guest, it would bring unnecessary worry. Smote grabbed the horn. He wanted to sound the alarm. He knew he should. But what if he was wrong? "If I ruin their day with a false alarm, the villagers may turn against me, Owl. What should I do? The people of Crim would not appreciate overzealousness. But what if ...?"

Smote shook his head, irritated at his own indecisiveness, and forced his mind to focus on finding the stranger. "Where is she, Owl? Where *is* she?" Smote peered in every direction. Heart pounding, he could only wait to see where the girl reappeared and hope his hesitation had not put the entire village in jeopardy. He could not leave to go searching. Since becoming the Watcher, he had never left the Tower, had been discouraged from doing so by Wise Woman Kess—for the sake of his health, she had explained. Being so dependent upon others made him feel even more helpless.

A boisterous argument at the Pavilion distracted him. It was the daughters of Storekeeper Brun fighting—again. Their father owned the storehouse and was a Tribunal judge. However, according to the Wise Woman, they were quite different. Nawhi was the responsible one. She brought his First Meal basket each day but she was not talkative. She left the food, exchanged the squat pot for an empty one, and retreated quickly. Her involvement with the festival meant his food would be further delayed. His stomach growled again.

It was said that Nawhi's younger sister, Zaela, though quite lovely, was as spoiled as month-old milk and her flirtatious ways had upset many. Her father gave extra storehouse provisions to those offended to avoid censure at Tribunal. However, Zaela's recent antics had required her to serve two months' penance by working for the innkeeper, Rauma.

The clamor of the young women arguing made Smote's head hurt worse than usual. But he soon had a bigger problem. More villagers began to gather. It would be easier for someone to hide in a crowd. Smote scrutinized the new arrivals. "Man carrying a vessel, no. Woman with three children, no. Old man with a cane, no."

The din of the two sisters mingled with noise from other villagers and colors of clothing began to blend. "No. No!" Smote groaned. He was failing when accuracy was needed most. "Calm ye. Calm ye," he said. But words could not calm his pounding heart. He opened the window slats as wide as possible and blinked his aching eyes. All at once, he spotted a dark patch weaving through the group, moving towards the Pavilion. "A hooded cape? Why would someone wear a hooded cape on a warm spring morning, Owl? It must be that girl!"

The shadowy figure weaved through the crowd. Caught up in celebration preparations, no one seemed bothered by the erratic movement. Suddenly, the caped figure rushed into the center of the Pavilion towards the squabbling sisters. A hand came forth from the cape, holding out an object. Was it a weapon? Smote could not tell, but Zaela screamed and Nawhi stood as though frozen, her mouth agape. Smote sounded the alarm, sick inside that he had been too late.

Chaos ensued! Zaela continued screaming. Smote saw the large Groggery guard jump forward. He knocked the object to the ground and pushed the intruder away from the sisters. The intruder stood with hands lowered in a sign of submission. Storekeeper Brun arrived next. He embraced Zaela. The villagers appeared uncertain whether to stay to see what was happening or flee for their lives. Leader Adris arrived. He picked up the fallen object, glanced at it briefly, and stuffed it into his pocket. The crowd hushed as he confronted the stranger. "Stand forth!" he demanded.

The hood of the cape was lowered. It *was* the girl! Gasps were heard throughout the gathering. Brun barely caught a swooning Nawhi before she hit the Pavilion floor. Zaela renewed her wailing. Leader Adris clutched his chest. As villagers scattered, rumors erupted, spreading in all directions.

"It is a ghost!"

"A ghost?"

"Yes, and Dark Menaces!"

"Dark Menaces are coming?"

"Yes, coming, coming. Run, hide!"

"There was a weapon. Leader Adris found a weapon!"

"She had a weapon?"

"Yes, I saw a weapon!"

"Did you see the weapon?"

"No, but I saw a ghost! Hurry, hurry. Run!"

"Hide your children! The Great Good is destroyed!"

Smote saw the innkeeper, Rauma, dodge fleeing citizens as she hurried to the Pavilion. When she reached the center, Rauma cried out, "Poor, dear child!" The girl in the cape held out her arms. Rauma pushed past her to console the shrieking Zaela instead. With that, the girl in the fur cape collapsed. She was roughly scooped up and carried away.

Stunned, Smote stumbled to his bed. He could barely breathe. The people of Crim had many superstitions. The one of Dark Menaces— forces of doom— that could descend upon a person, confounding them until the even worse Vast Vex could complete their ruination, had not made sense to him before. Now he understood. Tormented thoughts like thorny thistles spiraled through his mind. Would they punish him for not warning them? Would they deny him food or the medicine he needed? Would they cast him out of the village? If they did, where would he go? A guttural groan escaped his lips as his empty stomach twisted.

A spark of denial pushed through the mental debris. "The girl did *not* appear dangerous, Owl!" he protested. Weak and pain-ridden, he agonized for hours, wishing he could fall into oblivion.

Owl tumbled to the floor.

Chapter 3: The Wise Woman

Wise Woman Kess was *not* happy. A sudden pounding on her door had brought a limp human bundle that was hastily dumped onto her bed by Gart, the doorkeeper from the Groggery.

Kess demanded clarification.

"Adris said to bring her here," the young man grunted, and promptly departed.

Kess stomped her foot in disgust. "Mizzafrizzaritz!" she exclaimed.

Strangers or troublemakers were supposed to be taken to the holding center by the front gate. If they needed curative care or a nit check, she went there. She gladly assisted all as needed, but *she* went to *them*. She had been tenacious about doing regular nit checks on the villagers to ensure that there would never be another lice outbreak, and now a possible carrier was not only discarded into her dwelling but dumped onto her *own* bed. She was *very* unhappy!

The figure—a female by sound—moaned and moved slightly, exposing the side of the head. Kess went over to investigate. Her mouth fell open, incredulous. The smelly person was not only on *her* bed but wrapped in *her* fur cape. How did that happen? The culprit had obviously stolen it from her dwelling while she was out on visits, and then in a twist of fate, had been returned wrapped in it. Kess stomped her foot again, "Mizzafrizzaritz!"

Determined to solve the mystery, she stepped forward and with a stirring stick began to check the girl's hair. The unkempt girl opened her eyes and upon seeing Kess began to cry. The tears were there. The shaking was there. But there was no sound. Kess gasped and stepped back in horror as a grimy, delicate hand came from inside the cape and reached out to her. The nails were filthy, the dirt-streaked arm was partially covered by a tattered sleeve.

Confusion flooded over the Wise Woman. Stunned, she said, "Taramae?"

This girl had been declared dead months ago. How could it be that she had returned not only very much alive but in such terrible condition? Kess clasped the hand of her young friend, and asked, as she sat on the bed. "Oh, child, dear child! Where have you been?"

The girl attempted to speak. When no sound came out, again she curled up into a ball and continued to weep silently.

She flinched when Kess touched her shoulder and kindly asked, "Look at me, child. What has happened?"

Taramae moved the cape lower to display her throat. A rough, deep scar encircled the lower part of her throat. It was badly in need of healing salve.

Kess shuddered. "Who has done this?"

Using hand gestures, the girl tried to explain but soon gave up in frustration.

"Calm ye, calm ye. We will worry about answers later. You are safe now. You are home. Let me fetch your mother."

Taramae shook her head, tears cascading down her face.

"Rauma has seen you?"

The girl nodded.

"Yet they brought you here?"

Taramae's shoulders drooped.

Suddenly Kess understood the complication. Months earlier, Rauma had insisted that her daughter, Taramae, be declared dead so she could receive Sorrow Tributes. It would be quite embarrassing for the girl to now be alive.

Kess patted the girl's shoulder. "Fear not. You may stay with me. Let us get you clean."

As she filled a basin with kettle-heated water, there came a harsh rap at the door. Before she could answer, Leader Adris strode inside. Cautiously, he stepped toward the bed.

15

Wise Woman Kess smiled. "What a surprise you have sent me!"

Adris responded gruffly. "Everyone is frightened! They will not gather. They fear she is a haunted soul bringing Dark Menaces from the depths of Under Earth, and that soon the Vast Vex will bring a plague upon them all."

Kess stood, arms folded, annoyed. "Does she appear deceased to you?"

With an imploring glance of her tear-streaked face, Taramae held out a dirty hand for him to examine. He had known her all her life. Surely, he would not deny that she was real.

The leader was repulsed. "It *does* look as if she crawled out of a grave."

Taramae was dismayed.

Leader Adris turned to the Wise Woman. "The villagers need calming. The festival must go forward. This matter will be settled at Tribunal tomorrow."

"Tomorrow?" Kess protested. "Be reasonable, Adris. She cannot speak! How will she defend herself at Tribunal? We need at least seven days to see if her health improves."

Leader Adris stared at Taramae again, his eyebrows furrowed. "Three days!" was all he would concede. He thrust the object he had picked up into the Wise Woman's hands and left.

Kess stomped her foot. "Mizzafrizzaritz!" She hurriedly latched the door to prevent more uninvited guests, mumbling under her breath about the leader's lack of character. Next, she looked at his parting gift. It was a crude, tightly rolled piece of dried leather about six inches long. A marking scratched inside simply read: *Help Me.*

Kess was heartbroken. The girl had desperately reached out to friends, only to be pushed away, then dumped like rubbish. Ashamed of the conduct of the village, Kess returned to Taramae's bedside. "So sorry, my dear. You deserved a more hospitable greeting. Such a bothersome man!"

Taramae pointed toward the Pavilion and raised her hands as if to ask why.

"Why Tribunal?" Kess began to softly wipe the smudges off the girl's face. "You know these people. They are good, but they have old-time beliefs—superstitions. I have tried to teach them otherwise—about SkyFa and the Great Good. But in uncertain times, they revert to old ways. Your arrival has awakened old fears."

Taramae shook her head sadly.

"I know. I know," Kess agreed, and attempted to gently clean the sore mark around the girl's throat.

Taramae jerked away.

"So sorry. So sorry!" Kess apologized and handed her the cloth. "Finish washing your face. I have a better idea for the rest of you."

In a corner of the dwelling, blocked off by a stack of wood, was an area where Kess did her private bathing. She filled a larger clay vessel with warm water, then returned to assist her weak guest to walk over. "We must find a way to prove that you are not from Under Earth."

Taramae smiled shyly. She motioned for Kess to step back as she moved off the bed and unwrapped the rest of her exhausted body from the borrowed cape. An obvious motherhood bump bulged under the ragged dress. Taramae tenderly touched her abdomen and shrugged.

"Mizzafrizzaritz!" Kess gasped. "How? Where? Oh, my!" Kess looked Taramae up and down, then sighed heavily, "If that does not convince them, nothing will."

Taramae smiled again. However, both women knew that although this might solve one problem, it created a greater one. This circumstance would upset the order of things and require further explanation. But how does one explain anything when one cannot speak?

Kess helped her shaky friend peel off the ragged clothing. She cringed at the welts on the girl's back and legs, and at how thin she was. It was as if all her nourishment had gone to the tiny one she was carrying. Kess helped wash the matted hair, secretly checking for nits as she did so. It would likely take several soapings before the girl's lovely, fair hair was restored to its original color, and years before her attractive braids would return. They appeared to have been sawed off with a dull knife. Ragged-edged hair remained to the length of Taramae's chin in the front and slightly longer in the back. Carefully, Kess washed the hair, trying not to bump the sore that encircled the girl's neck. It was all Kess could do to keep from weeping— and gagging.

Who had done such a thing to this beautiful girl? Kess turned away and swallowed hard to stifle her anger and grief. "You finish here while I prepare some food." She hid her own tears as she worked. She had to remain strong if she were to help the girl prepare for Tribunal. But how?

After the bath, Taramae seemed delighted as she pulled on one of Kess's clean old dresses. Kess placed the food on the table, retrieved a healing balm from her shelves, and crossed to Taramae. "This will ease the suffering," she assured, as she lightly touched the ointment onto one of the tender places on Taramae's neck.

A disapproving groan came forth.

"Forgive me, dear," Kess apologized. "But your suffering gives me hope."

Taramae was confused.

Kess explained. "I have heard groanings. You *still* have a voice. With teas to quell the swelling of your throat, you may yet be able to speak—and you will *need* to."

Tears filled Taramae's eyes once more. Kess was right. She must be able to defend herself at Tribunal if she would be welcomed back into the village. That she might be able to speak again seemed a mere hope. Comment or protest had been choked out of her months ago. She had to fight now if she would regain her home—and keep her freedom. Taramae devoured the food in front of her and drank the healing tea.

Late for her daily village rounds, Kess gave further instructions as she prepared baskets with other teas, salves, and herbal breads. "At present you *must* stay inside. You need rest to gain strength. Later we will prepare a Tribunal petition."

Taramae nodded, drowsy by the rush of nourishment. She began to swoon.

Kess helped her to the bed, then continued to prepare for necessary visits. Within minutes the girl was asleep, just as the Wise Woman had planned. "Rest now, little one. All may yet return to the Great Good," Kess sounded optimistic, though even she did not know how it could. She picked up a lamp that she would need before near-dark and left her dwelling in shame.

Kess had never used her knowledge of plants to harm anyone and always kept her book of potions and cures hidden to avoid any accusations of sorcery. But that day she had steeped sleeping leaves into the tea for Taramae. It would not hurt her, but it was necessary to ensure that the girl did not wander from the dwelling. It was for her safety, Kess rationalized. But there were other reasons. Now that Taramae was back, the obstacles would be profound. "I am too old for such intrigues," Kess mumbled. "Mizzafrizzaritz!"

Chapter 4: Curious Crim

The Wise Woman's first visit was to Old Soul Nadee, the last of the adult settlers from Crim's the early days. Nadee had witnessed the evolution of the village and loved to tell the stories. She had been Kess's mentor but in past months her heart had been failing and Kess did not know how to help her. Grief added to the woman's decline, and Nadee had had more than her share.

Knocking lightly as she entered the elderly woman's dwelling, Kess called out, cheerfully, "I brought the tea that you like, and the bread. There is a different soup today."

"You are too kind," Nadee nodded as she shuffled from the resting room in back.

"It is not a fanciful meal, but it will ..."

"Keep me from starving?" Nadee chuckled, as she finished the sentence. "How many times have I repeated those words to others? It meant there was little meat in the broth."

Kess was embarrassed. "It is likewise the case today. I hope to bring better tomorrow."

"Do not fret. You have been busy," Nadee sympathized. "Sit for a while and visit. It might help to unburden yourself."

Kess sighed, "Alas, I cannot stay today. Many are needing attention."

"Is one of them a ghost?" Nadee asked, between sips of soup.

"You heard?"

"It was hard not to hear such hysterics. I have been waiting all day to hear the cause."

Kess hesitated. As Nadee's apprentice she would have loved to tell all and glean from her teacher's wisdom. However, considering Nadee's health, it would be too great a burden. So, in her role as Wise Woman, Kess approached the subject carefully. "Perhaps it would be best told another time?"

"It would not! A delay would be maddening. Tell me now, friend."

It was useless to delay. With a deep sigh, Kess announced, "Taramae has returned."

Astonished, Old Soul Nadee blinked several times. "What say? How can it be? She was pronounced dead, drowned in the river."

"She was not dead. She was stolen."

"Stolen?"

"Yes, and it has taken all this time for her to return."

Nadee's face brightened. "Was *he* with—I mean—did she return—alone?"

Kess nodded sadly. She knew Nadee was hoping for news regarding her grandson who had gone missing around the same time. "She is alone, and not well. Whoever was keeping her left bruises and scars."

Nadee was aghast.

"She finally escaped. How, I do not know. She is terribly weak."

"Has she told of the vicious villain?"

"Taramae cannot speak. She was strangled and has swelling in her throat."

Nadee quickly became a nurturer. "Have you tried myrrh oil?"

"Yes, but only once thus far, and clove tea."

"Repeated dosing may benefit."

"Hopefully so. She *must* speak to defend herself at Tribunal."

"Tribunal? Why ever would there be a Tribunal?" Nadee spat out a puff of air. "Adris! Sounds like his doings."

"You are correct. He wants proof that Taramae is not a ghost."

"A ghost?" Nadee spat air again. "He knows it is not so. He merely desires to demonstrate, once again, that he is master of Crim."

"It is true. Now you know my course and why I must leave. There is much to prepare."

"Dah ye, my dear. Please come again soon. And try adding turmeric to the girl's tea for the swelling."

"Will do. Will do."

"And add more meat to the broth?" the old woman teased.

Kess chuckled as she closed the door. She was sorry that she could not stay and chat further, but evening was approaching, and she needed to hurry to the Tower.

A group of children gathered by the Tower door, talking in hushed, excited tones. Kess snapped her fingers and pointed to the ground. They knew what it meant. All of them lined up and respectfully waited while the Wise Woman quickly performed a nit check. When she finished, she scolded, "Baird. Banaya. Take your friends and go home."

The siblings left without argument. The other children meekly followed. There would be much curiosity now that the Watcher had blown the warning horn, and those two waifs would quickly discover how to profit from it. Baird, age eleven, and Banaya, age eight, had become very resourceful with enriching themselves while at play.

After their mother died in Heb, their father, Ori, moved the family away from that dreadful place and began management of the Groggery. He worked late into the night and often slept during the day. Therefore, the children had plenty of unsupervised hours for mischief. Kess was amused by their creativity, but it was important that their scheming not involve the Watcher.

Children gone, Kess obtained an old key from a crack in the door jamb and unlocked the Tower door. She lit her lamp and holding it well ahead, ascended the steep staircase where she fetched a key for the second door from a raised shelf. "Wise Woman here," she announced, as she tapped on the door.

It was common for her to be welcomed whenever she visited. Her patient was healing well and always seemed pleased to see her. However, that evening when she tapped, there was no answer. Kess knocked louder. No response again. Worried, Kess pushed the door open and stepped into the small living space. The musty darkness felt and smelled like a dungeon. She set her lamp on the table and lit the one that had been left there. The space brightened considerably.

Smote sat crosswise on the bed, his back against the wall, seemingly unaware of her presence. Kess touched his knee, shaking it lightly. "Good eve, friend."

"Have you come to banish me?" Smote asked, in a dull-toned voice.

"Banish you?" she asked, concerned that he might be sinking back into the time of delusions that he had experienced when first brought there.

"I failed. They will want me to leave."

"Failed? How?"

"The stranger hurt someone. I warned them too late ... too late," his voice choked.

"No, no, friend. No one was hurt," she assured, as she picked up the little owl from the floor and placed it on the shelf above the table.

Smote shook his head, "There was screaming. People running." He turned to Kess pleading, "I swear, she did not seem dangerous!"

"Who?"

"That girl. That strange girl. She did not seem dangerous! But she must have been bad. They carried her away. *Is* she bad?"

Kess knew such excitement was not good for him. Perhaps he would lose interest if it appeared of little consequence. She began taking the contents out of the basket. "You had no food this morning? How terrible! And no change of squat pot, I can tell. Phew! This is not acceptable. I will have to scold Nawhi."

Smote shakily arose from the cot and crossed to the table. "I asked, *is that girl bad?*"

"Nawhi? No, she is not bad, but her head seems always to be in the clouds."

Smote was impatient. "Not Nawhi! That girl in the cape. Do not say you cannot remember. They took her to your dwelling!"

Kess hesitated again. "Oh—*that* girl. She is ill, and I am tending to her," she said, as she laid food out on the table. "Come, sit, you must eat. Then I will clean your wounds."

Smote appeared relieved. But again, he insisted, "Is she *bad?*"

"No, she is not bad. But the villagers are afraid."

"Why are they afraid of a child?"

"She is not a child. She is a small young woman who has lived here all her life." The Wise Woman took a deep breath. There was only so much that she dared tell. She began slowly. "A while ago the girl went missing. Many in the village believed she was dead, even her own mother. Therefore, when she returned suddenly, the villagers became frightened because they thought—they think—she is a ghost and worry that she will bring a curse."

"A curse? And this was her home?"

"Yes."

"And she was good before?"

"Yes, very good."

"But now they think she is bad?"

"They fear that her presence might summon the Vast Vex to the village if she stays."

Smote's shoulders sagged. If they could so easily turn away someone who had lived there before, how easily might they turn him away? If they did, where would he go? Cautiously, he asked, "What will they do with her?"

"Tribunal will be held. If we can prove that she did not float into the village from Under Earth, they will probably let her stay."

"What say?" Smote snorted in disbelief.

Kess repeated. "She was declared dead. For her to come back raises suspicion that she has come from Under Earth to haunt the village. It is greatly feared."

Smote caught her hand as she was about to apply salve. His face brightened. "She did not ascend from Under Earth! She came in a wagon!"

Kess's eyes widened. "A wagon? What wagon?"

You said she cannot talk "The serpent wagon with the dirty man and the two big oxen. The girl was hiding in the back and climbed out when the man went to see the leader."

"Tarce?" Kess spat out the name. "That miscreant! Why they let him into the village, I will never know. And you truly saw this?"

Smote turned, bravely resolute. "Yes! Take me to Tribunal. I will testify that she came in the wagon."

Once again, the Wise Woman sorted items on the table. It gave her time to think of an explanation that Smote might accept, as he happily considered a solution.

"I will go down there—you can help me walk—and I will tell them that she is not a ghost because she came in the serpent wagon. Therefore, they do not need to fear and she can stay in the village."

"It would not be … Um … I am not certain that …" Kess stumbled for reasons as she resumed putting salve on her patient's scabs, then finally settled on, "It is a generous offer, but would be too difficult for you to walk down the steep stairs. We do not want to risk a fall when you are making such progress. And the strain, yes, the strain might bring the fevers back. I will tell them at Tribunal what you saw. It will help, I am sure."

At first, Smote was disappointed, yet accepted the reasoning behind the answer, saying, "You take good care of me—of everyone. Dah ye, Mother Kess."

Kess nodded appreciatively but finished quickly. "I must go but will return tomorrow. Do not fret further. Eat now and rest."

Wise Woman Kess did not care to be outside after nightfall, but she had one more stop to make.. When she pounded on the door of Leader Adris, she could hear rowdy voices inside. Apparently not everyone had cancelled their festival celebrations. No one answered when she knocked the second time. She thought of barging through his door like he had done through hers earlier in the day; however, she considered herself more civilized. Still, she grew impatient and knocked even louder.

"Yessh?" The leader's voice slurred when he opened the door. He was obviously well-aled. Like a silly oaf, he belched. "Kessh! Come in. Come in."

Knowing that no serious conversation was possible with him in this condition, she declined. "Dah ye, no. But as judges, we must talk before Tribunal."

Adris almost dropped his flask. "How can we talk? You said she cannot talk."

"She cannot."

"That girl is not a ghosht." he whispered.

"You are correct. She is not a ghost." Kess spoke precisely so his befuddled brain could comprehend. "We must decide what to do, for her sake, and for the village."

Adris began to ramble. "If she *is* a ghosht we can make her go away. We could shay shoo, shoo, ghosht, and be done with her."

"Adris, get your wits about you!" As he was about to take another gulp of ale from a flask, the Wise Woman grabbed it. "No more of this tonight! You must think clearly!"

They tugged back and forth on the container until some of the foul fermented foam splashed onto her cape.

Adris burped in her face and giggled. "I like this game!" he said, running his hand down her arm.

Kess pushed him away in disgust. "Do not trifle with me, fool!" she said, as she wiped her cloak in an attempt to remove the stench. "I will return tomorrow after Last Meal. Tell Brun to meet us here, and no more ale tonight!"

Adris shushed Kess as though it were a secret, sneakily closed the door, then yelled, "Hey, everyone. The Wize Wooman says, 'Have another drink!'"

A boisterous group cheered.

Kess stomped her foot and walked away. She was exhausted and longed for rest but Taramae occupied her nice soft bed. She had an old cot and an extra blanket. However, the discomfort would be measurable. "Mizzafrizzaritz!" she lamented six times as she walked home.

Chapter 5: Dreams and Honey Cakes

The heavenly smell of food roused Taramae from sleep. Wrapped in a blanket of fur, she felt warm and relaxed for the first time in months. She dozed between waking and slumbering, afraid to move for fear the charmed feeling would fade away. Moments later, she drifted back into the enticing realm of memories.

Laughter. Her dream always began with laughter. Taramae knew the sound well. Friends from her childhood ran across the meadows of her mind, beckoning her to play once more.

Good-natured Molay, the clothing maker's daughter, loyal Nawhi, oldest daughter of Storekeeper Brun, dutiful Drayis, heir of Leader Adris, and his clever, orphaned cousin, Jeric composed a rowdy group of not-naughty but noisy children whose relatives had prominence within the village. There was not a quiet moment in Crim whenever they gathered to play. Once the crops were season-strong, the children were allowed to run between the field furrows, taking their clamor with them. It was in the time of the Great Good, where nature and man were in balance.

In her sleep Taramae ran freely with them for a time, as she had done years before. However, her friends were soon far ahead, and she could not keep up. The harder she tried, the heavier her feet became. She could barely lift her legs. Taramae called out for them to wait but they did not hear her. The girls ran in one direction. The boys disappeared into a murky mist.

Taramae could see consuming clouds in the distance. Dark Menaces were coming! She tried to warn her friends but could not find them.

Taramae gasped for air as another harrowing nightmare burst across her mind, exploding all other thoughts in its path. Awake or asleep, it was always the same.

"Do you want to speak or breathe?" It was more of a hideous taunt than a question as the formidable Heska of Heb held Taramae by the throat, stretching her neck so high that the girl's toes barely touched the floor. The key on Heska's treasury necklace hit her in the face. "Quit your begging! Since that idjit, Tarce, brought you here against your wishes, it makes it awkward for me to send you home right away. I do not want to hear about who will come for you or what they might pay. You are here until I say you can leave, Shovo. That is your name now—Shovo! It means slave. You work; you eat. You speak; you die. I may just rip your tongue out. I have done it before to those who disobeyed and tried to argue their way out of punishment. It was rather entertaining, though they did not agree. Would you like that?" the foul-smelling harpy asked. She pressed her fat thumbs deeper against the girl's larynx as she shook her captive like a stray cat. Taramae relived the sensation of suffocation as her arms flailed the air.

Two warm hands grasped her left arm and lowered it. Taramae flinched. Hands? Her dream had never ended with hands before. She pulled away.

"Calm ye. Calm ye," a little voice said.

Taramae struggled to open her eyes. When she sat up quickly, a dizzying wave hit. She groaned and lay back down.

The warm hands patted her arm once more. "Calm ye. Calm ye," the soother repeated.

She turned to view the face of her comforter. A child—a little girl stood by the side of the bed. Her uneven auburn braids framed the tiny brown speckles splashed across her cheeks, and there was a front tooth missing when she smiled.

"You are supposed to eat now. The wise lady will be back soon."

Taramae smiled back as she slowly unwrapped her cocoon of comfort and stood. The girl offered her a steadying hand until, after noticing Taramae's protruding stomach, she suddenly gasped and bolted out the door.

Kess caught her in flight. "Wait, Banaya, wait! Do not be afraid. Come back inside and eat. This is Taramae, and she, like you, has a special story. Let me tell you her story."

27

Banaya agreed hesitantly. With one finger, she drew a circle in the air in front of her face and touched the tip of her nose. It was something she did to ward off evil. She could be safe now and would listen. After all, she was quite hungry.

Wise Woman Kess placed the meal on the table wondering how much she dared tell the child without too much being revealed to the village before Tribunal. Taramae's defense would come from the precise telling of the events that had brought her to the current predicament. She needed all the sympathy it might garner because she could not speak, and as one of the Tribunal judges, Kess would only be allowed limited assistance.

A crucial piece of information was missing regarding the pregnancy. Due to the manner of Taramae's disappearance, Kess was not certain who the baby's father was, and the last thing she needed was for rumors to prejudice the village. Banaya would have to be convinced to keep the secret. However, now frightened, she would be harder to persuade.

Banaya ate without looking up. Kess decided to use a different tactic. She spoke to Taramae first. "Banaya and her family came to Crim while you were away. She has a brother named Baird, and her father, Ori, became the ale maker at the Groggery when Old Sleff died."

Taramae remembered Old Sleff fondly and was sad to hear of his passing, but she smiled. She could tell that Kess was attempting to build a bridge of familiarity between her and the girl.

Banaya quickly looked away.

Kess continued. "Taramae, please serve Banaya another honey cake."

Taramae passed the plate across the table. The child hesitated, then grabbed another of the delectable pastries, circled her face and touched her nose.

"Banaya is one of my special friends. She comes to help me every day. She is learning to read and when she is twelve, she hopes to become my tyro."

The missing-tooth grin reappeared.

Taramae looked at Kess, her expression cloaked in sorrow. She too was to have apprenticed with the Wise Woman at age twelve. The opportunity had been denied after the Wild River tragedy. Her mother had never forgiven her and had chosen a different life path for her.

Kess noticed her sadness but continued. "Taramae is another special friend, Banaya. She has lived in Crim all her life. I was there when she was born. She has *always* been good. Many people liked her. Then one day, a terrible man stole her away."

Taramae was surprised. She had not been able to give information about her abduction, yet somehow Kess knew.

"Everyone wondered where she had gone. They thought she had drowned in the river."

Banaya caught her breath. "It is a bad place! Ghosts live all around it. We are told not to play there, but Baird goes fishing every day. You should speak with him."

Kess was alarmed. "Yes, I will speak with him. Nothing good *ever* happens at the Wild River," she warned, and proceeded with her story. "Happily, Taramae was not drowned, but she had to be brave for a long time, especially when the people who stole her were very unkind. Finally, one day she escaped and returned to our village. Unfortunately, people of Crim now fear she is a ghost. They want the village to feel safe again, so, Tribunal will be held. But Taramae was hurt badly while she was away."

The Wise Woman motioned for Taramae to lower the top edge of her dress to show the sore mark around her throat. Embarrassed, she complied. Banaya gasped, her hand flew up to cover her mouth.

"Taramae cannot speak now and needs friends to help her. Someone who knows of *other* reasons why the people might be afraid."

Banaya grinned mischievously. She and her brother often invented scary stories about ghosts so they could sell shiny pebbles as protective charms. It was how they purchased treats from the storehouse.

Apparently, the Wise Woman had an inkling about this activity and shook a scolding finger, then smiled and continued. "And because Taramae cannot explain what has happened, we need to be careful that no one knows about her tummy surprise yet. It is very important!"

Banaya's face clouded again. She glanced away. Taramae looked at Kess, questioning.

"Banaya might be afraid of you because of what happened to her mother." Banaya's lips began to quiver.

"You see, when they lived in Heb, Banaya's mother was also expecting a baby. However, because she did not have the help she needed, both mother and the infant perished. Banaya and her family are still sad. I believe she is afraid to be your friend for fear that something similar might happen to you. But she does not have to worry. I will be with you."

Tears rolled down Banaya's face. Taramae bit her lip to hold back tears. Her frail frame shook. She was especially glad to be back in Crim for *that* reason. She was keenly aware that Heska only cared about the child she was carrying. Once the pregnancy was discovered, they beat her on the legs, instead of across the back, and at times gave her better food to eat. But Taramae knew that if she delivered her baby in Heb, there would be no preserving of her life if difficulties arose. It was another reason she was grateful to be home!

Bond of empathy established, the child walked around the table and once again patted her new friend's arm. "Calm ye. Calm ye," Banaya comforted. Then turning to Kess, she asked, "How can I help her?"

"There may be a way," the Wise Woman said. She accompanied Banaya to the door and whispered into her ear.

After Banaya left, Kess busied herself clearing the table. She was stalling. She had to get details from Taramae if she was going to assist at Tribunal yet she feared what the answers might be. Proving that Taramae was not a ghost was not the biggest problem—the pregnancy was. The Rules of Honor had been established when Crim broke away from the hostile life of Heb. Those laws were to promote a respectable society and a pregnancy without a Pairing did not fit within customary social parameters. Change was uncomfortable, and according to the opinion of most, often unnecessary. But villagers would not be without compassion regarding Taramae's situation. There was a child's life to consider. Still, Kess's Tribunal presentation needed to be calculated for the greatest effect.

Lost in thought, Taramae walked around the cottage looking at things with an air of familiarity. As she passed the bookshelf, she ran her hand along the books and straightened a unique picture that hung on the wall. It was unlike any picture Taramae had ever seen and she had always marveled at it.

It was not drawn in the charcoal and earth-tone clays of common paintings. It had vivid colors. A pairing present from her husband, the Wise Woman treasured it. All Taramae knew of him was from gossip she had overheard her mother tell, that he came to Crim with the Givens to help and teach in the village, and that he walked away early one morning, never to return. Taramae was advised not to mention it, that it would be unkind to press for details. Kess proudly displayed the picture rather than to hide it away as a family embarrassment. Respectfully, Taramae wiped a whisp of dust off the corner.

Next to that hung a small drawing on a stretched piece of hide with a frame made of four sticks lashed together. It depicted two birds flying side by side. The style, though immature, showed potential talent. Taramae knew the artist well—Jeric. The picture was also a gift to the Wise Woman, for befriending him when others had shunned him. Taramae touched it softly.

Jeric, my Jeric, she cried out in her mind. Was it her fault he had died? For months, she had tried not to dwell on his death. Grieving took away the energy that she needed to perform shovo tasks. If efforts slacked there was punishment. Therefore, she had packed away memories of her Pairing and focused on one thing—how to escape from captivity before Jeric's child was born.

Heska's husband cowered in her presence, and with good reason. Whenever he leered at Taramae with a lustful eye, Heska promised to rearrange his body parts. It was deterrent enough, and the only kindness Heska had ever done for her. Now that she was home, Taramae could unbind the box that held her emotions hostage. Arms wrapped around her middle, she breathed deeply and swayed. She did not notice Kess walk up behind her. When Kess touched her shoulder, she jumped, crying out, "Ahhyee!" Surprised, Taramae made the sound again, "Ahhyee!"

"Good! Good!" Kess cheered. "The healing teas must be helping. Come, have another cup. We need to prepare for tomorrow."

"How?" Taramae mouthed the word.

"We will find a way," the Wise Woman answered, hoping that her own doubts would not betray her counterfeit confidence. She prepared the tea and returned to the table. While Taramae blew the tea to cool it, Kess carefully asked, "Was it Tarce who set you free?"

Indignant, Taramae shook her head, pointing to the infected scar around her neck.

"So sorry—so sorry! I am just sorting necessary information. It helps to know. So, if it was not Tarce who helped you escape, who else?"

Taramae held up two fingers.

"Two people? Oh my, that sounds like a deal of good fortune."

Taramae nodded, vigorously. The amazing circumstances of her escape had unfolded so unexpectedly that she barely believed it herself. As she stirred her tea, Taramae momentarily became lost in the swirls of memory. One stranger had aided in her release from the filthy, lightless wood closet where she had spent many captive days and all her lonely nights. He took her part of the way to Crim where she hid in a grove of trees near the Crossing hoping to walk the rest of the way home in the morning without being discovered. It was cold. The darkness was full of strange noises, and she despaired.

Suddenly another stranger, quite mysterious in appearance, discovered her crying and scared. Calmly, he said, "Save your tears for the joy that is to come," and held out his hand.

Every ounce of her tortured soul was apprehensive, yet she felt compelled to take it. Immediately, Taramae felt comfort beyond any she had felt before. He advised returning to Crim in the wagon of Tarce—which contradicted all common sense to someone trying to run away that terrible person.

However, the kind man promised, "It will work for the Great Good."

She had felt an unusual trust towards him, so complied with his instructions. Yet, because the whole experience was difficult to fully describe, she would be careful to whom she mentioned all the aspects lest others think she had gone mad in captivity. As she sipped her tea, Taramae's thoughts returned to the present.

"May we continue?" Kess asked softly. She needed to ask tough questions if she were to mount a proper defense. Fear of the possible answers caused her heart to beat rapidly. "Please forgive me, my dear, but I must know. Is Tarce the father of this baby?"

The cup crashed. The tea splashed. Taramae's face reddened. Her eyes narrowed as she hit her fist on the table. She clutched her throat as if the anger locked inside was about to explode. She stood up so fast that the chair fell over backwards. She paced the room, flailing her arms in frustration. How could she explain? Words had abandoned her. There were only scars and pain and nightmares. Tarce, the father of her baby? The mere thought sickened her. How could anyone even imagine that she would allow such a thing to happen? She would rather die!

She moaned as if a thousand screams plagued her brain and paced about the room looking for something to throw.

The reaction scared Kess.

Taramae suddenly stopped when she reached the corner where Kess's treasured pictures hung. As she stood, breathing heavily, the fury began to diminish, taking with it fumes of enraged energy. Composure replaced chaos. Taramae tenderly lifted the drawing of the birds down from the wall, returned to the table, and handed it to Kess.

"Yes, this is Jeric's artwork." Kess paused, looking from Taramae, to the picture, and back again. "Are you telling me that Jeric is the father of this child?"

Taramae nodded, eagerly.

"How can this be? Your mother denied the Pairing."

Taramae went to the bookshelf. She pulled out a heavy book that held with a collection of writings by the first settlers of Crim, turned past the pages where births and deaths were recorded, to an original copy of the Rules of Honor, and one page further to where four additional laws had been written into the village charter: Village Defense, Village Beliefs, PermaDevo, and PairCompe. She pointed to the third provision, *PermaDevo*.

Kess read aloud. "*A couple may make an unannounced Pairing Promise at the Sacred Stone with exchange of the man's clan token in case of impending war, or if devotion exists on both sides and family permission has been denied three times. The girl must be at least eighteen years of age. A village elder must also be consulted.* You did this?"

Taramae confidently concurred. She had been denied Jeric's love more than three times. She just had to get to the age requirement before her mother forced an unwanted betrothal.

Kess was surprised that the girl had dared to go against her mother. The woman's determination to find a prosperous Pairing for her daughter was no secret. It was delayed only by her inclination to keep the girl working at the inn night and day.

"But which village elder gave ..." Kess began to ask, then stopped, remembering a time three years earlier when she had explained PermaDevo to the young, despairing couple. Jeric and Taramae had seemed so upset with another parting about to take place that Kess remembered saying, "Do not despair! When you are of age, my permission will be granted." That seemed to reassure them. However, not having heard more concerning it in the following years, Kess assumed they had given up the notion. She had no idea that they had merely hidden their intentions and waited for Taramae's required age. This revelation was at once encouraging and dismaying. Kess gathered her nerves to deliver sad news. "My dear, people believe that Jeric tired of the Givens watch and ran away to the Peaks People."

Taramae shook her head. She knew he had *not* run away. He was gone. Bound and gagged in the wagon used to take her away, she had witnessed Tarce hit Jeric on the back of the head with a heavy stone as he had tried to rescue her. There was a rush of additional footsteps, and agitated grumblings from both perpetrators as they dragged Jeric's lifeless body to the Wild River and rolled it in. The sound memory made Taramae cringe.

The girl was clearly traumatized, but without details Kess did not know how to explain Taramae's situation at Tribunal. Carefully, she asked, "And you completed the Pairing Promise and made the solemn Commitment?"

Taramae shyly placed a hand on her abdomen. The Commitment had clearly been made.

Kess was very encouraged. "Of course. This may be all we need. Where is your token?"

All traces of joy disappeared. Jeric's clan token, a beautifully engraved, golden sphere on a braided leather cord had been hung lovingly around her neck by Jeric at their Pairing, only to be used by Tarce to choke her into unconsciousness the night of her abduction and then removed. She did not know what had become of it. Was it dropped among the rocks or had it fallen into the churning water as Jeric was dragged into it? She could not be certain. While in Heb as shovo, she had covertly searched for it among

Tarce's belongings when he was away, but to no avail. Taramae pointed to her neck and shook her head.

The Wise Woman felt Dark Menaces gathering about them. No token as proof of the Pairing Promise meant that Tribunal would be a bigger challenge but she tried to sound optimistic.

"We will find a way to communicate further when I return. For now, drink more tea and rest, rest, rest!"

"Poor girl!" Kess mumbled, Taramae's life was enshrouded with Vast Vex tragedies. Even in love she had been thwarted and for Jeric to be a part of this was so incredibly sad. If only Taramae still possessed the Pairing Token, it would have solved everything!

Chapter 6: The Wise Woman at Work

Exhausted from the enervating emotions and lack of restful sleep in recent days, the Wise Woman stretched her back and groaned, "Mizzafrizzaritz!" However, because her routine was vital to many people, she needed to push past her own discomfort.

First, she took soup and honey cakes to Old Soul Nadee, who eagerly asked, "Has the girl been able to speak yet? Are the teas working? You can give her more if necessary. Has she divulged who helped her?"

Kess longed for advice from her knowledgeable friend regarding Taramae's dilemma, but had no time for a lengthy discussion, therefore disclosure was best delayed. Kess shook her head. "She did have help. But with no voice, details are not possible yet. Perhaps there will be more to report tomorrow."

The second stop Kess made was to check on Taramae's friend, Molay, who was also expecting her first child, and nearer her time. She had Paired with Asa the hide tanner and needed a balm for blisters from handling furs with tannery acid.

"She will get used to it," Asa assured their guest.

This visit required diplomacy. If she told Asa that elements in the tanning liquid were not good for the baby, he would likely see it as a sign of potential weakness in his offspring. After all, he had been around it all his life and was a man of size and vigor. Kess had to appeal to him on another level.

She beckoned him across the room where they could speak confidently. "My friend, if your wife's hands are sore from harsh workings, how will she caress in the tender time?"

Asa's eyes widened, shocked at the Wise Woman's bluntness about such personal things. His face turned red. Molay glanced shyly in their direction.

Kess spoke loud enough for her to hear. "Molay is well known for stitching lovely garments. Perhaps her talents would best be used making goods from your beautiful furs and leather. Brun would gladly sell such at the storehouse."

Asa's countenance enlivened with the thought. "Dah ye, Wise Woman."

As she put a healing ointment on Molay's hands, they spoke of birthing plans. When Nadee was the Wise Woman, she had firmly believed that besides support women, there needed to be support men. Kess had maintained the tradition of having the husband brought in during the final pushing to brace a woman's shoulders for added strength. Glances were averted for the sake of her modesty, and lest the sight of blood might prove too affecting. A swooning man is unwelcome at a birthing.

"You are carrying lower today. It looks to be soon. Are your supporters prepared?"

"Yes, Wise Woman," Molay responded with confidence.

"It is good! I will return. Call upon me when your time comes."

"May I offer a piece of fur?" Asa asked.

"No, but I will gladly accept leather scraps."

Asa agreed, though he did not understand why an older woman who did not sew would ask for leftover cuttings. He motioned to the bundles in the corner. She took three large pieces, planning to trade them at the storehouse for what she needed.

As Molay escorted her to the door, Kess paused for a moment, "Have you heard? Taramae has returned."

Molay was instantly alarmed. "Do not speak of her here!" she shushed and quickly motioned for Kess to leave.

The next dwelling that Kess went to was that of a family with a new child. As the village Wise Woman, she officiated in the Naming Ceremony of each newborn within the first ten days of a child's life. It was another established custom of Nadee's which no one had challenged, so Kess continued enjoying it. However, she added her own flair. Before the observance began there was a nit check of all participants. She did it to safeguard the village and did not charge extra for the service. Then, if parents desired a specific designation, she would consider it. However, the final decision would be hers. This quelled many arguments between Pairings and hushed intrusive relatives.

That day, after the nit check was accomplished, Kess listened as the mother of the child spoke, humbly, "We are plain people. We do not expect a grand title. We thought, perhaps the name Arbil."

The child's scrawny, puckered face meant the unfortunate thing would have enough challenges in life without enduring a dreary tag. Therefore, the Wise Woman touched her forehead as if in deep thought, then suddenly looked surprised. She leaned closely toward the parents and whispered her blessing. "This is a Child of Promise. She will bring your family great joy. Love her dearly. Teach her kindly, and above all, keep these words to yourselves, lest they provoke the jealousy of others," she said, with a wink. With that, Kess stood upright and announced, "Her name will be Harmony, for she will have a gift for peace."

The gathering seemed pleased.

Kess loved being the Wise Woman, especially in moments like these— helping the precious little ones to a sweet beginning by encouraging their parents to cherish them. She did not stay for the family feast, but took their offering of a single coin, a thick slice of sweet cake, and left.

"Must remember to write that name in the book," she reminded herself. Over the years there had been many naming opportunities, and she did not intend to give the same name twice. To have more than one child with the same name in the village would be confusing. Some of the names Kess invented on the spot. Others seemed to be inspired. When parents had differing opinions, Kess tried to bring unity.

As she walked toward the Tower, another Naming Ceremony crossed her mind. The forest master, Ven, and his wife, Rauma, had argued for five days before calling upon the Wise Woman to intervene.

"Taraysa!" Rauma had insisted.

"Maezen!" Ven answered firmly, though grinning mischievously.

It was obvious to Kess that the man did not care as much about the name as he did about having a say in the process. The Wise Woman had presented in the same way, touched her forehead as if in deep thought, then suddenly looked surprised. She leaned closely toward the parents and whispered her blessing. "This is a Child of Promise. She will bring your family great joy. Love her dearly. Teach her kindly, and above all, keep these words to yourselves, lest they provoke the jealousy of others," she said, with a wink. With that, Kess stood upright and announced, "Her name will be Taramae."

Ven clapped his hands. "It is done!" He gathered his tools and went off to work.

Rauma seemed less convinced as she provided a coin offering and a small vessel of honey. She had complained, "Taramae is an odd name."

"It is a unique name for a child of noble character."

Rauma seemed satisfied with that explanation. But Kess had not lied. From the very beginning she had felt that Taramae would be blessed with inner strength for an exceptional destiny. It was a good thing. She needed it, especially now!

Taramae had survived many hardships and needed to be protected. She was not the only one. Kess had pledged to help Taramae with a Tribunal petition. However, as one of the judges, Kess had to proceed prudently. If there was a claim of bias, her own standing within the village could be jeopardized.

The Wise Woman arrived at the Tower later than usual, hoping the delay had not added to the Watcher's anxiety. As she waited at the top of the stairs, Kess could hear his foot dragging when he crossed to the door. "Pleasant day to you," she happily greeted when he opened it.

He corrected her, "Pleasant day to you, *Smote!*"

"Must I call you that?" she protested.

"Does it not fit?" he asked, laughing as he raised his hands to frame his scarred face.

Kess rolled her eyes, and gave in. "Pleasant day to you, *Smote.*"

"Pleasant day to you, Mother Kess."

The Wise Woman loved the personal reference he had given her. Having been denied motherhood, she enjoyed hearing the endearment. She noticed the bare table. "They haven't brought your food?"

"That Nawhi girl came earlier. She is nervous and never speaks. She brought corn mush and dry bread and changed the squat pot. The water was forgotten."

Corn mush, dry bread, and no water? Kess was disgusted. She would speak to Storekeeper Brun about it. He was responsible to provide sustenance for Smote. It was part of the agreement. How was this man to heal without proper nourishment? He needed meat, fruit, and certainly more water.

Kess handed Smote a flask of healing tea but knew it was not enough liquid for a whole day, especially with warmer weather coming. She couldn't hide her displeasure about the man's poor circumstances. "I will see that you have better meals," she promised. "You will be pleased with what I have brought today." She lifted the sweet cake from her basket.

"Wonderful!" Smote exclaimed, pinching a corner from the cake to sample.

Kess caught his hand before he snitched another. "First, your treatment."

Smote groaned like a juvenile. He knew it was necessary to smooth the creams and ointments on his mending head and back, but any pressure on the sharp, tingling skin added to the constant pain. He sat as still as possible and tried a diverting conversation. "I love cake! Was there an occasion today?"

Gently patting ointment on his face, she said, "A Naming Ceremony for a baby—a girl."

"Did you name her Smote?"

"No! It would be an awful name for a girl."

"Yet, it is a good one for me. I surely had a better one once. Unfortunately, it seems to have been misplaced. Perhaps you could ask the villagers if they have seen a spare name lurking about. Though by looks, they would likely agree that *Smote* fits me best."

Kess winced at the levity regarding his memory loss and was tempted to scold but instead, asked, "Do you keep teasing and delay the treatment and the cake, or do you want to hear of the Naming Ceremony?"

"Hard to choose," he laughed, then flinched as she touched a sore place on his scalp.

"I named the little one Harmony. She needed a pretty name."

"Because she is an ugly baby?"

Kess tried to be diplomatic. "Her loveliness has not yet revealed itself."

"So, she *is* an ugly baby."

The Wise Woman dabbed another spot.

"Ouch! Careful, careful! I will quit teasing," he half laughed. "It is a good name. Now, please tell me the name of that other girl."

"What girl?"

40

"The girl in the cape at the Pavilion."

Kess teased back. "Oh, *that* girl. She already has a name."

"And *what* might that be?" Smote asked, strains of frustration in his tone.

Kess stalled. "I am going to leave extra salve. Apply some as needed. I may be late tomorrow. It is Tribunal day."

"For the girl who is not a ghost?"

"Yes."

"Whose name is …?"

Kess finally gave in. "Taramae. Her name is Taramae. What do you think of that one?"

Smote appeared to absorb the information for a few seconds, then shook his head slightly. "It is a good enough name," he shrugged. "What will they do at Tribunal?"

"They will decide if she is fit to stay in the village."

Smote looked dejected. "They may soon make such a judgement about me."

Kess knew it was time to change the subject. Removing parchment pages from the basket, she presented them with a flair. She had hoped that drawing might give Smote something else to do in the night and perhaps spark a memory.

Smote was grateful for the new pieces. "I finished the other you brought." Proudly, he handed her the drawing. It was an animal picture with two words scrawled across the bottom.

Kess was amused and amazed. Were his language skills returning? "Well done!" she praised, then testing, asked, "What do the words say?"

Smote was curious. "Words? Do you think they are *words*? It seemed only lines that I felt inclined to put there," he admitted, and pondered what the lines might mean.

Kess tried not to show her disappointment. "Perhaps the picture could be hung on the wall for you," she suggested as she scanned the barren interior, again embarrassed that they had not done better for this man. It was depressing. "I will strive to make your surroundings more comfortable. For now, I must go."

Smote hated to be alone. "You could stay and share the cake," he offered, taking the owl off the shelf, and placing it into his pocket.

"You enjoy it, dear. I will share another time. There is much to do."

Downcast, yet accepting, he thanked her, "Dah ye, Mother Kess. Please return soon."

She packed up the basket, patted him on the arm, and left.

Worried that he had upset her, Smote watched from the window as the Wise Woman went to her next task. She was his main link to the outside world, and he could not bear to lose that connection. "You tease too much!," he scolded himself, as he sat on the stool by the window, slowly eating cake while watching the gate being closed.

"The gatekeeper rolls each hefty rock out of the way and brings each heavy wooden side to the center. He gathers his strength and pushes the latch into place. He flinches, then shakes his hand. He checks to see if the gate is secure. Why does he do that? He just locked it. Now the gatekeeper goes home."

Smote sighed. "Did we ever have a home, Owl? We must have had one somewhere, with a more purposeful life than this. I have tried to remember. Nothing is there. Do you remember?" He pushed further into the realms of remembrance. "And what of those lines on the pages? Mother Kess said they are words. What do they mean, Owl? I can almost see it, and then it shatters. I can reach out to grab it and then it slips away. How does one solve a puzzle when so many pieces are missing?"

Smote ate the last bite of cake. His thoughts turned again to the girl in the cape. "I should hate her, Owl." he said. "She frightened the village. Now they will believe their Watcher is incapable." He could feel a rising discomfort in his temples. He shook his head trying to erase it. He needed more time to think before the pain hit.

"What was that girl's name? Kess called her Tara—Tara—Taramae? Yes. Do you suppose she is a wanderer like me?" For a moment, the thought made him feel less lonely. Suddenly a bolt of brain pain forced him to stop pondering. As Smote watched the last of the sun streaks fade, he groaned, "Please, Crim. Please allow her to stay."

Chapter 7: No Pity

Taramae was sitting at the table drinking more of the healing tea when Rauma suddenly marched into Kess's dwelling without knocking. Repulsed by her daughter's appearance, she spewed forth a verbal blast. "Runaway! Gone for months. Leaving me to manage the inn alone. Not caring one whit for my burden. Explain yourself!"

Taramae wanted to explain but could not. She touched her throat and lifted her hand in a helpless gesture.

Rauma mistook the lack of response for an insult. "Nothing to say? Returned only to disgrace me? 'Child of noble character'—ha!" she scoffed and stomped out.

Taramae was astonished. Emotions pummeled one another like the raging waves crashed onto the jagged rocks of the Wild River. As a slave, she had sometimes imagined what the reunion with her mother might be like. She had expected there might be anger at first for the unannounced Pairing but had hoped it would resolve into forgiveness, so they could be a family once more.

She had a family a long time ago. In those days, her mother smiled, and sang to little brother, Aven, and her father came home from working in the forest smelling of freshly hewn trees. He would chant as he swung her in a circle, "Taramae, Taramae, bright as a summer's day. Sunbeams in day and stars at night. Catch, before they fly away."

There was always a high lift and spin at the end. Taramae would squeal in delight. Her mother would giggle, even while hushing, "Shush you two. Aven is sleeping."

Back then there was laughter, the teaching of words by the fireplace, learning about marvels in the night sky, prayers at the Sacred Stone, stories about SkyFa, who watches over all, and warm, honeyed milk before bedtime. The Great Good was secure.

At times, Taramae found small, hand-carved animals hidden under her pillow. There were seven in the collection and each was a cherished possession. "Dah ye, Pah!" she would exclaim and wrap arms around his well-tanned neck.

When her mother said, "You spoil the child, Ven!" he humored her with a carved bead for her necklace, and would dance her about, saying, "Growing up comes quickly enough. Do not wish it on her sooner, wife."

Then one day, when Taramae was eight years old, all happiness left. A ferocious lightning storm felled a massive tree and with it Ven, the forest master. Taramae remembered vividly how the Placers came, four men from the village whose calling it was to respectfully prepare the dead. They wrapped her father's body in cloth and placed it deep in the ground in a field called The Last Rest. After the grave was finished, friends and family could come and place tributes at the gravesite. Taramae wanted to throw herself down upon the mound and cry her heart out.

Sensing that possibility, her mother grabbed her long braid, and whispered, "Do *not* embarrass me!"

The Placers positioned a large stone upon the grave which was simply etched *Ven*. Any joy her mother had had seemed buried at the Last Rest, and the stone, an etched covering of her heart.

For three weeks, Sorrow Tributes were delivered to their dwelling by caring villagers. From some came soup or a loaf of bread. From others a ladle or a span of cloth. Rauma seemed most grateful when storehouse coins were offered. Taramae's friend, Nawhi, came every day with her father to deliver those to Rauma.

Nawhi understood Taramae's heartache well. There was a stone at Last Rest with her mother's name on it, the result of a tragic fall from a wagon two years before. Yes, Nawhi understood.

So did Jeric. Every day, he brought Taramae something. Sometimes it was a flower, sometimes a shiny stone, or a sweet treat. "I know how this feels," he would say, and quietly leave. Certainly, he did. His parents had died of mountain fever, leaving him in the care of Adris, an uncle who resented his presence, and sent him to live with his grandmother.

During the sorrow tributes, Taramae was not allowed to play outside. She did not care. Listless, she played with four-year-old Aven. But she knew to pray to SkyFa in a childlike way, and held Aven whispering sweet stories of Pah and sharing her special animals with him. He liked the rabbit best, so she gave it to him. He always carried it in his pocket.

Taramae did not understand then that a mother must move forward to find a way to support her children. Once the tributes ended, Rauma would be on her own. One day, after Jeric left his tribute, her mother snapped a dishrag close to her face and scowled, "You will never have a Pairing with that boy! Do not even imagine it. He will always be poor. Both you and Aven must Pair well or we will not survive."

At age eight, the last thought Taramae had was that of a future spouse. Jeric was ten and just a friend. Still, she did not want to lose him. But she *had* lost him. Taramae could barely breathe when recalling the devastation of it all.

Kess's last stop of the day was to meet with the other Tribunal judges. She doubted that she could yet entrust details about Taramae to Leader Adris or Storekeeper Brun but hoped to ensure their cooperation. Unfortunately, Brun and Adris had already discussed the preferred results of Tribunal by the time she arrived.

"Might the girl choose to leave?" Brun asked.

"She must!" Adris insisted. "She is a trickster, a disrupter. The villagers will not settle down until she leaves. We must make the ghost disappear."

Kess looked at both men with disgust. "Where is she supposed to go? She came back for a reason. How could you make the judgement before you hear what happened to her? It is not the way of Tribunal!"

"The villagers are in turmoil. Her presence disturbs the tranquility. She must leave!" Adris insisted.

Kess was appalled. "The villagers have more heart than you think. Once they hear her petition, they will accept her, unless you instill prejudice before Taramae's story can be told."

"You are already in her favor! How can you be impartial when you are clearly under her spell? Perhaps we need a new judge?" Adris challenged.

Kess glared. "Perhaps Crim needs a new leader! You are being childish! There is no spell, no ghost. It is dangerous thinking!"

"Stop—stop, both of you," Brun demanded. "Arguing will not resolve the matter. Kess is right. We must hear the petition in front of the village. We must be fair."

Kess took a deep breath. "Dah ye, Brun. She has been grievously injured and has come home for help. We *cannot* cast her out."

"We *cannot* cast her out," Adris mocked her alarm. "We have heard this excuse from the Wise Woman before."

Kess realized it was unwise to divulge more information at this time. Adris had a way of twisting things to his advantage. She would save the telling to gain the sympathy of the villagers and bring pressure on the judges to make a correct decision. She needed to change the direction of the conversation.

Turning to Brun, she softly said, "The Watcher needs better food and more water."

Brun nodded.

Adris bristled. "The Watcher was supposed to be gone by now. You guaranteed me that he would not last long."

"He is healing."

"He is *another* problem! You should not have brought him here, Brun."

"It was the right thing to do," Brun defended. "It was our responsibility."

Adris sneered, "How is it our responsibility? We do not even know the man."

"Nevertheless, we should be grateful that the Wise Woman has proven so capable."

Adris challenged her again. "I am not convinced. Is it an example of her capability, or of her vanity? Is it the healing arts or use of sorcery?"

Kess fumed. She wanted to yank what was left of his hair off his fat head, or better yet, to find some sort of sorcery to make the rest of it all fall out. Instead, she chose to leave and closed the door assertively behind her.

Adris was pleased to have rattled the Wise Woman's composure. He thought she was too confident for a mere woman, and her popularity within the village was something he envied. But her extreme interest in the girl's case left him suspicious. "I am telling you, Brun, that Taramae is a trickster!"

Brun commented honestly, "You are the only one she has ever tricked. Everyone knows that Taramae rejected your Pairing Proposal when she was younger and gave the gifts you sent to Rauma, claiming they were sent for her. I do not blame her. Have you looked in the mirror?"

"You would not win a beauty prize either!"

Brun laughed. "Yes, but at least I know it."

Adris mumbled, spitefully. "By doing what she did, that girl has caused a glut of trouble. Her mother still pesters me!"

"You might accept the woman. Rauma is a pleasant sight."

"She is too cunning. She wants prestige. And how can you say pleasant? She never smiles. The best qualities of the mother went into the daughter long ago. It will not work to have Taramae here. I wish they would both disappear!"

Brun warned. "Careful, friend. We must judge impartially in this matter."

Adris plucked a gray hair from his beard. "We will see about that."

"Mizzafrizzaritz!" Wise Woman Kess mumbled through tightened teeth and kicked three stones as she walked home. Her lantern provided limited light on the path ahead. Her quiet, predictable life had been turned upside down. It was too much excitement for her liking. She did not regret Taramae's return, had always felt a motherly connection to the girl, therefore the challenge of presenting the tangled details of Taramae's predicament weighed heavily on Kess. It would have been much easier had she been able to discuss it with the other judges ahead of time. They could have tactfully explained things to the villagers. Now, that assistance was nonexistent. The leader's pride had gotten in the way.

Kess knew plenty of Adris's secrets and would have loved to mock him publicly for his selfishness. However, doing so would not help Taramae. She had to save the girl without alienating those who would also have a say in the decision. The burden rested solely on her shoulders, and those shoulders were very tired.

"Mizzafrizzaritz!" Kess mumbled a third time and kicked another stone.

"Ouch!" came a cry from the other side of the path.

"So sorry!" she called out and lifted her lantern higher.

Rauma, the innkeeper, grimaced while rubbing her forearm.

"Are you injured, Rauma? Here, let me look at you."

Rauma jerked her arm away. "Leave it!"

Realizing how close they were to her own dwelling, Kess was suddenly hopeful. "Have you come to see Taramae? I am certain she would love to see you. It would be a benefit at Tribunal if the village sees how you support your daughter."

As Rauma pushed past Kess, she spat out the words, "My daughter is dead."

Taramae was lying on the bed when Kess arrived home. Silent sobs shook her body. Rauma had been there. All Kess could do was pat her shoulder. "Calm ye, my dear. Rest. Tomorrow the sun will shine again."

She hated to see Taramae suffering and anguished as she fixed something to eat, wondering why people hurt their loved ones. Since her father's death, Taramae had been the target of her mother's unhappiness. After the Wild River incident, it became vindictiveness. Kess, who had never been blessed with children, simply could not understand how people could be so cruel to theirs. No wonder the girl has nightmares, Kess thought. Forlorn and frazzled, she finished her tea and went to bed.

Chapter 8: Tribunal Day

S mote was on high alert. Like a hawk on its perch, he watched every detail of the morning, determined not to fail at his post. Tribunal day was an early morning event, and as a matter of security, he wished they would keep the gates closed until it was over. They did not.

Soon after the gate was opened, a donkey cart came inside. A young man was seemingly the escort of a sizeable woman with an imposing demeanor. They did not go to see Leader Adris as was the custom for outside merchants. Instead, the cart was halted by the shaded side of the Pavilion, out of the main view of the villagers arriving. The man got out immediately and stood at attention near the animal's head.

"This is very unsettling, Owl. Do we trust these strangers? Why do they pause covertly?" Smote watched closely and held the warning trumpet at the ready.

During tea and toast that morning, though Kess appeared calm, she was sick with worry. "It will all work for the Great Good," Kess reassured Taramae, after explaining the Tribunal plan. The words were as much for her as they were for Taramae. "You look lovely, dear. Do not forget the cape!" That said, Kess had to leave. As a Tribunal judge she must be sitting in place on one of the ruling seats before the accused was brought forth.

"Pleasant morn to you, Gart," the Wise Woman greeted the reserved young man from the Groggery as she left her dwelling. "You may go in."

Gart acknowledged her with a nod and went inside. It was the custom for those appearing before Tribunal to receive an escort to the

Pavilion—another mark of how serious an occasion it was to be. Somberly, Gart walked beside Taramae. She did not recognize him. He had arrived at the village while she was away. He seemed to be a little older than her, but the bushy beard made it difficult to tell. He was solemn but not hostile to her, once even catching her arm as she stumbled over the hem of the clumsy cape. What a sight they made, this slight, fur-wrapped bundle and the stocky, tall man known for his gruff manner of keeping order at the Groggery. The villagers stared as Taramae took her place to be judged.

Gart helped her step up onto The Pedestal. Standing higher provided villagers with a better view of the accused person. No one wanted to be sent to The Pedestal. It was meant to be a deterrent to others to avoid the humiliation of Tribunal. Taramae knew it well, had seen others stand there, and had been there as a child. She hoped her shaking knees would calm so she would not fall nor faint from the heat of the cape. She lowered the hood piece. That helped a little. Banaya stood close by, next to her brother, Baird. She gave Taramae an encouraging smile. That helped even more.

Timidly, Taramae looked around the Pavilion. Her mother was standing indifferently near the back, more curious than caring. There was no support there. She looked for her best friend, Nawhi, but could not see her anywhere. Zaela, of course, was in the front row, arms folded smugly, awaiting the judgement. It was unnerving.

For a moment, Taramae thought she saw a shadow by the window of the Tower. Was someone watching over her? The absurdity of that possibility made her smile. As a child, she had been taught by her father that SkyFa watched over all. Yet for months in Heb she had wondered if her silent pleadings were reaching Him. She wanted to believe. She needed help from the heavens more than ever. But a shadow in the Tower was not quite what she was hoping for.

First to address the crowd was Leader Adris. "Dear people of Crim," he greeted, with an air of stern superiority. "We are grateful to see so many of you come to witness the helms of justice. It is crucial to the sanctity of the village that matters of concern be settled through rational judgment, that Dark Menaces are dispelled, and our lives may once again go forth in peace and happiness."

Villagers murmured in agreement.

"This is an unusual situation. You see here a person who has mysteriously entered our village, causing alarm. We will discover the truth and determine the necessary consequences. However, for some inexplicable reason, the girl cannot speak. Therefore, Wise Woman Kess will help with her defense. That being so, to make it impartial, the Wise Woman will now recuse herself from the final judgment."

Brun was surprised. Kess was furious. She had expected Adris to undermine her somehow but did not anticipate that he would overuse his authority in a way that could not be argued publicly. The appearance of unity among adjudicators must be maintained, therefore, Kess acknowledged the leader as she stepped forward. However, she was not smiling and kicked the leg of his chair as she stood to speak.

Kess looked intently into the gathering. She looked every adult in the eye. As their Wise Woman, she was privy to many confidences. They were well aware of what she knew about them. She expected their full attention. Lastly, she looked at Taramae and began. "Dear friends of Crim, I struggle to find the words to tell you about this beautiful young woman, Taramae, without offending the ears of the tenderhearted."

The crowd murmured. Several children were sent away from the Pavilion. The adults stepped in closer. Zaela elbowed the person next to her who had gotten too close.

Kess took a deep breath. "Several months ago, Taramae was here, in this very place, cheerfully helping prepare for the next day's Gathering Festival. Then she suddenly disappeared. When some of her clothing was found by the river, it was told ..." Kess looked in Rauma's direction, then clarified, "It was *believed* that she had drowned. However, it was *not* true. Taramae had been stolen!"

Gasps could be heard throughout the crowd.

"She had been kidnapped!"

More gasps and murmuring. Even Zaela was wide-eyed.

"Yes, kidnapped, by a repulsive man previously trusted in Crim. He took this lovely girl and she was forced to be a slave. She was treated so poorly that she lost her voice. That is why she cannot speak to you today." Kess motioned for Taramae to reveal the mark on her neck.

Some cries were heard. Adris shuddered.

"Taramae cannot speak, but she was brave! Stolen and wronged, she suffered beatings and starvation."

There were more gasps from the crowd.

Kess made the most of the moment. "Yes, beatings, *and* starvation! Yet Taramae did not give up hope that one day she might return home to Crim, to the people she loved, where she could be safe once again. Would you not want your daughters to be so valiant?"

The villagers nodded.

The Wise Woman went on, saying, "However, when she arrived in Crim, she was not greeted with compassion, but with suspicion. Before knowing how she had suffered, or learning of her courage, some claimed that she was a ghost, and feared her presence would bring a curse. She was accused of having a weapon." Kess looked directly at Zaela, who had spread the rumor.

Zaela, seemingly not paying attention, admired her own fingernails.

"But it was not a weapon, was it, Leader Adris?"

"It was not," he verified, though he did not appreciate being called upon as a witness, nor that empathy for Taramae was building.

"Our leader has just confirmed that there was no weapon. Allow me to tell you that it was merely a scroll of leather upon which was written, 'Help me.'"

Cries of "Oh no!" circulated through the gathering.

Kess sadly said, "Now some want to call her a ghost and cast her away in her time of need."

Many villagers gazed at their feet, ashamed.

Adris loudly intervened. "Yes, but how can you be certain that she is *not* a ghost? She may be using trickery to deceive even you, Wise Woman. Two months ago, people began hearing frightening voices in the wind, raising concerns of Dark Menaces. It might have been her. Then she suddenly appeared at our Clearing Festival to destroy the joy of the day. It sounds like the workings of the Vast Vex to me."

Kess scowled at him. "She did not return by the power of the Vast Vex! She returned to the village by hiding in the wagon of the scoundrel who stole her months before—Tarce of Heb!"

Disapproving grumbles spread through the crowd. Many, especially Storekeeper Brun, had seen Tarce that day and noticed him acting more oddly than usual at the Groggery before he hastily left the village.

Next, Kess turned to Banaya. "As for the frightening voices—it seems that children who are desirous to have a sweet treat or a new toy, can be very inventive. They might find a way to convince other children—and a few adults—that shiny pebbles have the power to dispel evil. To make this even more believable, they may enlist the assistance of another child to make distant eerie noises to help with the convincing."

The Wise Woman winked at Banaya. The girl shrugged, embarrassed. Baird slugged her on the arm for telling and stomped out of the Pavilion.

Some in the crowd chuckled. Some felt duped, including Zaela.

"Inventive minds such as these should not be punished but rather be taught how best to use their imaginative skills for the *benefit* of the village."

Leader Adris interrupted again. "You still have not proven that Taramae is not a ghost, and ghosts can be banished."

The Wise Woman looked directly at him and asked, "Can a ghost have a baby?"

"What say?"

"Can a ghost have a baby?" Kess asked, stressing each word.

"Of course not!" Adris huffed.

This was the moment the Wise Woman had been waiting for. She motioned for Taramae to drop the cape. As soon as it fell, the motherhood bump was immediately noticeable. The crowd gasped again.

"Disgusting!" Zaela said and left in a huff.

"We ... uh, we ... will adjourn to discuss this de—development. I mean this ... this situation," Adris stammered. "Tribunal will proceed in one hour. All children are excused from further discussions." He emphatically motioned to Brun and Kess. "Follow me!"

Tribunal was usually swift and decisive. This had never happened before. The villagers did not know what to do. Should they go home? Should they stay? They began to talk amongst themselves. The children ran to play. Some threw their little shiny stones at Banaya before they left. She withstood their pelting fearlessly, smiled at Taramae, and then ran to join them.

Gently, Gart assisted Taramae to step off the Pedestal. "I am so sorry that I dumped you onto the bed. I did not know," he apologized.

She nodded, then rested upon the judgement seat typically reserved for Kess. No one spoke to her.

"This is very unusual, Owl. I hope that nothing is wrong. Taramae appears to be quite weary. Why does no one offer her a drink of water?" Smote mumbled, annoyed.

Once at his home, Leader Adris accused, "A baby? You knew about this!"

"Yes, and I would have told you had you been congenial during our last discussion."

Brun was worried. He was the one who had dealings with Tarce of Heb. It was because of his trading at the storehouse that the merchant was allowed into the village. "And the father?" he asked nervously.

"The father is Jeric."

Adris was totally taken aback by the news. "Jeric? How? He has been gone for months."

"And did he not leave about the same time the girl disappeared?"

"He did," Brun verified. "But Rauma denied their Pairing."

"Yes, and because of her mother's continuing disapproval, they held a secret Pairing Ceremony at the Sacred Stone the morning of the last Gathering Festival."

Adris's mind was racing. He knew that Taramae and his nephew had been friends since childhood but had believed that after their punishments they had no longer associated. Like others, he had assumed that Jeric had merely grown tired of being a Givens keeper and had left the village. Adris was still angry that Jeric's token—a family heirloom—had been removed from his personal treasury. Now he knew why.

"Can she prove the ceremony?" Brun asked, hopeful. A clandestine Pairing would explain many things and make the necessary judgement simpler.

Adris's attention refocused. "Yes, if they had a Pairing, where is Jeric's token?"

Kess frowned. "It was ripped off her neck. Did you not see the scarring? The last time she saw Jeric …" Kess hesitated. "She believes he was killed."

"Killed?" Adris had not considered that possibility. Neither did he look upset. Brun looked away sadly.

Adris paced as he pondered what to do. The laws of Crim had few provisions for instances like this. Perhaps a temporary broadening of the laws might qualify in this event. Otherwise, it would mean expulsion from the village, and now that Kess had successfully solicited sympathy for the girl, it would not be easy to cast her out.

"Neither of you knows how difficult it is to be the leader of this village!" he huffed.

Brun clarified, "That is why we have three Tribunal judges."

"Yes, but I am the one who has to make the difficult, final decisions and there are so many ungrateful people."

"Perhaps recently, now that you have begun collecting taxes."

Disgruntled at Brun, Adris continued, "I have done nothing but maintain order. If we start making exceptions for a pregnant, unmarried girl, where will it end?"

Kess stomped her foot. "Pregnancy is not a disease! Besides that, we are not talking about a stranger. We are talking about a dear girl—married or otherwise—who was born and raised here, carrying your own nephew's child!"

Suddenly Adris' scheming mind churned up a better solution. Few, if any, of the villagers had even read the laws. While unfortunate, it made Tribunal declarations easier. Therefore, Adris knew he would be able to do what he pleased, unchallenged. He almost laughed as he dismissed the Wise Woman, "Leave. We will make our determination."

His unexpected joviality made Kess *very* concerned.

As the villagers assembled once again, Smote observed that the donkey cart had moved to the back of the pavilion, blocking an easy exit. "I do not like it, Owl," he said and prepared to blow the warning horn at the slightest indication of trouble. He could see most of what was happening but could not hear the conversations clearly. Exasperated, he stomped his foot.

Once again Taramae ascended The Pedestal, uncertain of her fate. She was terrified. What would she do if they turned her away? Where would she go?

Leader Adris addressed the crowd. "Dah ye for your patience. We have weighed the evidence and have decided that Taramae of Crim is *not* a ghost. Therefore, she is welcomed back into the village."

Taramae sighed heavily, teetering slightly.

The villagers seemed to approve.

"It is done," Adris declared, with finality. Then, as required at Tribunal's end, he added, "Does anyone deny consent?"

From the back of the Pavilion, Heska of Heb yelled, "I deny consent! I have rights here."

"No!" Taramae cried out in a weak, raspy voice.

His view obstructed, Leader Adris demanded to know, "Who calls this?"

Brun hesitated. "I believe it is Heska, the wife of Tarce."

Adris, who had had past dealings with the woman, pretended not to recognize her. "Come forward, quickly. What is your claim?"

Heska stepped down from the cart and harshly pushed her way through the villagers to get to the judges. Once there, she took an arrogant stance. "I claim PairCompe. The child is *mine*."

Taramae nearly fell off the Pedestal. Gart steadied her.

Wise Woman Kess was adamant. "You have *no* rights here! Tarce inflicted great harm on Taramae, likely with your assistance. However, he is *not* the father of the child."

Leader Adris glared at Taramae. "Is the fathering in dispute?" he demanded to know.

She shook her head decisively, no!

Turning to Heska, Adris announced, "Woman, you have no claim. Return to Heb. Your business is no longer—"

Heska interrupted. "Adris, you idjit! You *cannot* dismiss me so quickly! What he did—taking the girl—Tarce was *paid* to do by *someone* in this village. I will gladly tell the name aloud unless my petition is heard. This information has great worth to someone."

A new wave of speculation flooded the village. Dark Menaces began to arrive.

Impatiently, Brun asked, "What do you want?"

"I told you. I want the child. You can keep the slave—I mean, the girl."

"Impossible!" Kess rebuked. She was at once torn between wanting to do a nit check on the woman before she infected the entire village, and simply yanking the thick, greasy hair out.

"It is not impossible if you do not care to have the details declared publicly this instant. My silence requires the trade of that child," she announced smugly. "My husband is a faithless reprobate, a wandering dog, and a coward. For these reasons he would never have attempted to steal the girl unless he had been paid well to do so. What happened on the way back to Heb, only they know. However, now that there is a child, it belongs to me."

Taramae stood, defiant. Once more, she struggled to speak. "No, no!" she insisted.

Heska sneered, raising her hand as if to strike.

Gart stepped forward protectively.

Leader Adris had had enough. "Heska of Heb, you will leave Crim immediately. You have no claim here."

"I demand PairCompe! It is within your laws. *If a child is born of infidelity, the wronged wife may claim it as compensation.*"

Adris was disgusted. "I know what it says. It is a seldom used provision. No one even remembers why it was put in the charter to begin with."

"You *must* honor it!"

"I *must* not!" Adris retorted. "Your compensation will be to keep your loathsome husband. If ever he dares to come to Crim again, he will be imprisoned."

"I will tell!" Heska promised.

Kess snapped. "Who could trust your words? Taramae is back. That matters most."

"She will not be here long. I have legions at my disposal!"

Adris commanded, "Do as you have been told—leave!"

Gart stood forth, imposing his height above Heska. Taking her by the arm, he pulled her away from the Pavilion to her donkey cart.

Heska was incredulous. No one had ever treated her like this. Most were afraid of her. Fear usually gave her the necessary power to do as she pleased. Her requests had never before been denied. She was flabbergasted that it had happened in lowly Crim, and began screaming, "Adris, this is not over! I will be back. I want that child! I will tell!"

Gart steered her bulkiness up into the donkey cart.

"Let go, nudgebutt! Of all people, you know better than to treat me thus," Heska snarled as she jerked her arm away. The threatening got louder. "Do you hear me? I will be back! I cast the Vast Vex on you all! I cast the Vast Vex on all!"

Heska seized the reins from the escort with the donkey and attempted to whip Gart. When he successfully dodged, she began to hit the guard. "You are a terrible guard—no help at all! You will walk back, idjit!"

The man looked stricken.

"Go!" Gart's deep voice warned them both.

Heska left the village screaming threats as she went. They would be sorry. Many people owed her favors and could be sent to do her bidding.

"That settles the matter," Leader Adris announced. "The woman has no claim. However, as an extra measure of safety for the girl, we will once again require that visitors leave all weapons at the armory upon entering. Brun, notify the gatekeeper."

Taramae smiled. Was Adris capable of compassion?

Adris could not resist the opportunity that now presented itself. His mind twirled with excitement as he added, "As we have affirmed, Taramae is welcomed back into the village. Nevertheless, based on the laws of the village, because there is a child involved, and the child's father is not able to claim it, and the fact that she is quite young, we require that, as a condition of her acceptance, Taramae must have a proper Pairing."

Taramae had not even considered *that* possibility. Her knees buckled.

Kess helped her sit down, protesting, "No! She still needs time to heal, and the baby will be coming."

Adris raised his hand to stifle dissent, "We are not without compassion. Taramae may stay under your care as needed until the child is born. Nevertheless, by the time of the Naming Ceremony she must have a husband."

Taramae covered her face with her hands.

Brun stepped forward quickly and interjected, "However, she may choose the man!"

Adris appreciated neither the interruption nor the clarification. By rights he should have been the only contender. He had no heir and Taramae *was* carrying a child related to him by blood. But for the sake of unity among adjudicators, he could not publicly contradict Brun. Instead, he waved his hand dismissively. "Fine. Tribunal is over. You may leave. Tomorrow, we begin the Clearing Festival anew."

The villagers cheered. Most avoided looking directly at Taramae as Gart walked her through the crowd towards Kess's dwelling. Zaela walked past her and shrugged her shoulder with a snubbing sound.

Taramae held her head up. She had nothing to be ashamed of. She appeared courageous yet was frightened beyond measure, glad for Gart's arm of support, and the haven of the Wise Woman's dwelling. But a Pairing? Taramae shuddered at the thought.

Smote felt hopeful. "The villagers cheered, Owl. That is a good omen, right? But Taramae did not seem happy. Why?"

Chapter 9: The Aftermath

Wise Woman Kess tried to reassure Taramae, as she prepared to leave for her rounds. "Do not despair. We will find a remedy for this problem. Lie down and rest."

But Taramae was not able to rest. Her thoughts swirled as swiftly as the currents of that malevolent river. She fought to keep them out of realms of despair. She had not believed in Dark Menaces as a child, but through a myriad of harsh experiences while growing up she could not deny their existence and certainly did not need bad thoughts to invite them now. She needed to focus on her future and that of her child. She was not surprised that Tribunal had resulted in stipulations for her remaining in the village. After all, her presence raised many questions, and Crim was a place of order. But a mandatory Pairing? It would be hard enough to have a baby without family support. To be required to choose someone for a Pairing within ten days after the birth seemed as cruel as her mother's attempts to barter her off for compensation a year earlier.

Taramae had barely been Paired the first time, had finally been able to be with the man she had loved for so long. How could she replace him with another? But what else could she do? Even if she could leave, where would she go? Heb was out of the question. She would not be safe there. Jeric had lived among the Peaks People, but she knew no one there. They might not welcome her either.

Dark Menaces began to creep upon her. Jeric! Jeric! her heart cried out. A whimper came forth. It stirred determination. She must have a voice to appeal for more time before Tribunal. She had to be able to say more than *no*. Taramae tried all afternoon to utter other words. The strain hurt terribly. "SkyFa, please help me," she prayed.

Kess was exhausted. However, completing her Wise Woman duties was a necessity. She tried to be as cheerful as possible, but everywhere she went someone talked about the Tribunal. It delayed her arrival at the Tower, making her more anxious. Smote also wanted to fully understand what he had seen from a distance.

Once more, Kess rehearsed the details. Like everyone else, Smote was surprised to learn about Taramae's child, but was bothered more that she was judged harshly. "What do you mean, she must have a Pairing or leave the village?" he asked, bewildered.

"It is what was determined. For the order of the village and the future of the child, she must choose shortly after the child is born. I argued against it, but Leader Adris would not listen. At least she may choose for herself."

"What of the baby's father?"

Kess paused. "She believes her husband is dead. She witnessed his demise. Her heart is broken, but she has been courageous."

Smote was worried. If they were so prejudiced against one of their own, how might they treat him one day? "She escaped to return home but is still not free?" he asked.

Kess began applying ointment to his sores. "There are a few good men in Crim. It may yet work for the Great Good."

Smote despaired. "What I told you of her arrival in the wagon did no good!"

"It did! It was very important. It helped me tell her story. Dah ye, Smote!"

"And what of the woman with the donkey? Her actions seemed suspicious and she was yelling about something."

After his reaction to the judgement, the Wise Woman did not dare tell the truth about Heska's demands. Further upsets might cause a decline in his health. "She is a lunatic who wanders into the village at times. It was best to insist that she leave." It was not a complete lie and was quite necessary, Kess believed.

By the time she was finished for the day, Kess staggered homeward. "Mizzafrizzaritz!" she groaned, hoping to have a soothing drink, and then go to bed. That wish would be delayed.

A large shadow loomed outside her door. Unsure, she slowed her pace until she could see more clearly. Regretting that she did not have a cane handy, she determined that she would swing the lantern and scream if necessary.

The shadow moved towards her. Kess caught her breath and prepared to swing boldly.

"I waited, to be certain she was safe," a deep voice said.

"Oh, Gart!" she sighed. "So kind of you. Truly kind. You may go home."

"No, I must go to work now," he said, and headed in the direction of the Groggery.

Taramae sat at the table inside. She smiled as the Wise Woman entered. A cushion had been placed on Kess's favorite chair. As she approached, Taramae lifted the pot and asked, in a triumphant, yet pain-filled voice, "T—tea?"

Chapter 10: The Tyro

Taramae did not attend the resumed Clearing Festival. She could hear celebratory noises outside, however, drained emotionally as much as physically, she had no desire to face renewed scrutiny nor cause uneasiness to the villagers. Instead, Banaya brought wildflowers to adorn Taramae's jaggedly cut hair.

She struggled to speak. "Dah ye! St—stellaria is fave … fave …"

"Favorite," Banaya helped finish, then promised. "Someday we will pick them together," She understood the needed caution. Everyone knew of the threats made by the horrible woman from Heb.

Taramae braided Banaya's chaotic, curly hair and shared some of the flowers. As they looked into the mirror together, a delighted Banaya beamed, "I must show my friends. But fear not, you are my most-friend!" She hugged Taramae tightly and gleefully ran out to play.

After Banaya left, Taramae peered into the mirror once more. It was the first time in months that she had considered her appearance with more than a passing glance. Her once-lively eyes were dull from distress, the skin on her face was chapped, and since the day that her then-lustrous braids were sawed off by Heska with a carving knife, Taramae hadn't paid much attention to her hair. It was too upsetting. Now, as she looked in the mirror, dismay filled her soul. No wonder the villagers viewed her as an apparition from Under Earth! In that moment, Taramae decided not to go out into the village ever again. She would spend her days in seclusion until the baby came, then raise her child away from everyone. She was sad. She was mad. Despair began to overwhelm her. Dark Menaces began creeping in.

She spotted her old dress in the burn bin by the fireplace. It was a repulsive reminder of her previous plight. Angrily she began to tear it into shreds. It felt good to see the torn fabric fall into pieces at her feet. When she had finished, she gathered the scraps and was about to throw them into the fire, when another hearthside memory came to her.

For special occasions when she was a child, her mother had rolled and tied her lovely hair in bits of cloth before bedtime so it might be curled. Could it be done now? Did she remember how? She looked again in the mirror at the uneven lengths of hair, then washed the longest strips of cloth and hung them up to dry. The other snips and strings she thrust into the fire with great satisfaction. Her skin would still take time and salves to heal, but if there could be a change to her hair, it would truly lift her spirits. With that, the sparkle in her eyes might return. There was no guarantee for any of it, but it was worth a try.

Word came from Gart that two suspicious-acting drinkers had been asking questions regarding her whereabouts at the Groggery. He had invited them to leave the village by the scruffs of their necks. Caution needed to be taken.

Within a few days, a routine was established. Every morning, Taramae combed her slightly curly hair and encouragingly gazed into the mirror. As she braided Banaya's hair, she practiced her fragmented speech.

In the afternoons, Gart watched from afar as Taramae accompanied Wise Woman Kess on visits to the afflicted or needy. What she had done to merit his protection, Taramae did not know but was glad of it.

On her first visit to Old Soul Nadee, she was met with loving arms. Cupping Taramae's face in her hands, Nadee exclaimed, "Thanks be to SkyFa—you live! It was awful when I heard otherwise."

"Good be back," was Taramae's breathy reply.

"And look at you!" Nadee gently touched Taramae's abdomen in several places. "Hmm," she mused, "this child is quite small. You need to eat more." Turning to Kess, Nadee advised, "She needs to eat more."

Kess knew it was best to graciously accept the advice of the one who had taught her, even when it was obvious. "She is getting used to eating again and will gradually improve, I am sure."

"Very good. Very good," Nadee approved.

"Baby be strong." Taramae said proudly. "Be strong like fa—" Taramae stopped short of saying *father*. She realized that doing so might cause their old friend more grief.

Nadee took both of Taramae's hands in hers, and spoke emotionally. "Never be afraid to speak of our dear Jeric. We have wonderful memories to share. You may come speak to me of him anytime."

Taramae was grateful. "S-someday tell s-stories to b-babe."

"Yes, there are scores of family stories to be told. They should be written down before I pass. Will you assist me?"

Taramae smiled but hesitated to promise. Only Kess knew why. Taramae had limited writing skills. After the Wild River verdict, Rauma had pulled her out of school to toil at the inn.

As they walked to their next appointment. Kess offered, "Perhaps we can record her stories together. You have a good memory of what has been told, and I have a suitable pen."

"Dah ye," Taramae replied softly.

At first other villagers grudgingly accepted Taramae. But soon her cheerful demeanor put them at ease. Taramae loved the visits. It gave her the sense of being the Wise Woman's apprentice that she had longed for as a child.

Taramae visited with another of her childhood friends, Molay, twice. When alone, Molay seemed pleased to see her and they talked of their babies with expectant joy. It was the first time Taramae had to ponder the forthcoming event with happiness. For months there had been only grief and the need for safeguarding. Reestablishing the relationship with Molay greatly improved Taramae's morale.

However, they arrived on the third visit as Nawhi and Zaela were leaving and Molay's husband, Asa, stood in the doorway, arms folded. Clearly Taramae's presence was not welcome. She excused herself, "I speak Nawhi. Will wait out."

The Wise Woman agreed.

"Are you well?" Nawhi asked.

"Voice g-gets b-better," Taramae answered. "C-come visit me?"

Zaela was aghast. "We will *not* be coming to visit! Nawhi, I cannot believe you are even speaking with this *person*!"

"She is our friend," Nawhi confirmed.

"She is not *my* friend! She has dishonored the village! We do not want to be seen with—"

Gart stepped forth from the shadows and placed his hand firmly on Zaela's shoulder. "Say no more," he warned.

Zaela spun around to face him. "Why do you follow her, Gart? She is damaged. Look at her—sickly, with child, and her hair is dreadful. Why does she wear flowers in it?" Zaela smirked. "Is she a princess? Yes, perhaps the princess of wretchedness!"

Gart held his finger up close to her face. "Stop, now!"

"I will not stop! Why do you defend her? You may not care what people say, but I do!"

"What will people say of *you*?" he asked and swooped her up into his arms carrying the loudly protesting young woman across the courtyard to the doorway of the storehouse.

Taramae and Nawhi laughed. They were not the only ones.

Gart carefully set Zaela on the ground. She made several more disparaging remarks regarding his size and character. When he smiled at her in response, it made her angrier.

Her father came outside. "What is all the noise? I am trying to run a business here!" he demanded to know.

Zaela made her accusation. "This giant carried me home like a child. I did nothing wrong. I told the truth about Taramae. She is a disgrace! Many have said so. At least I had the courage to say it to her face. This—this lunkish brute told me to be quiet and when I would not, he carried me home like a child. Like a child! People are laughing. I am humiliated! He must go before Tribunal!"

Brun quickly discerned the situation. "Zaela, go inside!"

She shook her finger at Gart. "I will be avenged! My father will see that you go before Tribunal." She stomped on his foot, and stormed off, slamming the door behind her.

Brun looked sternly at Gart for a moment and, when he was certain Zaela was not watching, he patted the young man on the shoulder. "Dah ye," he said, and returned to his business.

As soon as Kess came out of Molay's residence, Nawhi seemed in a hurry to get away. She excused herself, saying, "I must go. Zaela throws things when she is angry. We cannot let her destroy the storehouse."

"W-will visit?" Taramae asked.

Nawhi nervously bit her lower lip. "I will try."

Nawhi's reaction made Taramae doubt that any visit would be made. How she had missed their childhood friendship! The two girls had had many wonderful adventures, like picking flowers, making muddy messes by the drippy side of the well, and confusing her little sister by pretending to be invisible. They comforted each other when Nawhi's mother and then Taramae's father died. They sang silly songs, whispered secrets about which boy their hearts were drawn to, ran with other friends out in the gardens, ate apples, and threw mushy fruit at each other.

Then one day, almost beyond all understanding, that terrible accident happened at the river and they were not allowed to spend time together as their grieving needed. But their friendship never died.

As Nawhi walked away, Taramae worried about how worn down she appeared. Nawhi was just as lovely as Zaela but her confidence, which had waned over the years, seemed to have withered further in the last few months. Perhaps overseeing Zaela's antics was too much to bear.

Going to care for others gave Taramae a sense of purpose. However, one part of their routine seemed peculiar. Whenever it was time to visit the Tower, Kess made an excuse to go alone. After the third time, Taramae began asking questions. "Why g-go alone T-Tower?"

Kess hesitated. "The stairs are steep, in bad repair, and the way is dark and drafty. It would be stressful, possibly even dangerous for you."

Taramae was not convinced and pressed for information. "Person is m-man?"

"Yes. Therefore, it may also be inappropriate for you to go."

Taramae was irritated. "Worked around m-men at inn. Why not do this?"

"Your health was better then and you will improve."

"He will n—not improve? What ails?"

Again, Kess seemed uneasy. "He is healing from terrible injuries."

"How you help?"

"I take extra food and apply ointments to his head and back."

"You heal m—many, yet this one n—not be well?"

"The outcome is uncertain." Then Kess scolded, "Taramae, quit pestering me about it. I will care for him. It is for the best. Leave it be. There is no reason to overtire yourself."

Chapter 11: Cobwebs

Two days later, in the early hours, there came a pounding on the door, nearly knocking it off the hinges.

"Who is there?" Kess called out, alarmed.

Taramae stood behind her, brandishing a cane.

"It is Asa!" the gruff voice answered. Another double thud shook the door.

Kess swiftly opened. "Stop, Asa, before you break my door down! What is needed?"

Asa began ordering the Wise Woman around. "Molay needs you. It is her time. She cries. You must come—now!"

"I will get my things."

"No. Come—now!" he demanded and made a grab for her arm.

Kess dodged his impatient grasp. "I must dress and gather supplies. Do you want me to help your wife?"

"Yes, you must hurry!"

"I will, but first, run around the Pavilion three times. It will bring fair fortune for the birth. Then bring two buckets of fresh water from the well to your dwelling one at a time, so as not to spill any. Can you do that?"

"Yes."

"Then go. Go! I will be there before your task is complete."

Asa ran toward the Pavilion.

Taramae helped Kess assemble the necessary items. She had never heard of fair fortune and was perplexed by Asa's assigned tasks. Finally, she asked, "Why send for run and water?"

Kess laughed and shrugged. "It will keep him busy while I prepare. I did not need him dragging me out by the braids. It takes a while for a first baby to be welcomed into the world. I know we have time. If I am gone long, please take the new broth and the brown bread to Nadee. Be sure to stir from the bottom of the pot to get some of the meat for her and see if the gatekeeper's hand is healing. Poor man keeps getting slivers."

"W-will do. Tell M-Molay, h-heart with her."

The Wise Woman nodded. "Will do."

When Kess had not returned from Molay's delivery by midday, Taramae was worried. Poor Molay! Poor Kess! They must be exhausted! Taramae felt powerless to assist them. The Vast Vex began to creep in when she imagined herself in that future situation. Staying busy helped to push the negative feelings aside. "SkyFa, please help them. SkyFa, please help them," she repeated as she smoothed her hair, filled the baskets, and went out on needed rounds.

She took the broth and bread to Old Soul Nadee, put clean linens on her bed, and listened as she told another story of earlier times. The sweet woman was pleased to have company and spending time there lifted Taramae's spirits as well.

Next, she took another sliver from the gatekeeper's hand and dressed the drainage from the previous one. His reaction was rather perplexing. Though he appeared grateful for the relief, he seemed disappointed that it was she and not Kess who had come to his aid. Taramae wondered if he had been using the hand injuries to get the Wise Woman's attention all along.

Those tasks accomplished, Taramae was about to go home, when she looked up and saw movement cross the open window of the Tower. She paused, walked a few more steps, and glanced up. She saw it again. Was he watching her? Shivers ran down her spine. She started quickly toward Kess's cottage when a different thought occurred. What if the man was in distress? If so, waiting for Kess would be miserable for him, poor fellow.

Taramae scolded herself, "Are you a tyro or a coward? You ought to see if the man needs help. Kess may not approve but will be quite fatigued and might appreciate having all the errands completed." Infused with bravery, Taramae decided to go.

The Tower had not been used for years. The need for a sentinel had ended with the truce after the Givens War. Why would someone with severe injuries be housed there? It was not an easily accessible accommodation. If there were safety concerns, why was he not being kept in the holding center? Wiser minds than hers had determined the necessity of using the Tower instead, but it made no sense to her.

Taramae hesitated before opening the first door. Kess warned that it was frightening. But hadn't she just been through the most frightening time of her life in Heb and survived? How could this be worse than that? Taramae took a deep breath, found the key to the outside door, and stepped inside.

It did not look as bad as she had imagined, according to Kess's description. It was eerily dim except for a small window at the top of the stairs letting in a sliver of sunshine. The stairs were not as steep or as rickety as she had been told. Even in her condition, it was easy to ascend to the second level, yet she had to be wary. The musty dampness made the steps slick and each of her footsteps slid slightly.

Ancient cobwebs waved frayed fingers at her with every slight breeze. Taramae brushed one away that clung to her frock. "Even s—spiders had sense to l—leave this place," she murmured. Her words became a ghostly echo, *"This place … this place …"*

Was this why Kess was so determined to keep her away? Or were the injuries of the man inside so alarming that Kess feared seeing such might prove traumatic? What would she do if the man was in horrific condition? Taramae braced herself for the worst. "N—no matter what, be s—strong," she whispered and timidly tapped on the door at the top of the stairs.

The echo came again, *"S—strong … S—strong…"*

Smote was at his post by the window when he heard the door. "Come in, Mother Kess," he called out.

A wave of afternoon sun illuminated the doorway as it opened, Smote was surprised to see that instead of the Wise Woman, it was a girl—the girl from the Pavilion incident. She held her hand up to block the sun and squinted to see him clearly.

"Hello," Taramae began, breathlessly cheerful, trying to calm her shaky voice. "W-wise Woman not c-come." She giggled upon seeing an unusual drawing on the table. She moved it aside to set the basket down. "Hope no b-bother," she said, shielding her eyes once more.

"It is no bother. It is nice to have other guests. I watch people all day long from my window, but few have visited here."

Taramae froze. The voice sounded familiar—*very* familiar. Her mind reeled with thoughts of the impossible. She pushed them aside. Was she dreaming? Was she delusional? Taramae did not turn, but instead, tilted her head, listening more intently, and asked, "How feel today?"

"I am somewhat better, but quite hungry. First Meal was late again, and less than needed. My stomach still grumbles. Oh, I am sorry! I should not complain," Smote apologized. He walked toward the center of the room to block the sun for her.

Taramae gasped. How could this be? When Smote was within arm's reach, she finally turned toward him. She looked up at him. She looked down. She blinked several times, looked up again.

"Are you alright, Taramae?"

Chills ran down her spine when he said her name. She gazed, mesmerized at his face, as though visually sorting pieces of a puzzle. The visage was almost unrecognizable, but the voice was unmistakable! She rushed forward, fully embracing him. "My love, it *is* you! It *is* you! I knew voice! I knew voice!" She began to sob, her head against his chest.

Smote did not mind the feeling. It had been a long time since he had been embraced in such a way. He did not actually remember how long—but it was not unpleasant. He patted her on the back. What else could he do? Obviously, she needed comfort. He supposed she was expressing gratitude for the information he had supplied for her case before Tribunal. "You are welcome," he said. "My name is Smote. It was an honor to assist in your defense."

Arms still around him, Taramae looked up at him quizzically. "What say?"

Even with tears streaming down her pale, scratched face she was a beautiful girl. He wondered if she did not hear the first time, so he repeated louder. "My name is Smote. It was an honor to assist in your defense."

Again, his guest seemed confused. "S—Smote?"

"Yes. And you are Taramae."

Her face brightened. Her arms tightened to hug him once more.

"The Wise Woman told me your name."

Taramae stopped. "She *t-told* you?"

"Yes. I am new to Crim. I have been the Watcher for a while, and saw you get out of the snake wagon when you came into the village. I told Mother Kess—that is what I call her—and she mentioned that it helped at Tribunal."

Taramae gazed into his face for several seconds. Was he teasing? Jeric had been known to do so at times. When there was no hint of jest, Taramae suddenly pulled back, embarrassed. She stood, barely breathing. She looked at the floor swaying slightly, then wiped her face on her sleeve and walked away. She began placing items from the basket onto the table. Through sniffles, she inquired, "How c-come to Crim?"

"They found me by the water. My ship must have been lost at sea."

"Ship?" Taramae considered his statement. No ship ever came near Crim. The currents were treacherous and the boulders imposing. Jeric would have known that. Smote, however, did not. More evidence that the man before her did not know who he was, let alone know who she was. To him, she was a stranger. She wanted to pull her hair out and scream, but it would bring unwanted attention from villagers. She bit her lower lip as it quivered.

Smote mistook her emotion for concern regarding his welfare. "Do not worry. The Wise Woman provides good care for me. Is she ill?"

"What s-say?"

"Is the Wise Woman ill? She usually attends to me."

"No, helps b-birth."

Smote glanced at her motherhood bump. "It must bring you comfort knowing she is here for such times."

Suddenly self-conscious of her condition, Taramae answered. "Yes, will need in w-weeks. Today mother is Molay." She said the name of their longtime friend slowly and watched for his response.

"Molay." Smote considered it briefly. "Hmm, I have not met her. I have had few guests." Suddenly, Smote remembered his shocking appearance and turned away. "So sorry—so sorry," he apologized. "I forgot how horrible I look!"

Taramae *was* fully disheartened by his appearance, but smiled the best she could, and lied. "N—not so bad. Please, c-come sit. I h-help you."

Usually when Smote's left foot dragged as he walked, he dealt with it. However, around this pretty young woman, he felt embarrassed. He could not control the foot, so he quipped. "If I was a dancer in my past life, I will need to find a new occupation."

She was dismayed by the joke but suppressed her sadness. "P-Past life?" she asked, as she applied the ointment the way the Wise Woman had taught her.

Her touch was soft, almost caressing. Smote did not mind at all. "Yes. I am someone from somewhere, but illness has stolen my real self. Now I am merely Smote."

When the girl paused, sniffling, he quickly changed the subject. "Will you please answer a question for me?"

Her voice was clogged with emotion. "W-will try."

"What is a Clearing Festival?"

Taramae glanced to see if he was serious, then answered. "Old time tra— tradition. Givens herd c-cleared from village. Take to s—summer fields."

"There was a herd in the village? That would be messy!"

"That c-cleared too. Taken to gardens. Then celebrate."

"I see no herd."

"Before, where N—New Side dwells are now. Out of village n—now." She prepared the basket to leave.

Smote tried to think of another reason to persuade her to stay longer. "May I ask you another question?"

"Yes."

"What is a Given?"

Taramae searched for words, then picked up Smote's amusing animal drawing. It was of a short, stout, furry creature with tall, curving horns and thin, tapering legs. She giggled at the words scrawled underneath and handed him the drawing. "Is Given."

Smote was baffled. "How strange! I saw that animal in a dream. It is a real thing?"

"A m-memory?" she asked, hopefully.

As Smote pondered, a look of pain crossed his face. He shook his head no. "Mother Kess says those lines are words. What do they say?"

Taramae could not help laughing. "It s-says, *they stink*."

Smote laughed aloud, "*Do* they stink?"

Taramae nodded, and they laughed together. She loved that sound, had missed it terribly. She hoped the lighthearted moment might bring back a remembrance of their times together. When it was apparent that it had not, she sadly said, "I must go."

Smote followed her to the door. "Being the Watcher is a wearisome task. These walls must tire of my mumblings. It is nice to speak with others. Will you return?"

She nodded and left. Covering her mouth with one hand did not muffle her anguished sobs as she slowly descended the slick stairs.

When Smote heard the echoes, he chastised himself. "You ugly smudge! You scared her away! Too talky. Too pushy. Mizzafrizzaritz!" he cussed, borrowing the Wise Woman's favorite expression. He walked to the window in time to see Taramae running awkwardly away. When it looked as if she might fall, the young man from the Groggery stopped her, took her arm for support, and walked the rest of the way with her.

"She will not return, Owl," Smote said, dejectedly. "She will not return."

Chapter 12: Hard Truth

It was nearly dark when Kess rushed to her dwelling to collect items for a quick visit to Smote.

"You may go home, Gart," she said, as she reached her door. "Dah ye for watching over her but I am sure Taramae is safe."

Gart shook his head no. "She cries on and on."

"Why? Did someone upset her?"

"No. She helped people and has been crying ever since."

"Helped people? Oh, Taramae must have completed my rounds. How nice of her. But why would that upset ..." Kess was immediately concerned. "Did she go to the Tower?"

"Yes."

"Again, dah ye, Gart. I will take care of her. Please go." Kess rushed to shut the door behind her. Jars of ointments and potions were scattered across the table where Taramae had hastily dropped the basket. She lay curled up on the bed, moaning.

"Where are you hurting?"

Taramae indicated her lower abdomen.

"No, no, no—too soon! Too soon!" She hurried to brew some raspberry tea.

Taramae groaned between swallows, then she suddenly accused, "Why n—not tell?"

"Tell?" Kess evaded. "Not tell what? I am not sure—"

"Stop!" Taramae loudly demanded, wincing with every accentuated word. "I WANT TRUTH! JERIC ALIVE! WHY NOT TELL? You like mother to me, now betray! I should leave." She swung her legs off the bed and attempted to stand.

"No, no, you must not leave. You must not! Please lie back down!" Kess cried out, as she caught Taramae's arm to keep the dizzy, groaning girl from falling.

As Taramae melted down in pain, she asked, in anguish, "WHY n— not tell, JERIC ALIVE?"

The weight of carrying entangled secrets crashed upon Kess, dissolving her last ounce of strength. She sat down on the bed. "*Jeric* is *not* alive," she whispered. "*Smote* is alive."

Taramae wailed, "He n—not know me!"

"He does not know anyone."

"His face, his b-beautiful face, g-gone! Poor, hurt b-body!"

"He has suffered much. The river tossed him over many rocks. He was barely alive when found. We have been caring for him the best we can."

"*WE?* Who *we?*"

"We can talk about it another time.

"*WHO WE?*" Taramae demanded to know.

Kess relented, "Only me, Brun, and Nawhi."

"Nawhi? Nawhi! Why she n—not *tell* me? My friend, n--not friend? Another betray!"

"Please stop saying that! No one has betrayed you. I have constantly defended you and did not want to add another disappointment to your troubles!"

Taramae's grieving continued, "He not know me! My love n—not know me! My heart b—b breaks!" She grabbed Kess's sleeve. "Make him r—remember me!"

Kess pulled her hand away gently and held it as she explained. "He *has* tried to remember, and he would try harder if we pushed him. But the added distress would be too much! Will you put *his* health at risk for your own sake?"

"I love him! I n*eed* him! N—Never hurt him!"

"You would not intend to, but it *would* happen. It is too much for his mind to bear! It is better that he exists as who he *is*, rather than run mad with grief over who he *was*, and what he has lost." Not sure that Taramae was convinced, Kess added, "And what of his safety?"

Taramae thought of how thoroughly locked away Smote was. "Not safe?"

"You heard Heska. Someone *paid* Tarce to steal you. If that person knows Jeric—I mean Smote—is alive, they might fear he could identify them, and harm him again. He was nearly killed the first time. Few people know who the Watcher is, not even Adris. It is best."

Taramae had not considered that. She rocked with discomfort and searched her mind to make sense of the happenings of the day. Jeric was alive. She had touched him, held him, heard his heart beating. An incredible dream had almost come true. For a moment she had felt tremendous relief. However, he had not returned her embrace. His comfort was that of a stranger.

Taramae's voice grew hoarse with each weeping word, as she asked, "What to d—do? What to d—do? Child has father, but n—no father. Taramae has husband, but n—no husband. N—Need Pair to stay. But still Paired. What to d—do?"

"First, you will rest and keep this baby from coming early. Then we will decide what must be done. It may yet turn out for the Great Good," the Wise Woman encouraged, wiping tears of her own.

Taramae was too exhausted to argue. Her body rebelled with shock and sorrow. It had taken years of planning to manage the Pairing with Jeric. They had been so careful not to show any interest or affection that might incur her mother's wrath or further interference. They had obeyed all the laws of the village, until they were finally able to pledge their love and make the commitment. Now she was supposed to forget all of that and find another man?

The child within her kicked harshly. Taramae pondered between spasms that even he knew this was all wrong. When at last too tired to cry another tear, she curled up on her side, one arm holding her stomach. As she drifted off, she caringly enquired, "How Molay?"

"Sore, but fine. Delivered a baby girl—petite and sweet like her momma. Asa could hold her in one hand."

Taramae smiled, imagining Asa's surprise. He had requested a big, burly boy, like himself. "Good for Molay!" As she giggled, Taramae's own baby moved sharply, bringing her back to the moment. She groaned in pain even after she fell asleep.

Kess picked the basket up off the table and put it in its usual place on the side cupboard. Once again, she had promised results she could not guarantee. Besides that, three Pairing Proposals had arrived for Taramae's consideration. Kess did not have the heart to tell her. A scroll of intent was attached to each one. Kess sat down, exhausted, she could not resist discovering who they were from.

One was from Ori, the Groggery keeper. The penning was sweet and childish, likely written with assistance from Banaya. Or perhaps, written *by* Banaya. Did her father even know about it? The second scroll was from Leader Adris. It was *not* a surprise. The direction his judgment had taken at Tribunal made it obvious that he had a personal motive for requiring Taramae to select a husband. If she wanted wealth and power, Adris was the logical choice, regardless of the age difference, though Kess doubted that anyone who married that infuriating man would *ever* be happy. She would not wish him on a stinkbug, let alone a friend. Nevertheless, the option had to be presented. Kess unrolled the last scroll.

It simply read—Gart. "Not Gart!" she groaned, then hushed to keep Taramae from waking. It was not that Gart would be the worst choice. He was more Taramae's age than the others, strong, caring, and hardworking but that was really all that was known about him. He had arrived in the village a few months earlier and had immediately gone to work for the ailing Old Sleff at the Groggery, keeping the peace when the ale flowed too strongly. His size and ability with a short sword made him a welcome addition to village security. He lived at Rauma's inn, had few possessions, and had proven trustworthy. That had to count for something. But how could he not support a wife and child?

The best choice was the most impossible—Jeric. However, Jeric was no longer Jeric and Smote had the least to offer of anyone. Who knew what he might become once he fully healed—if ever. It would be unwise for Taramae to gamble on her future—and that of her child. But how could Taramae let go if there was even the tiniest thread of hope? There were many possible regrets. There had to be a better choice, but at the moment,

Kess's drained brain could not find the path to it. "Mizzafrizzaritz!" she grumbled, checked on Taramae once more, tacked a warning sign onto her door, and went to bed.

The sign on the door read: *No Guests Allowed!*

"Surely, they cannot mean me!" Adris fumed, as he knocked loudly and attempted to turn the door handle.

Gart was about to stop him when Kess came outside, wrapping a shawl around her night clothes. "SHH! *NO ONE* may enter!" she whispered, firmly. "She needs *complete* rest. The baby almost came early. It was very bad! The girl must be left in peace if she and child are to survive."

Adris protested loudly. "I need to see her! I must speak with her."

Kess pushed her stern finger into his shoulder and shushed him more emphatically. "She needs you LEAST of all! GO away NOW!"

"She has not answered my offer."

The withering look that Kess gave him nearly melted the crooked whiskers off his chin. Adris stepped back. Perhaps this *was* serious. He became alarmed. Without a baby, his strategy to obtain an heir related by blood would be thwarted, and Taramae would not be desperate for a Pairing. He understood the Wise Woman's caution; still, as leader, he could not bear being denied entrance wherever he chose. So, sounding as official as possible, Adris spouted, "She must respond within seven days. It is the custom!"

Kess's glance sent daggers as she shut the door.

After Adris left, Gart tapped softly on the door.

"I said, NO guests!" Kess reiterated, as she swung open the door. Her demeanor softened when she saw it was only him. "You do not need to wait outside, Gart. I do not know how long the healing will take."

"I just wanted to ask if you need anything?" he whispered.

"No. Dah ye, Gart. Go home and rest."

Gart nodded but stayed a while longer which was for the best. He stopped Rauma from barging in. She had heard a rumor about Taramae and was more curious than concerned. When Gart insisted that no one was to go in until the Wise Woman said so, Rauma stared at him. He had been staying at the inn for months, and this was the first time she had seen him less than cordial. Now the serious dark eyes, the firmness of stance, the proud way of holding his shoulders reminded her of someone, though she could not quite place whom. She went away wondering if it was someone from Crim or from her past in Heb.

Gart caught Banaya as she was ready to knock and shook his head. She was terribly upset when she was not allowed to see Taramae. She was about to circle her face and touch her nose when he gently explained that Taramae was having serious problems and needed peace and quiet—even from friends. It was a distressing reminder of what had happened before her mother died. Banaya felt she had to do something.

Walking a short distance outside the gate, she picked the prettiest flower that she could find and took it to the Sacred Stone. Holding it against her heart, Banaya pleaded, "SkyFa, Taramae needs you," and placed the flower on the earth in front of the shrine. She was not sure if she believed in SkyFa. Her mother had, and it had not helped. But Taramae believed it, so it might work this time.

On the way back through the gates, an inspiration came over her. Running door to door, she told villagers that Taramae needed their support in whatever way they could give it. Throughout the day more flower tributes were left at the Sacred Stone, and little gifts accumulated outside the Wise Woman's dwelling. Though some villagers still felt uncomfortable around Taramae, certainly no one wanted her or her child to die.

Chapter 13: Uncovering Courage

For three days, Taramae lay in bed, afraid to move. Barely eating, drinking special teas, and rising only if absolutely necessary. Every twinge of pain caused her to worry. To make matters worse, there had been no recent movement from the baby. She *could not* lose this baby! There was still six weeks to go. The more she thought of the consequences, the more her heart raced, making her very tired. She was grateful that the Wise Woman was keeping others away. She did not need witnesses to her despair.

Dark Menaces plagued Taramae. She thought of Jeric becoming Smote and wept. She thought of the deaths of her father and little brother Aven and wept. She had never been allowed to fully grieve their loss. She thought of her mother's stinging rejections, the blame foisted upon her as a child, and the aching loneliness she had suffered.

She remembered the day when Jeric had been sent away to be a Givens keeper, which meant that she would see him only twice a year from then on, in brief, stolen moments.

"You will forget me," he had mourned, during their last moments together.

"Never!" she had promised as she gave him a small wooden owl, one of seven hand-carved gifts from her father. "He does not speak but he is a good listener."

"Good riddance!" her mother hissed, after he had gone. "I told you long ago, you will never be Paired with that boy. Perhaps a Givens stampede will dispense with him."

Stunned, Taramae had asked, "Did you arrange this as my punishment for losing Aven?"

"I do not wield the power in Crim. But I do not disagree. Now that I have the inn, you will have no time for frivolity nor melancholy."

For these memories and more, Taramae wept. She wrapped her arms around her middle and pleaded with SkyFa that the tiny one not be born too soon.

It had taken so much effort for Jeric and her to keep their Pairing a secret. The waiting, the notes, the slight touching of hands in passing. Then, when she was finally of age and on a morning when her mother would be sleeping off heavy celebrating, they had met at the Sacred Stone and exchanged Jeric's clan token. Their two days of tender time together had been so precious, finally to kiss and embrace. Taramae sighed.

Their plan to run away to the mountains was only foiled when Jeric sneaked back into Crim to retrieve something. If only they had been together when Tarce came to steal her away. Jeric would still be alive. Depleted of tears, Taramae slept. She lay motionless, barely breathing. The Wise Woman did not attempt to wake her.

On the fourth day, as Taramae was rousing awake, a firm, calm voice came into her mind, "Save your tears for the joy that is to come." Taramae was confused until she heard it again and recognized it as that of her second rescuer.

She still marveled at the providence of her escape. Before Heska was to leave for the mineral baths for two days, there was a screaming fight with Tarce and she hit him many times. After she left, Tarce planned to kill Taramae to ruin Heska's plan to obtain a child. He was threatening to dump her off the cliff at Plateau Falls when the first of two tender mercies occurred. A tradesman who rarely came to Heb for supplies just happened to come that day. Suddenly the door to the wood closet that she was locked in at night was flung open.

"I told you, she is a rare find, light hair and eyes, of sturdy stock from Crim. Just for today, because you are a special customer, I will sell her cheap! She knows how to work and will not be with child much longer. If that is a problem, you can get rid of it."

The man seemed appalled at the sight of her but said he would think about it and offered to buy drinks of Heb grog and return for his purchased goods later. Early the next morning, while Tarce slept off drunkenness, the man returned, and unlocked the wood closet. He whispered that he would be passing by the Crossing, halfway to Crim, and offered to take her that far if she wanted to go. He did not smell of grog nor feel unsafe. It was a split-second, possibly unwise decision, but she was in definite danger if she stayed. Once a safe distance away, she had tried to thank him, but not having spoken in months, there was no voice.

The man, however, nervously talked all along on the way. His was the span keeper at the stone bridge for the Peaks People. He had not been to Heb for three years, but the day before had suddenly felt inclined to go. Perhaps it was for the Great Good, he said, and apologized that he could not take her farther. He had to return to his post at the bridge. He left her by a grove of trees near the Crossing with a flask of water and a small blanket. She hid in the trees and planned to begin walking the next day but huddling in the darkness was more frightening than she had imagined. She cried and prayed as she shivered, waiting for the dawn. Then came the second tender mercy.

A man with long white hair suddenly appeared nearby and beckoned to her, saying, "Save your tears for the joy that is to come. If you desire to return home, come now. Tarce is looking for you but has gone with a tent woman for the night. You must come now."

Taramae had feared recapture more than anything. Still, there was something different about this man. His countenance was kind. He held out his hand. "Please do as I say," he advised, as he gave her bread and led her toward Tarce's wagon.

Horrified, she pulled away, looking around to see if Tarce was hiding somewhere, ready to pounce on her. In whispers, the mystical gentleman reassured her that all would be well as he helped her into the wagon to hide under some fur pelts, and then he was gone.

"Save your tears for the joy that is to come," he had said.

Taramae tumbled the thought about in her mind once again. How could tears be for joy? And how could she find joy amidst such tragedy? She was about to renew her lamentations when a new thought, a wave of fortitude, came into her mind and lifted her spirits. For months, in an act of defiance for being denied any display of emotion, she had found comfort in the dark nights by singing *the Hope Song* in her mind. *Loo, aloo, loo, little child, the hope of Mother's love, loo, aloo, loo little child, so full of Heaven's charms. May you in safety rest, under my heart be blessed, loo, aloo, loo, little child, 'til safe within my arms.*" She had not crumbled then. Heska's viciousness had just firmed up her determination to survive. Could crying make her stronger now? It could not!

She needed to be quick-witted to cast off the Dark Menaces. If she had learned anything from her mother, it was how to move forward when all seemed hopeless. But *she* would do it differently. She would be fearless yet still have a place in her heart for her child. The remembered exhortation had given her courage. Her fearlessness led to resolve. And with that, the baby within moved once again.

Chapter 14: The Drumbeat

The Wise Woman had stayed near Taramae leaving only briefly for the most needed visits. Old Soul Nadee understood the situation and gave other suggestions for Kess to try in order to keep the baby from coming early. Kess wished she could share more details about what had happened to so upset Taramae but felt it best not to. If Taramae's young heart could barely withstand the shock of the Smote revelation, how much more devastating might the news be to the older woman whose health had been frail for years?

Kess still believed that the fewer people who knew about Smote, the better. It was necessary for her to make daily visits to him but shortening them was a challenge. He peppered her with questions every time.

"What will happen to Taramae now?" he asked first.

Kess tried to hurry with the application of salves, but the haste caused him additional pain, so she slowed down. "Taramae will receive those who have made Pairing Proposals. Each of them will explain what comfort and security they can provide for her and her child. They may expound upon their lineage, so that she is assured an honorable heritage for all future children."

"Will they speak of love?"

"If they have tender feelings for her, none will be expressed until she has decided upon the practical aspects. There is no touching unless she reaches out a hand for them to hold. No other affection is allowed until after the Pairing Ceremony."

The thought of another man holding Taramae's hand made Smote's stomach lurch. He felt angry yet knew that he had no right to feel so. A drumbeat of confusion throbbed in his head.

Aware of the agitation, the Wise Woman changed the course of discussion. She had noticed new drawings on the parchment pieces previously left for him. Did Smote understand the significance of the large stone, the young woman, and the river scene? "It appears you have been sketching again. Tell me of your creations."

He shook his head. "Another time."

Kess was about to place the drawings back on the table when she noticed that there were words written on each. Did he understand their meaning? Kess devised a test. "My eyes are rather tired today. I cannot read what you have written."

Smote took the drawings from her and impatiently answered. "This one says *stone*. This one says *girl*, and that one says *water*. It seems that words are coming back to me, but for what purpose—what benefit?" He threw the pictures down on the table. "Will people purchase pictures with words by the Watcher to decorate the walls of their dwellings?" he asked, sarcastically. "I think not!"

An inspired thought came to the Wise Woman, and she asked, "Are you able to form words into phrases?"

"If I concentrate. But it is very tiring."

"There is one possible benefit, if you be willing."

"What say?"

Kess then explained that Taramae had been asked to record the events of Old Soul Nadee's life. "Sadly, though Taramae has a vivid memory of the stories, she cannot accomplish the pencraft."

"She did not attend school?"

Kess took a chance that the explanation might unlock remembrances. "After the Tribunal judgment, Taramae was pulled from schooling to work for her mother."

"A judgment? Was she not a child?"

"Yes. But it is a long story, and you are hurting, so perhaps …"

"Tell it now, please. It will provide something other than pain to ponder."

Kess motioned for Smote to sit on his bed. She pulled the stool close and took a deep breath. "One day when Taramae was ten years old, she and a group of friends gathered at the gates for an adventure while their parents prepared for another festival. Her friends Nawhi and Molay were there, as well as two older boys, Drayis and Jeric."

Kess paused to note any response to the names mentioned. When there was none, she continued. "Taramae was allowed to play if she took her little brother, Aven, with her. Zaela tagged along with Nawhi."

"That would cause a problem," Smote said, recalling how the girls were often seen fighting in the village.

"And it did. Zaela was a mischief-maker even then. She knew that Drayis held a tender place in her sister's heart, so she deliberately sought to gain his attention.

"It was later told that a quarrel ensued between Nawhi and Zaela, complete with slapping and braid yanking. It took Taramae, Drayis, and Jeric to pull them apart.

"Little Aven stood with Molay close to the river's edge happily throwing rocks into the turbulent tide. At one point, Aven reached for a shiny stone, stumbled, and was swept into the torrent. Molay screamed, but it was too late. The others turned from the fray in time to see the child disappear beneath the swirling surface.

"Then, disregarding the hazardous rocks, Drayis and Jeric jumped in to save their little friend, and were also swept away. Moments later they resurfaced downstream—without Aven. Drayis helped the choking Jeric to shore, then returned to dive under one more time. He never came up again."

"How terrible!"

"It was! Astounding shock came over the village. When pleadings to SkyFa by the water's edge did not produce the bodies of the two boys immediately, Dark Menaces took control, prompting some to return to old superstitions. Weeping, wailing, and the pounding of drums went on for days. When that failed, a high wall of stones was placed on the shore as a memorial, and a warning to others. Those were the saddest days ever recorded in the history of Crim. But what happened afterward was cruel."

"What happened?"

Kess stood for a moment to stretch. "In their bitterness, two of the parents convened Tribunal. Never before had children been brought forth for such a reckoning. But Leader Adris made an exception because his son, Drayis, was one of the drowned, and he deemed the remaining children reckless. Henceforth, after the weeks of sorrow tributes they were moved into their grown-up responsibilities. The severity of penance varied greatly. Nawhi and Zaela were allowed to finish their schooling, but afterward both became workers in their father's storehouse, something they were already accustomed to doing. No school for the others. Molay began daily to learn stitchery from her mother in order to make clothing. Jeric and Taramae received the harshest punishments.

"Jeric was a promising student, a favorite of the schoolmaster, but he was denied an apprenticeship and was instead sent to the monotonous existence as apprentice to the Givens keeper, away from the village for months at a time. Taramae's mother had saved enough from previous sorrow tributes to become the innkeeper; therefore Taramae, who was to have learned healing arts from me, became a servant at the time-worn inn."

"How was that fair?"

"It was not! Nadee and I fought against it, but to no avail. Taramae's own mother agreed, and no one else would stand up against the grieving Adris. Two children lost their lives at the Wild River, and others lost their freedom because of it."

Smote was filled with sympathy. "Has this girl not had *enough* trouble?"

Kess sighed. "Truly, she has. I am trying hard to help her. I have an idea, but it would depend on your writing skills."

"You want me to write?"

"Possibly. See what you can remember and we will discuss it when I come tomorrow."

Upon her next visit, Kess saw that there were lines and lines of sentences—some more coherent than others—scribbled on the backs of drawings and any scrap of leftover parchment available. Smote appeared exhausted but pleased.

Kess shared an idea, "Now that you know why Taramae cannot write well enough to record the stories for Nadee, I wondered if, when your words become clear, she told the tales for you to write down, and Nadee's history could be written at last. It would prove quite taxing for you but be beneficial for future generations. Of course, this would be when Taramae is well enough to make several visits. So, dear Smote, consider it, and tell me if you approve."

Smote's expression brightened. "I approve. I approve very much!"

When Kess returned from her errands that day, she was relieved to see that Taramae's demeanor had greatly improved. She wondered how the idea about working with Smote would be accepted by Taramae. "I believe you can do this. Your speech is progressing, and it will give you more time with him, with the hope of recognition."

"I will do!" Taramae answered enthusiastically. She willing to consider any stratagem that might bring Jeric back to her.

"It is good. However, these efforts may not change anything. The damage was quite severe." Kess warned, her face becoming stern. "And no matter how much we desire it, there may never be a miraculous outcome. At *no* time should memories be forced upon Smote! If any are to come, they must be from *his* mind."

Taramae agreed, though she knew that would be the hardest part.

"Good, good! Rest a while longer. Your health must be secured first."

Taramae understood. She was so grateful that the cramping had stopped.

"In the meantime, and I hate to mention it, but I am bound by tradition—you must go forward with the appearance of consideration of the Pairing Proposals," the Wise Woman said, and apologetically placed three Pairing Proposals in front of Taramae. "It will keep the curiosity of others at bay until an outcome with Smote can be determined."

Taramae shook her head. It felt overwhelmingly awkward as she looked at the scrolls. She hated to give anyone false hope. On the other hand, there was still a possibility that she might need to accept one of the proposals laid before her.

Chapter 15: Pairing Visits

T he next morning Ori, the Groggery keeper, came with his daughter, Banaya, when it was time for her daily hair braiding. He was an able-bodied man, of moderate height and hardy health, handsome in a rugged way with light flecks of gray just beginning to weave through his chestnut-colored locks. His was the first Pairing offer Taramae had received, and he felt the need to clarify it.

He had worried that Taramae merely tolerated his daughter out of pity, and his pride could not bear that. However, as he sat across the table from them as they chatted, combed, and plaited, Ori realized there was genuine affection. Once the hair task was completed, Banaya gleefully posed in front of him and danced to display the finished look. "Beautiful!" he praised, "Now, go play while I speak with this lady."

Banaya hugged Taramae. "You will like him," she said confidently, then skipped outside.

Upon her exit, Ori apologized, "I feel I must explain."

Taramae shook her head, smiling. "No need. Wise Woman told offer from daughter, not father. Please, not be angry with her."

"I will not scold. She knows what she wants but is too young to understand what anguish might be stirred up by having a new baby around. You see …" Ori hesitated. "Her mother, my Naya, died having a child."

Taramae shook her head. "So sorry."

"Dah ye," he said, then added, "My children need a mother. Banaya has great fondness for you and needs help with her hair and learning. Baird needs a reason to spend less time sulking at the river. There is necessity on their behalf. However, I am not ready for another wife. My heart is ..." Ori stopped before emotions surfaced.

Taramae looked away. "I understand."

Ori considered the young woman in her pitiable situation and changed the direction of the discussion. "Banaya wants to cut her braids."

Taramae turned back around, horrified. "No! Must not!"

"I agree, but she wants shortened waves to match yours."

Taramae shook her head. "It was not choice for me. She should stay braids. Best for children's hair like hers."

"I agree. That is why I said she must wait until she is fourteen years old to cut it."

"Why fourteen?"

Ori chuckled. "It was the first number that came to mind."

They laughed for several moments, and then Ori remarked, "You have a fine skill with caring for hair."

"Dah ye."

"Perhaps others might come to you and pay some."

Taramae had not considered that possibility. "Will think on it. Dah ye for visit."

Ori arose to leave, then paused. "I said it is too soon for me to obtain a new wife. But if it would help you avoid a miserable option, you may consider this Pairing Proposal valid, and I will be honored."

Taramae nodded.

Leader Adris arrived as Ori was leaving. He displayed annoyance at not having been Taramae's first suitor. Taramae was upset that Adris was one of those coming to visit her at all. This man, of gray beard with flecks of food upon it, had been the cause of much heartache in her life. The thought of a Pairing with him gave Taramae the urge to retch.

As a child, she had feared him. When their group of friends gathered, Adris had suspiciously looked over each from head to toe before allowing his son to play. Drayis always seemed glad to be away from his father's prideful ramblings about the leadership role the boy would play in the future. However, Drayis was more curious about the past, trying to understand why his mother had left. There was a melancholy about him, but he was a true friend, and in a crisis, had willingly sacrificed his life to save another.

Adris had never forgiven the surviving children and his actions had ruined Taramae's life and Jeric's. Now he wanted to Pair with her? Again came the urge to retch.

Adris's words were sticky sweet. "I know you are anxious to get this matter settled. Believe me, I am also." He provided his best alluring grin. "Be assured that when our Pairing takes place, you will have many things to make your life enjoyable. Clothes, jewels, servants." He touched her hand across the table.

Taramae pulled it away. Those with a Pairing Proposal were not allowed to make advances unless the woman indicated that it was welcomed. She certainly had given *no* indication and folded her arms. What a strange offer, she thought. In Crim society there were not supposed to be *servants*, but it was well known Adris treated those he employed as such. He was also offering the clothing and jewels his first wife had left behind.

"Where Shayza?" Taramae blurted out.

"What say?"

"Perhaps wife wants clothes, jewels back."

"Preposterous! She is dead."

"Truly? It would be bad if first wife comes back after new Pairing." Taramae felt her question was valid.

"She is *dead*, I tell you! And despite what you have heard, she did *not* run away. Why would you mention such a thing? It is not appropriate! I am offering comforts, likely more than deserved, and you dwell upon gossip of the past. Shayza was ungrateful for luxuries. You have never had nice things. I thought you might appreciate them. Let me know when you are willing to consider this matter seriously!" he snapped, slamming the door as he left.

Gart paced nervously outside. Usually, he performed his duties with quiet confidence, but what he was about to ask filled him with trepidation. What if Taramae said no? He would be humiliated. It would not only ruin the opportunity he was seeking but spoil the relationship with Taramae that he had worked so hard to establish. He mulled over all possibilities and paced.

Taramae could hear Gart outside. She feared his proposal most. How could she say no to someone who had been so supportive of her? It would spoil their friendship and possibly cause the loss of her protector. But she could not rightfully accept his nor *any* offer so she was relieved to see his hesitation. Perhaps he would change his mind. She hoped so.

A timid knock finally came.

"Come in, Gart."

He nervously rolled his hands as he cleared his throat to speak. "Taramae ... I have come to ask—"

She stopped him. "Please sit, friend. We *are* friends, right?"

Gart nodded as he sat down by the table. "Yes, we are friends."

"Do we say truth?"

"Yes," he agreed again.

"Then, say truth, Gart. Do you want Pairing with me?"

Gart's face flushed red. "No."

Relieved, she asked. "Why send offer? Just to be kind?"

Gart looked down and shook his head. "No. To be selfish."

Taramae was perplexed. "What say?"

Again, Gart hesitated. "You have needed my help, and I will always give it, no matter what you choose today. But it is *my* dream that needs *your* help."

"My help? How?"

Gart was embarrassed. "Can you—would you—pretend a false love?"

"Confusing me. Speak plain."

Gart stood and paced once more as he struggled with the request. "You know that I stay at your mother's inn."

"Yes."

"Zaela was sent there for flirtatious attention to a Paired man. The wife would not accept offered recompense from the storehouse but insisted on a working penance."

"Good! Zaela needs learn work. She spoiled."

Gart shrugged. "But she *is* beautiful."

Taramae was afraid of what Gart was about to say. "Go on."

"Zaela smiled at me every day as she assisted with cooking or cleaning. Sometimes I held the broom."

"Sometimes you do sweeping *for* her, true? She uses charm to get her way."

He shrugged, embarrassed. "She was tired and appreciated my help."

"No. She has talent for wriggle out of duty." Taramae shook her head. "Poor friend, with Zaela in your heart!"

Gart chuckled.

"Better to choose Nawhi. She is kind-hearted, works hard, also lovely, with no conceit."

"I considered her at first, but she has never smiled nor spoken to me and walks as though carrying a heavy burden."

"Heavy burden is Zaela!"

Gart grinned. "Yes, but from the moment I met Zaela ..."

Poor Gart! Taramae shook her head empathetically. "Not fond of this torment for you, but how can help?"

Gart winced as though warily preparing to repeat the unsavory question. "Could you pretend a false love?"

Taramae raised her hands, questioning.

Gart sat back down and proceeded hopefully. "If another beautiful girl were to find me appealing, Zaela might see me as worthy and in time, I could make a Pairing Proposal to *her*."

Though the prospect of fooling Zaela was enticing to Taramae, she felt badly that Gart yearned for the favor of such a troublemaker. Zaela did not deserve a young man as exceptional as he. "She break your heart," Taramae warned.

Gart stood confidently. "Not if she treasures me. First, she must see that I have value. You do not have to accept my Pairing offer, but if she believed you might ..."

With an apprehensive smile, Taramae agreed. "I will help." The scheme might work to advantage for both, though it would require careful presentation if it were to be believed. Still, Taramae felt sorry for Gart. He was in love with a whirlwind.

Chapter 16: The Book of Nadee, Part One

As she walked to the Tower carrying a satchel of parchment, a new taper, and ink, Taramae recalled the Wise Woman's strict instructions. "At no time should memories be forced upon Smote! They must be from *his* mind." There was so much Taramae wanted him to remember and time was running out. Yet despite her impatience, she knew she must abide by the counsel.

It had been eight days since she had last seen Smote and much had happened. She was both nervous and excited. But first she must deal with another matter. Gart was waiting at the tree garden near the Tower. "Good morn, Gart," Taramae greeted him loudly, with a flirtatious smile to make their pretended attraction more believable.

"Good morn," he said, tenderly placing a flower in her hair before they sat on the bench.

The remainder of the conversation was spoken in quiet tones, as suitors might do. "I must tell you something," Gart whispered. "Two more of Heska's men were here last night inquiring about your whereabouts."

Frightened, Taramae glanced around.

"Do not worry. I sent them away speedily, but we must be vigilant."

She giggled as though he had said something clever in order to continue the pretense. "People watching," she said, smiling, through mostly-closed teeth.

"Good. Someone might tell Zaela," he answered, smiling, through mostly-closed teeth.

"We hope or be fools," Taramae giggled again.

Gart laughed, then asked about the satchel. Taramae quietly explained that Smote was scribing Nadee's life story as she told it.

Gart disapproved. "Someone else should do it! It is too upsetting for you to go there."

"No. Will be for Great Good," she assured him, yet truthfully, Taramae had misgivings of her own. Healing teas and practicing conversations had improved her speech, but what if Smote would still be unable to understand her? Gathering courage, she said, "Must go now," and slipped away to the Tower.

Smote saw her approaching the Tower. "She is coming, Owl. She is coming!" he whispered with a mixture of enthusiasm and apprehension. "It will be wondrous to work on the history with her, Owl, but what if it makes her ill again? And what if I cannot remember which words to write?" He had been practicing handwriting as more words came back to him. "Steady on, Owl, steady on!" he said, and into his pocket it went.

Taramae was out of breath when she reached the top of the stairs. She could hear Smote's dragging walk as he came to open the door. Jeric had always been agile. Being crippled would have been a great hardship for him. Smote seemed to accept it.

"Good morn," he greeted her in a gentle tone.

"It is fine morn, Smote," she said, her eyes sparkling, her light hair attractively curled. She appeared mother-radiant.

When Taramae caught him admiring her, he quickly complimented, "The flower is lovely."

"Dah ye." She handed him the satchel and looked around for a place to sit.

Smote offered her the stool but he needed to sit on it as the scribe. Sitting on his bed would be awkward, if not inappropriate, so Taramae decided to stand. "Where to begin?" she sighed.

"Perhaps at the beginning?" he answered, smartly.

They laughed, and the story unfolded.

As Taramae calmed, speaking became easier. "When Nadee was twenty and five years, she was a healer and wife from troubled country of our first fathers, far across deep water. It was beautiful there, but full of wars."

"Why were they fighting wars?"

Taramae shrugged. "Nadee say someone take something. Others fight to get back. Some men plot. Other men die. Women cry. It goes on and on. No one recalls first reason."

"Foolishness!" Smote said, only jotting down a few words.

"Nadee and husband want to follow Rules of Honor, to live in peace. They plan for better life across deep water with his cousins, Vrray and Larus, who work for a king that would not want them to leave. They know nothing of ships. Sea trader named Hebarcet was secretly hired to take to new land. He was crude man, lived by no rules, but loved his family, also tired of wars.

Larus was gardens keeper for palace. Knows working of land and seeds. Vrray had wealth as crafter fine metals for royal family jewelry. He paid trader for prov—provis ..."

Penning briefly paused, Smote helped her. "Provisions?"

Embarrassed, Taramae cleared her throat. Vocal exertion was still daunting. "Too hard for you understand. I should leave."

"No, no. It *is* understandable."

"But you only write some words, not all. Is unclear?"

Embarrassed, Smote chuckled, "It is quite clear. It is me who has the challenge. I am writing notes now and will write long sentences later. My present memory is quite good. My past memory is long gone."

The remark about his past memory made Taramae sad. Smote mistook her expression.

"Do not worry. I will get it all down. Let me recount. You said, when Nadee was twenty and five years, she was a healer and a wife. Her family lived in a beautiful country that was plagued by wars. Her family joined with others to leave. Having no knowledge of ships, they hired a man of questionable character named Hebarcet to take them. Is that correct?"

Taramae smiled and continued. "Hebarcet was to buy all supplies but said needed more money. Vrray sold last possession—beautiful ruby earned making statue for king. Gem buyer guessed leaving was reason for fast trade. Also wanted to go new land. Said he will pay money if can bring daughter. She only ten years, does not eat much. Vrray agreed."

"The merchant had a daughter?"

"Girl, named Kess."

"Ohh." Smote appreciated the connection.

Taramae continued. "One morning when still dark, Nadee and husband gather with Vrray's family, Larus with wife and son, others who keep secret, the merchant and Kess at harbor. They take few belongings. Afraid king's guards would stop from leaving.

"At harbor, brothers' group saw *two* ships ready, one for them, one for Hebarcet's family, and friends. No time to argue. They decide all can go if Hebarcet people follow Rules of Honor in new land."

"Rules of Honor?" Smote asked.

"Ancient laws for living in peace, from SkyFa legends."

"SkyFa?"

Taramae was dismayed. Her father had died before she could learn more about SkyFa but Jeric had taught her more of His ways. He loved the SkyFa legends. Smote however, knew nothing of them. She tried to explain without emotion. "SkyFa is Spirit Father of all. He lives in best peace beyond sky, answers prayers. Rules taught to all for many years."

Smote appeared skeptical. "If warring countries believed in the Rules of Honor, why did they fight?"

"When they fight for power and lands, fathers of fathers forget Rules of Honor."

"Hebarcet was not a man of rules. Why would he agree to follow such in the new land?"

"It was deceit! Hebarcet found spy who said he would tell soldiers they were leaving. Put a knife on man's throat to kill. Vrray saved man and gave the ruby if man promised not to tell. He grabbed it and ran away. The ships sailed."

Taramae walked around, arching her back in an uncomfortable stretch. Standing for a long time was miserable. That, as well as the laughing, and the baby pressure had brought about another urgency.

Smote saw her fatigue. "Shall we stop?"

Taramae fought the discomfort. "Soon." She continued. "The ships were upon deep water for many weeks. Sometimes heavy waves, up and down, up and down. When they stop at first land, Nadee's husband and others explore. He bitten by poison crawlers. Ships did not stay. Nadee could not save husband. So sad, but she must go on. People needed her.

"Not much food was left. Hebarcet said they had no food to share. Ships stopped again at land of forests. Not much flat land, but some people stayed.

They name it Timber Isle. Others sail again. People get sick. Nadee was helping, but all needed food and fresh water. Larus's wife, and small son, Adris, very sick.

"Adris? As in the grown leader now?"

Taramae nodded. "One more day and almost night they saw this land. Vrray wants to call new land Zarhoma, after realms above where SkyFa lives, but too weak to explore. Hebarcet said his people will make it safe. Two days pass. Larus's wife and more die. Young Adris sicker. Nadee tended him all the time as if her own child. They fear Hebarcet was killed. Finally, guides come to take them to port. All glad to be off deep water. But soon find Hebarcet is ruler of new land. He has food and fresh water if they agree. Called new land by his name and took best places for his people. Vrray and Larus people were too weak, had to accept."

"Evil man!" Smote scowled.

Taramae nodded and stopped to stretch her back again. The talk of ships on rough water and pregnancy pressure was having an effect on her bladder. She looked out the window to divert her attention. What she saw made her smile. The rendezvous with Gart had been noticed. Zaela was down by the tree garden railing at him. Taramae could not hear the words, but the tone was grating. The plan was working! She delayed departing.

Smote interrupted her musing, annoyed. "I knew Hebarcet could not be trusted!"

"Yes. He said they must pay tributes and be loyal to him. The man who pretended to be spy did it only to get the ruby for Hebarcet. He became a real spy on brothers group."

Taramae stopped. She needed to leave *urgently*. "Must go! Will come tomorrow!"

"Did I do something wrong?" Smote asked.

Taramae half-whimpered a quick excuse, "No, must rest *now*."

"Of course, of course. Rest well."

"You too," she said, closing the door quickly.

Smote heard groaning echoes as Taramae walked down the stairs. He stood at the window and watched as she waddle-walked towards the Wise Woman's dwelling. The man from the Groggery met her and they quickly walked the rest of the way together. It appeared to be a kindness, but it bothered Smote. "We should be the ones walking with her, Owl."

Chapter 17: The Book of Nadee, Part 2

"How was your visit?" Wise Woman Kess was anxious to know.

Taramae stirred her tea, sadly. "Hard to do. It hurts much to speak."

Kess placed a comforting hand on Taramae's shoulder. "We feared it might be thus. But you are getting better at it every day."

Taramae nodded. "Telling stories to Smote that Jeric told to me troubles my heart. He remembers none." Taramae stopped. "Will you tell Nadee about Tower? She mourns so!"

"How could it help her? Would it not break *her* heart more to know that he lives, but does not know her, and may never."

Taramae sighed. "Not sure. But she would want to hear. Perhaps more will come of effort tomorrow. But must have chair to sit on!"

The next day, Taramae repeated the same pattern as the day before. She met briefly with Gart at the tree garden, where he made a big fuss over the honey cake she had brought him. Others noticed and would likely tell Zaela. "Glad you are happy, but guard your heart, friend," she warned.

"If I do not try, I will always wonder what might have been possible. It is my life. I must take the reins," he said, determinedly.

Taramae agreed.

"Is the storytelling going well?"

"Slower than hoped. Some words hard to say." Taramae sighed.

"You are improving. Do not despair. He needs to be patient."

"He is good. It is enjoyable there—mostly."

Gart considered her reaction. "Perhaps *your* heart also needs to be guarded?"

Smote eagerly greeted her at his door. He pointed to the chair Nawhi had brought with his First Meal basket. "A chair, a real chair! I have been here for months and only received a stool. Someone must favor you!" Smote bowed low as though beckoning royalty to be seated.

Taramae giggled, then sat down as regally as possible for a heavily centered near-mother.

Smote chuckled, then said, "Please tell me how Nadee and friends escaped from Hebarcet! Curiosity has pestered me all night."

"Sorry to disturb your sleep."

"No, no. I was merely intrigued by what happened."

Taramae smiled. "I try speaking better. It is good prac—prac ..."

"Practice? I think you are doing fine. Take your time. I am a patient sort," he said, readying paper and pen.

"Dah ye, Jer—" she stopped short and corrected herself. "Dah ye, Smote," she said, hoping he had not noticed.

Looking at his notes, he said, "You were telling about the spy. I have been angry about that traitorous man all night. Please start there."

Taramae smiled and obliged his request. "The man became a true spy on the brothers' group and reported if they spoke of rebellion or pray with group."

"What a scoundrel!"

"Yes. Before long, people mix beliefs and customs. Many choose to follow Rules of Honor. Some choose to believe ways of Hebarcet with Vast Vex and Dark Menaces. He sent his spy and guards to punish those who did not believe his way. They burn all SkyFa writings."

Smote shook his head, "Disgusting!"

"True. But the brothers' group made secret writings of the Rules of Honor they remembered. Hid them from Hebarcet. Only gave a small scroll to trusted ones."

"Do you know the rules?"

"Most. Parents were given scroll when became new settlers in Crim. But Pah already knew. He was raised in ways of SkyFa when boy on

Timber Isle. As young man, Pah left Timber Isle where there were lots of trees, but few women. He paired with Mah in Heb. She was from Vast Vex belief."

"Their beliefs did not match?" Smote asked, having a private reason for his query.

"No, but they loved much, so the difference not a problem. I was born in Crim. I learn Rules of Honor from Pah when young. Mah did not mind."

"What are they?"

It had been years since she heard the special rules spoken at home. Rauma had never forgiven SkyFa for taking her husband and son, therefore such discussions were forbidden.

Taramae remembered the rules as best she could and quickly recited. "Rules say, Honor SkyFa. Honor family. Honor life. Honor Peace. Honor Pairings. Honor truth. Honor neighbor. Honor love." She took a deep breath, pleased that she had recalled them so well.

"Have the people followed them?"

"Most try. There is Tribunal when big mistakes are made, and banishment if people break Pairing vows."

Smote considered the answer for a moment and then returned to the scribing. "And then what happened?"

"Before long, other trade ships found this land. All prospered. They built settlement and mostly live in peace for five years under Hebarcet rule. Nadee taught ways of healing, accepted the Pairing Proposal of Larus, became mother to Adris, and had a baby boy named Narus."

Taramae paused to see if the name of Jeric's father brought any reaction.

"Narus. Narus," he repeated, then shook his head. "Another odd name."

There was no spark of recognition. Taramae turned away to hide her disappointment.

Smote continued, "How did they escape Hebarcet's control?"

Taramae winced from a kick within. She stood to change positions. "One day, Hebarcet sick, nigh to death. Wild living, harsh drink hurt his body. His shaman could not help. Hebarcet was frightened. He called for Wise Woman Nadee. But she would not help unless he swore oath that when were healed, people who want to leave can be free, not punished. Vrray wrote down the promise and Hebarcet signed it."

"Then Hebarcet died?"

"No! Wise Woman Nadee is great healer! Still, took weeks before Hebarcet well, but he kept word. Said the settlement was getting crowded. They could go, even take some supplies. Some Heb people wanted to leave and some wanted to stay. In the brothers' group it was same."

Smote listened patiently as Taramae explained how provisions were gathered and the day for the exodus was determined. Vrray and Larus had not been allowed to explore past Plateau Falls, so they were not sure where they were going.

"After two days walking they came to a place—now called the Crossing."

"Only two days from Heb? That is not much of a separation," Smote said, sarcastically.

Taramae was annoyed. "Past Crim there is much forest, unknown land, possible wild animals. Could they explore with women, children, and old ones? No. They needed to settle."

Smote appreciated the logic. "Of course, sorry."

Taramae continued. "Vrray wanted to go into the mountains to look for ore and gems. Larus wanted flat land for growing food. Some say brothers had fight. Nadee says there was no fight, just worry about being safe apart.

"Vrray group crossed the stone bridge above Wild River and went into mountains. They call selves Peaks People. Larus's group moved three times. Some say he was unwise leader. Nadee says Larus wanted best soil. One day past the Crossing they choose here."

Smote shuffled through his drawings and handed Taramae one of a large rock and that strange animal. "What of these?" he asked.

"The rock is a Sacred Stone, special to Crim. Very big. Taller than me, and wide." Taramae stood with both arms outstretched. "Sharp on sides, mostly flat on top. Your drawing is correct."

Smote considered the drawing once more. "A stone can be sacred?"

She nodded and continued the tale. "When Larus's group found this place, that rock was in the way. They tried to move it and failed. When they dig, the soil under was crimson color, not like other soil around. After much digging, the sky darkened and there was booming crash. Larus said, 'This stone must be sacred to SkyFa. We will not try to move it ever again.'

"Larus counted the people—sixty-three. He walked sixty-three strides from the Sacred Stone to where gates would be and called place Crim for crimson soil under the stone and they began to build fortress."

"Hmm! Tell me more about these Givens animals," Smote requested.

Taramae walked around, stretching. "Sorry. Son is too restless. Will talk tomorrow."

"How could I deny a request from your son?" Smote smiled. "I will look forward to your visit on the morrow."

The next day, though eager for the visit, Taramae increasingly felt the strain on her body.

"You were speaking about the first settlers of Crim," Smote reminded her.

She sat and continued the story. "Not much time was left in first growing season. Little food for winter. People were scared. Brought tributes at Sacred Stone and prayed mightily."

"SkyFa did not answer?"

Taramae was highly annoyed. "Sometimes SkyFa answers by sending others! Should I keep telling?"

"Yes, of course. I apologize."

She cleared her throat. "One day, a herd of those, what you call, strange animals came over h—horizon led by a man with long white hair. He helped them build a large pen to keep the animals nearby and taught them how to use for meat, milk, and fur. They named the animals *Givens* for belief that they were given from SkyFa to help in the time of great need."

"What became of the man?"

"He stayed for few years to help build the village and help with war. Then left."

Smote seemed impressed. "How do you know these things?"

Taramae hesitated. "My Jeric taught me. He learned much from Nadee. He is—*was* her grandson. He came to live in Crim from Peaks People after a mountain fever killed his parents." Taramae choked up. "He would have been great schoolmaster."

Smote saw that recalling upset her, so quickly asked, "And what is this Givens War that I have heard tell of?"

"A story for another time. My son tires of sitting," Taramae said, as she stretched her aching back. Smote saw the baby bulge shift. She stopped to rub it, and half-laughed, half-whined as the baby inside kicked her hand.

Smote's eyes widened. "You can feel it?"

"Very much." Taramae thought about letting him feel the movement. After all, it was Jeric's child. Nevertheless, it was not Smote's child. Therefore, such intimacy might not be appropriate. Such complicated thoughts made Taramae's head swirl.

"You did the telling well today," Smote complimented her.

Taramae smiled. "Dah ye. I must go. Will return tomorrow."

Chapter 18: Misery

The next morning Taramae felt absolutely miserable. She wanted to scream and throw things. To make matters worse, the heat of the day arrived earlier than usual, and the constant ache in her hips from carrying her child lower was undeniable. Adding to that, Banaya was whiny and fidgety and would not sit up straight. The hair session did not go well and she was sent out to play with lopsided twists more than braids.

Taramae considered not returning to visit Smote, however, decided to take fruit and the honey cake that she had made to share but did not want to stay long. Smote did not deserve a cranky guest and she was feeling her crankiest. With no smiles to passers-by, Taramae trudged to the Tower. Gart was not at the tree garden. Unfortunately, Zaela was.

When Taramae arrived, Zaela walked up face to face. "What is this you are doing?" she demanded to know.

Ignoring the question, Taramae looked around. "Where is Gart?"

"He is throwing another rotten rogue out of the Groggery. You seem to attract unscrupulous men to the village. Again, I ask, what is this you are doing?"

Taramae felt too testy for such annoyance. "Going to the Tower."

Zaela was exasperated. "Not that! It is terribly inappropriate, but not surprising that you would be doing such a thing. What I meant was, why such flirtations with Gart?"

Normally, Taramae would have enjoyed the opportunity to sow seeds of mischief with the girl, but not today. "Gart is my friend," she answered, as civilly as possible. "Perhaps more someday."

"Perhaps more someday," Zaela mocked her words in a whiny voice, then scowled. "Has he sent you a Pairing Proposal? Some say it is so."

"It is so. Why not? Gart is strong, of fair looks, a Pairing would be enjoyable."

"It is not right!" Zaela stomped her foot.

Taramae struggled to respond courteously. "Why does it matter to *you*?"

"It is not right!" Zaela repeated, looking as if she might strangle Taramae, but instead stomped off a few paces, then turning, yelled, "My father says that runaway—that misfit, Jeric, is the father of your disgraced child. What if he comes back to claim it?"

That was it! Taramae's last thread of tolerance snapped. She boldly waddled up to Zaela face to face and proclaimed, loud enough for all the village gawkers to hear, "He is *not* coming back! You know *nothing*! You are a spoiled, gossipy girl! How *dare* you slander my precious child or his wonderful father! I will choose whom I want to choose, even if you do not approve of it and scream till the rooftops crumble!" With that, Taramae lifted her chin and marched unapologetically to the Tower door.

She was still fuming and out of breath from her angry ascent of the Tower stairs when she entered Smote's chamber. It was gaggingly stuffy inside. There was no cooling breeze, and to make matters worse, the squat pot had not been taken out that morning. Nausea crept up her throat with dirty fingernails. The pressure of the pregnancy and the jostling up the steep stairs caused her to desperately *need* a squat pot, but she could not even consider using the odiferous one. She was prepared to cancel the session. But there was Smote, so pleased to see her, and obviously embarrassed about the condition of his lodgings.

Taramae handed him the fruit and bread and tried to hurry the writing along. Watching him work, it was as if Jeric sat before her eyes acting as scribe, and yet it was not him. One frustration stacked upon another as Taramae opened the window wider to claim any trace of fresh air available. The village below was peaceful. She resented it. How dare they be so serene when she felt tormented? She sat down, forcing herself to continue the story, speaking quickly, often covering her mouth.

After an hour, Smote looked up. "Does this sound correct? You said Hebarcet became angry. He thought that after a year in the wilderness, the people would come begging him to return. When they did not and had unexpectedly prospered, he was determined to regain control or destroy them. He sent a message to Crim claiming that the Givens should be his because they came from the land, and all the land belonged to him. Leader Larus ignored the demands. Instead, he and the villagers worked faster to finish surrounding the village with the tallest walls and strongest gate possible.

"Hebarcet was furious. He sent an emissary to threaten Crim. Instead, the man defected, making Hebarcet even more angry. He called for all able-bodied men from his village to meet for Heb grog, whereupon they were conscripted and told to prepare to leave for battle in two days.

"When Heb was quiet for the night, the owner of the groggery, a man named Sleff, locked his business, and sneaked away on his feeble mule to warn old friends in Crim of Hebarcet's intentions. He knew he could never return.

"The people at the Crossing were also glad to receive word about Hebarcet's impending rampage and, knowing that he would likely punish all in his path, they prepared to hide in the forest as soon as his army was in sight. Sleff sent a young man to warn the Peaks People.

"By the time Hebarcet arrived outside the walls of Crim, all inside were prepared for battle with rocks and slings, staves and swords." Smote stopped. "You said that the people here hated war, that they fled from it in other lands. Yet at times I see that they are armed?"

Taramae pondered a moment, trying to shift positions to ease discomfort. "They tried for peace alone, but Hebarcet took over easily because they came with few weapons on ship. They learned a hard lesson and would not be fooled again. Weapons come from Peak's metals trade. Pah told me once about the armory. He said, 'You hope to trust others, but always prepare.'"

Smote nodded. "Wise words." He wrote down several lines and continued. "You said that Hebarcet and two hundred men set up an encampment outside Crim. On the first day they shot intimidating arrows and beat drums while Hebarcet shook his long, metal staff, and threatened Crim. They did not respond. Next, a large log on a wide cart was rammed repeatedly into the gate. It was scarred but did not fail. Hebarcet was enraged.

"He had a wagon full of large stones brought that could be slung into the village. The first sentry tower was damaged and two of the Givens were killed in the pen, but the walls held. Hebarcet was answered with a barrage of stones and a slew of arrows. Many of his men were injured and ran away in the night. On the fourth day, Hebarcet tried to have the Sacred Stone pried from the ground to roll it against the gate, but it could not be moved." Looking to Taramae for approval, Smote asked, "Does that sound correct?"

She nodded, saying, "Your words are much stronger than mine. It reminds me of … Taramae stopped.

Her discomfort was obvious so Smote hurried. "What happened to Hebarcet?"

Taramae wanted to scream, "You know what happened! You were the one who told *me* of Nadee's stories in the first place. Quit hiding in your head and remember!" Of course, she could not say those things but restraining the intense emotions and the smell caused her stomach to knot. It took great effort to control herself. She stepped to the window to take a deep breath. It did not help the stench.

Taramae sat back down very carefully, resolved to tell the best part of the story quickly and leave. "When Hebarcet's men fail to move Sacred Stone, he beat them with his staff and made them lift him up to stand on it. He called for Dark Menaces to plague the Crim people. There was no answer. He demanded the Vast Vex destroy the walls of Crim. Again, no answer. He went crazy, yelling at the Vast Vex again. Still no answer.

"Dark clouds gathered. Hebarcet shook his staff and cursed SkyFa, saying, 'If you are there, SkyFa, I command you to bring destruction! You are their god and I own them. So you must obey *me!*'

"A huge flash came from the sky. It knocked him off the Sacred Stone. He flew high into the air and landed on his neck in a patch of thorns. It was end of Hebarcet."

Smote seemed amused. "Perhaps the Vast Vex did not care for Hebarcet's demands and sent the lightning."

"Perhaps it was SkyFa."

Smote looked warily at her to see if she was serious. She obviously was, so he did not scoff at the belief, but rather asked, "And the war was over?"

"Soon. Hebarcet's son vowed more fighting. He changed his mind when army of Peaks People arrived. He came before Tribunal and promised no more war. He would not be the leader of all. His village would be called Heb, and would trade for Givens meat and other things. Larus and Vrray agreed. And it has been so since."

"And it has been so since," Smote repeated, as he wrote several more words. "You have told well," he complimented her. Then he looked up, sadness in his countenance. "Now that the story of Nadee has been completed, you will not come to visit."

Taramae was bothered. "It is *not* complete. There are more stories to tell."

"She told you more?"

Taramae knew better than to disclose too much, but in her present state of intense irritability, she could not resist. "No, *she* did not tell."

"Oh, yes, now I remember. You said Jeric told you the stories." Smote was suddenly excited. "I think I knew him!"

"What say?" Taramae asked.

"I think I met your Jeric!"

"You *met* him?"

"Yes! Dark hair, light eyes, about as tall as me, perhaps not as thin? I believe he was on the same ship that I was on."

Taramae's shoulders fell. There was the mention of a ship again. He insisted on believing that he had been a sailor. Exasperated, Taramae twisted the front of her frock, almost tearing it. Was she ever going to reach the place where Jeric lived in Smote's mind and free him? Her extreme vexation burst all constraint and through gritted teeth, she asked, "If you were a sailor, a stranger to this land, how do you know to write the language? How do you know how to draw pictures of Givens and Sacred Stone? Do you *ever* wonder?"

Smote paused, considering. His mind searched for an answer. It caused a terrible jolt. He stood, head shaking, his balance off, legs weakened. Taramae stepped forward to catch him before he fell and helped him to his bed. He lay down, forearm across his forehead, eyes closed.

"Forgive me, forgive me!" she cried.

"No, I should be sorry. I did not mean to frighten you," he apologized. "This happens at times. It will pass. It will pass. There is medicine on the table."

Taramae moved the writings, searching for the potion that the Wise Woman had left. She noticed that amongst other drawings were profiles of her face, and of her standing by the window, hand across her protruding belly. She was on his mind; however, she was on Smote's mind, not Jeric's.

Taramae was ashamed. Her impatient ploy to help him remember had failed. The Wise Woman had warned her that doing so might cause him harm, and she was right. Taramae apologized as she mixed the potion with water. "I am so sorry, Smote! I stayed too long and talked crossly." Tears raced down her face as she helped him sit up to drink.

"No, it is good that you see this, that you understand how it is with me," Smote whispered. As they looked eye to eye, he had the strongest urge to kiss her. His feelings for her had grown but he could not tell her. He had nothing to offer. Anguish made his head hurt worse. He lay back down, and rolled away from her, his face towards the wall. "Will you return tomorrow?" he asked, faintly.

Other stories would have to wait. "Perhaps it would be too soon. You should rest."

"No, *please* come!" he insisted, trying to sit up again, then groaned from the effort and lay back down.

"Calm ye. Calm ye, dear Smote." Taramae said as she smoothed a lock of hair across his sweaty forehead. "I will return."

When Taramae hurried to Kess's cottage needing to change wet under-clothes, terribly upset about Smote's putrid living conditions, and his reaction to her comments, Kess knew it was time to intervene. "This scheme to help the Pairing survive has been a gamble from the beginning," she sadly admitted. "Perhaps it was not wise after all."

Upon entering Smote's room with extra medicine and nourishment, Kess severely scolded Nawhi, "Take this repulsive receptacle away, girl, and never let it get this bad again!"

Smote lay curled up on the cot. As she touched his back, he startled awake. "Come, eat," she entreated. "There is warm soup and bread. Then I will apply more ointment. It will ease your discomfort."

Smote slowly arose, groaning. "Why did you send her?"

"I hoped it would cheer you to help with the writing. I am sorry that it was unpleasant. I will tell her not to return."

"No!" Smote blurted out in earnest. "I *must* see her again. I feel drawn to her, as if—" He shook his head, which made it hurt more. "As if—I do not know—but there is something."

"Do not worry about it now. Come. Sit."

Shakily, Smote crossed to the stool by the table. With headache pounding and his strength depleted, he considered the food for a moment, then waved it away. As the Wise Woman softly applied the medicine to his head and neck, he asked, "How will she fare?"

Kess paused, unsure of how to answer without causing further distress. "What say?"

Smote was annoyed that she was not following his line of thinking and asked again. "How will Taramae fare after her child is born?"

Kess paused once more. Perhaps the truth was the kindest response after all. Gently she replied, "She will choose a Pairing, or she will leave the village."

Smote's shoulders slumped. "Are they good men?"

"Yes. Some have better character than others. Some are poorer than others. But all are capable and willing."

"Does she care for them?"

Kess sighed, again determining how best to answer. "Taramae will never care for anyone as she did for the father of her child. But she will likely accept one. Unless …"

"Unless? What say?"

"Unless she pleads before Tribunal for reconsideration of the verdict, to ask that a Pairing not be required."

Smote turned and grabbed Kess's hand. "She must plead! She must plead! She cannot be forced to choose."

"Why?" Kess asked, wondering if this was a moment of memory return.

Agitated, Smote pressed his forehead with both hands, "I do not know. I DO NOT KNOW! But she *must* not be forced to choose."

"Calm ye. Calm ye. There is still time for her to decide. You must trust that she will do what is best. Now rest, dear friend. Rest." She assisted him back to his cot and administered another draught.

Smote drank it and lay down, entreating, "I must see her again. I must!"

"You will," Wise Woman Kess assured him, and covered him gently with a blanket.

Chapter 19: Slamming Doors

Taramae was quiet the next morning while braiding Banaya's hair. She pondered the events of the day before, especially her own response when Zaela mentioned Jeric's possible return. "He is *never* coming back!" she had angrily replied. How strange it was to hear herself say the words.. She did not want to accept that Smote would never become Jeric again, but it felt inevitable.

Her body and soul ached for Jeric. She cared for Smote, enjoyed her time with him, yet he was not Jeric. Could she come to love Smote for who he was *as* he was? And would he be able to love her as she was, child and all? If not, what could she do? The time for decisions was approaching fast. She missed her father's wisdom. She could not speak with her mother. The Wise Woman was there for discussions, but no one could make the decisions for her.

"I made a poem about the village," Banaya said, proudly. "Do you want to hear it?"

When Taramae did not respond, Banaya tugged on her sleeve. "I said, I made a poem."

"What say?"

"Never mind. You are far away. Does the Tower man trouble you?"

Worried, Taramae asked, "What do you know of the Tower?"

Banaya was annoyed. "Everyone knows there is a man in the Tower, and you visit him every day."

"Who knows?"

Banaya answered, impatiently. "*Everyone!* He watches from the window. He blew the warning horn when you returned. *Everyone* knows."

Taramae was alarmed.

"People talk at the Groggery, and I listen from our sleeping loft. They think he has a dangerous sickness. No one wants to go near him. They think he brings Dark Menaces. They say you are foolish for going to see him."

"Do *you* think I am foolish?"

"No—I think you are brave! But when you leave there, I can see you are sad and tired. Why do you go if it is not good for you?"

"I go to help the Wise Woman. She helps many people. Some need extra care, like Old Soul Nadee and the Tower man. I take healing balms to him. He is not dangerous. He is lonely and injured but knowledgeable in the ways of words. He is helping to write a story about Old Soul Nadee and the beginning of Crim."

"A story? I like stories! When it is finished, will he go away?"

A sickening feeling came over Taramae. What *will* happen to Smote in the future? If the village could not accept him, would he be pressured to leave? Apprehension descended upon her.

"*Will* he go away?" Banaya asked again.

"I hope not," Taramae responded. Finished with the braiding, Taramae placed her hand gently on the girl's shoulder. "Banaya, it is important you not speak of the Tower man to others. It would be unsafe, and I would be sad if he is hurt again."

"Again?" Banaya asked. "Who hurt him befo—" she started to ask when there was a sudden, loud knock. "I will answer it, but then I want to tell you something." She scampered to the door.

Banaya stood silent at the sight of Leader Adris. He pushed past her. "I have come to see Taramae, girl. Go home."

Banaya ran past him quickly to Taramae's side, wrapping protective arms around her.

Taramae patted her back. "It is fine. You may go play." She leaned down and whispered, "Please, keep our secret. We will speak again."

Banaya whispered back, "I made a poem."

"Very nice. You may share it with me tomorrow."

"And I wanted to say, your words are much better today."

"Dah ye, sweet friend. Now go."

Banaya frowned as she walked past the leader. She made the sign of a circle in front of her face and touched her nose.

"What an odd child!" Adris smirked. "Is she the daughter of the Groggery keeper?"

"Yes. She comes every morning for help with her braids."

Adris sniffed as if smelling something foul. "She must learn to do them on her own. When we are Paired, you will not have time for other children."

"I will always have time for friends." Taramae spoke politely, though feelings of past animosity began to simmer.

"We will see," Adris said. "Did you think upon my proposal?"

"Yes."

"Might you accept now to avoid further delay? You cannot consider the other offers in earnest. Both are poor men."

"How do you know who they are?"

Pridefully, Adris answered, "I know everything that goes on in this village. You have no true choice. Will you go back to the inn with Gart and become your mother's servant once more? Will you raise an innocent baby in the loft of the Groggery with drunken men lurking below, and have other ruffian offspring to care for? You need rest and comfort now, not hard work, my dear. If we complete the Pairing, you could come to my dwelling tomorrow for repose until the child is born. He would happily be my heir, and possibly the leader in the future, if there are no other male children. It is a tremendous prospect!"

Taramae was astonished at the gall of this man. A tremendous prospect? The promise of being deposed by younger siblings? "Drayis was always sad," she said. "Why would another child be happy? And what if this baby is a girl?"

"Some think I pushed Drayis too hard to follow my example, but they are wrong. His mother's absence—I mean, her death—made him occasionally downhearted. But he was given everything, why would he be sad? And if this baby is a girl, we will simply try again, right?"

Taramae almost threw up in her mouth. She was not in the mood! How could Adris pretend to care about her happiness now? He never had before. Such arrogance!

She wanted to be done with this conniving caller, to return to the Tower. Smote had been so stricken when she left yesterday. Besides that, the conversation with Banaya still echoed through her thoughts. She took a deep breath. "I do not know whom I will choose."

Adris was angry. "I am telling you, girl. There *is* no choice! Are you so lost to sense, so overwhelmed with maternity that you cannot think clearly?"

"Enough!" Taramae seethed, her fist hit the table. Anger caused her to tremble, her speech to break once more. "My c—condition forces me to think even *more* c—clearly. All decisions are for happiness of my child. You c—cared nothing for his father, denied wealth and love to orphan of own blood. You c—cast him away, ruined his future vocation for accident n—not of his doing. How can you be trusted n—not do likewise to son? How c—could I look upon you each morning without c—contempt for pain in my life caused by the false charges brought at Tribunal? How c—can you imagine there would be af—affection when such memories pr—prevail? You are the one lost to sense!"

Adris was thoroughly insulted. He was not accustomed to being spoken to thus. He was about to reply with similar harshness, but her shaking demeanor warned against it. "You are too impassioned to discuss matters further," he reproached. "When you amend your thoughts, I will forgive this moment of unbridled emotion." He abruptly left.

Forgive? Taramae looked around for something to throw against the door. Her head was spinning, her heart racing. She would *never* Pair with this man—even if she had to live under a rock! She collapsed onto the bed and pounded a pillow.

Adris cursed all the way home. He was furious that Taramae kept bringing Shayza into the conversation. She was gone, that was all that needed to be said! His lips clenched with emotion that forced admitting. He felt humiliated beyond reason. This girl, this Taramae, it was none of her business! It was none of anyone's business! He knew what they had said about him. The chant they used to call out in drunken humor at the Groggery: *'Leader, Leader, foolish man, thinks he will be king one day. Bought himself a pretty wife and then she ran away.'*

What about all the good he had done? Keeping order in the village? The trade treaties he had successfully negotiated that had brought prosperity to

Crim? All of that went down in a hail of drunken mirth at his expense, mocking one of the most painful moments of his life.

Yes, Shayza had left. He was actually surprised. He had given her nice clothing and jewelry bartered for with the most reputable tradesmen. It had taken him years to hone his business skills but he had earned respect and it meant a lot to him. Due to his prestige, Shayza had status in Crim in a way she never would have had in Heb. It was not his fault that she had few friends and craved attention from him that he was often too tired to favor her with. He had no idea what else she wanted. So yes, he was surprised when he found the bitter letter she had left.

He pulled the rumpled letter from a drawer. It read: *"You promised me riches and love but have given me baubles and loneliness. Love withers in the shadow of power. You never wanted my companionship, only a son to brag about and teach your ways. You have achieved that honor but you know nothing of fatherhood nor compassion for others. I am leaving before two lives are ruined. Do not seek after me. You may say that I am dead, for my heart is nearly so from disappointment and despair. But know that if you harm our son, in any way, I will hear of it and there will not be respite from the endless torment of Under Earth demons that I will curse you with. –Shayza"*

She did not need to send any demons to him. The first came when he tried to explain the unexplainable to a distraught child. The boy's tender demeanor was never the same after his mother's abandonment. There was a letter intended for his thirteenth birthday. It said that she had never forgotten him and still had love to share. She thought he would be old enough by then to strike out on his own and come to find her. Adris had burned it. He could not have his son leave him too! But it had not mattered. Drayis never lived to be thirteen, and Adris's own inner demons continually harassed him about the mistakes he had made. At least people had some decency after that, and the *Leader, Leader* chant ceased.

But now, Adris had a chance to start over. He would not make the same mistakes. He would be the kind of father that Drayis had needed. Looking through his son's belongings, the lone toy was a ball. Other expensive things Drayis had given away. He had made the ball himself. A wad of fur tightly covered with layers of leather strands. Drayis kept asking him to join in a throwing game that he and Jeric had invented but Adris felt it was too undignified.

Now Adris held the ball to his forehead and wept. "I promise you, son, that I will do better next time," he said aloud, and placed the ball on a shelf near his bed as a constant reminder of the pledge he had just made. He had to have another chance—another son! If only that girl—that stubborn girl would relent! Adris marched over to the inn to once again demand that her mother bring more pressure to bear.

After Adris left, Taramae felt trapped and furious and hated feeling so. It diminished her courage, drained her of the energy needed to stand up for what she wanted for herself and her child. She wanted to run to Jeric for comfort, to feel reassuring arms wrapped around her, renewing her strength. It felt like madness to think she would never have that again. Dark Menaces began encroaching. Taramae forced focus from her fears. She *must* spend more time with Smote. It would help her confirm necessary decisions before the child was born. One way or the other, she must move forward with her life.

She washed her face, put on a clean frock and prepared to return to the Tower when another knock came on the door. Warily, she opened it. "Mother?" she groaned, holding her lower back. Taramae was surprised Rauma had returned. Their last encounter had ended harshly.

Rauma's hardened demeanor seemed to soften upon seeing Taramae's painful stance. "You should sit down," she said gruffly, as she pushed past Taramae to enter.

Perplexed, Taramae said, "Come in. May I offer you some tea?"

In her usual disgruntled tone Rauma said, "Fine. Bring the tea. Then sit. We must speak."

With anticipation, Taramae stoked the embers of the fire to reheat the kettle. Her mother had never been a tea drinker. She must have something serious to discuss. Was there hope of reconciliation?

As Rauma stirred honey into the cup of steaming liquid, her eyes studied every inch of Taramae across the table. Then she spoke. "Adris just came to see me. He was terribly upset. Why have you not accepted his Pairing Proposal?"

Taramae's hope for a reunion vanished. "Are you now his envoy?"

"He is adamant!"

Taramae gathered strength for another battle. "He is *always* adamant about *something*. Why does everyone bend to his whims? Besides that, I thought *you* liked him. Why are you so easily giving him to me? Did he reject your advances again?"

Rauma looked away.

"Oh, I see. What sum has he offered? You have never denied a bribe and you sold everything from our life before."

Rauma retorted, "Do not be ungrateful. We have survived on what I could raise, wherever I could get it and you were of little help!"

"Of little help!" Taramae responded, visibly upset once again. "I served day and night at the inn. I was treated as a servant, not as your child. And when I *died*, as you claimed, you received Sorrow Tributes—again. None of that helped?"

"But you left!"

"I was stolen! It was no choice of mine! What did you choose? Simply to forget and move on? Did you look for me, or even wonder what became of me? Or did you simply place a stone next to Aven's at the Last Rest and collect the tributes?"

Rauma slapped her hand on the table. "I searched!"

"When? For how long? For a minute? For a day? And how far? I was in Heb—four days away, shovo to Heska all the time. No one ever searched there. Not even once!"

"Your belongings were found by the river. Everyone believed—"

"People believe what they want to believe—to have done with the matter." Taramae wiped tears away roughly. She would not cry for this woman. Anger swelled. "You are the *one* person who should have searched to the ends of the earth for me—but did *not*—and when I was miraculously able to return home, you rushed past me at the Pavilion to comfort Zaela, of all people. That selfish sham!"

"She was fair company for a while, but not the best worker. I was just trying to be nice."

"Nice? When were you nice to *me*? And I worked hard!"

Seeing Taramae's unhealthy distress, Rauma tried to calm things down before answering the charges laid against her character. "I cannot mend the past. You have suffered, and my remorse will not erase it. But you have an opportunity now to have a better life."

Taramae's eyes flashed in fury. "How could I Pair with such a man?"

"He cares for you and for the future of your child. He has much to recommend him."

Taramae scoffed. "Adris has *never* cared for me. He wants to claim my son."

"True, but in return, he would provide rest and comforts."

"Comforts? He wants to give me his dead wife's clothing and jewelry. Would you wear those? Does it not invite Dark Menaces?"

Rauma winced at the distasteful suggestion, then shrugged. "There are worse things. Would you prefer to live in squalor at the Groggery?"

"Why must I choose either?"

"It is the way of things."

"Not all ways fit every life!"

"Then what will you do?"

Taramae took a breath, now was her moment to venture a new concept. In a near-pleading tone she said, "I braid hair well and I am learning to curl. Perhaps I could raise this child at the inn and care for the hair of others."

Rauma scoffed. "There is no such vocation!"

"There could be. New ideas can be considered."

"It is doubtful. You hate the inn. You ran from it, abandoned me!"

"I ran away from an arranged Pairing! I overheard you many times speaking with men about me at the inn, taking offers with ale at the Groggery. Can you deny it? I left with Jeric—my dear love—before I was given away."

Rauma's face twisted with anger. "I *never* would have given you away! It was mostly done in jest. And where is this dear love of yours when you need him now?"

Taramae's lips quivered. "Jeric is no more."

"In truth? Adris says that Jeric has deserted you. Adris wants to shield you from shame. He also requests that you no longer make visits to the Tower. He is afraid that the villagers may think your behavior inappropriate for that of the leader's wife."

"Horrid lies from a horrid man! Another stitch in his cloak of corrupt cloth!" Taramae's anger rekindled. "You are a shrewd woman. Can you not recognize such cunning?"

"It sounds like the best offer."

Taramae was flabbergasted. "To how many *others* did you offer me?"

Rauma paused before admitting, "There were several. Old Sleff was especially keen on the idea," she smirked.

Taramae was horrified. "Old Sleff? He just died!"

"He was not seriously considered. On the other hand, a prosperous inheritance would have been secured with only a short time of being inconvenienced by him."

Taramae's mouth fell open.

"Do not look at me like that. I spoke to men about you because men would speak to me—if about you. I never intended to force a Pairing. Why would I let go of my best worker? I am merely a lonely woman. I enjoyed conversations—and free drinks. You did not need to leave."

"I *did* need to leave. We had waited many years. Our joy was brief, but complete."

"Complete? With Jeric—an orphan with no more prospects than to be a Givens keeper?"

Taramae defended. "He could have been a great teacher. He was robbed of the opportunity by lies and bitterness at Tribunal, like me!"

"It is done. It cannot be changed. You can still do better with Adris."

Taramae gave up. It was no use. She tried one more approach, by appealing to her mother's profit-loving side. "I could do better with you at the inn, to return as your daughter, perhaps even a partner, to help, but not as a servant."

"You would rather do that than live in luxury at the leader's house? Think of your child, you foolish girl!"

"I *am* thinking of my child! I want him to be as happy as I was before the Vast Vex took Pah and Aven. We will have joy and, laughter, and songs, even if it is in a tent at the Crossing."

"You would never be safe there, hounded day and night by Heska's henchmen. Perhaps you *should* give this child to her and begin again without fear of retribution."

Taramae threw her spoon across the table. It clanged loudly onto the side of her mother's cup. "Would you give *your* son to that cold-hearted witch? No! Then why your *grandson*? Imagine his life—abused by Heska, or the revolting, perverse Tarce." Taramae stood, pointing to the door. "If you would wish such misery on a child of your own blood, leave—now!"

The entire village heard the door slam.

Chapter 20: Stellaria

Smote was still drained of energy from the previous day yet looked forward to another visit from Taramae.

"Why is she late, Owl?" He worried until he heard a light knock at the door, and called out, "Enter and welcome!"

As the door creaked open, a small face peered into the room. The child gasped at the sight of him, but bravely held out a hand, "I picked you some wildflowers."

Smote's heart melted, "Dah ye! Such a great gift. Come in, come in. Who might you be?"

The girl circled the air in front of her face and touched her nose, then valiantly announced, "I am Banaya, daughter of Ori, sister of Baird, friend of Taramae!"

Smote stood as tall as possible and valiantly announced, "I am Smote! I am not a daughter or sister of anyone, but also a friend of Taramae."

Banaya grinned, then resumed her serious demeanor. "I am more of a friend!"

"Why do you think that?"

"She tells me stories."

"She tells *me* stories."

Banaya frowned. "We have shared meals."

"*We* have shared meals."

"She braids my hair."

"Alas, I have no braids," Smote sighed, and shrugged. "You win!"

Banaya giggled. "Then I am her most-friend!"

Smote laughed too, as she walked around him, looking up and down. "It is true. You have no braids," she giggled again, then she wrinkled her nose and sniffed. "I guess you have never been to the bath house."

Smote laughed. "Do you recommend that I do so?"

Banaya nodded. "You would like it. The water is very warm and comes from deep in the earth. Old Soul Nadee lives by it. She is nice. Her dwelling is small, but she is a small lady so perhaps it is enough." She walked to the window. "Woezy!" she exclaimed. "You can see almost everything! The inn. The storehouse. The Groggery. That is where I live. I sleep in a loft on the tallest part of the stack bed. My pah sleeps on the lowest part. My brother sleeps in the middle. Sometimes when sky drums boom, I sleep on the bottom bed by my pah. I do not like sky drums. Do you like sky drums?"

"No."

"Me neither! Did you know that there is a tall hill above the Wild River called the Plateau Falls? And it has a waterfall that sounds like sky drums! They say the Vast Vex lives under it."

"I did not know that," Smote said.

Once again distracted, Banaya said, "Oh, look! Leader Adris is walking from the Wise Woman's cottage. He went to visit Taramae. Taramae does not like him, and I do not like him. He told me to go away before I could tell my poem to her."

Banaya paused in her village viewing, looked him up and down again, then plainly asked, "Who hurt you?"

"What say?"

"Taramae said I must not speak of you to others, or someone might hurt you again."

"Taramae said that?"

"Yes. I told her the villagers are afraid you have a dangerous sickness, and she said, 'He is not sick. He is hurt.' So, I ask, who hurt you?"

Smote forlornly shook his head. "I do not remember. I was found by the river. I must have fallen off my ship and been lost in a storm."

"Ships cannot go on that river," she said, absentmindedly gazing out the window. Then turning back, she said, joyfully, "I made a poem."

Turning the conversation back to clarify, Smote asked, "Ships cannot go on the river?"

"No. Not even little boats. There are too many rocks and swirlings. No one is supposed to play there. The Wild River steals children! My brother, Baird, goes to catch fish. He does not catch many, but sometimes he snags other things."

Smote sat down by his table and pressed his fingers to his forehead. Confusion crossed his mind. What there was of memories was jumbled. Now recent assumptions made no sense.

"Are you ill?" she asked, coming to his side.

Smote shook his head. "No, no. I am fine. You said something about a poem? Would you tell it to me?"

Banaya cleared her throat. "It is called 'A Visit to Crim.' You are the first to hear it."

"Such an honor!"

"Please do not interrupt." She took a deep breath and began. *"Crim is friendly. You can believe me. Come inside and you will see."*

She interrupted herself. "They were nice to us when we moved here from Heb. That is not a friendly place!"

"Oh, and when did you come …" Smote started to ask.

"Shh! I will continue. *When you walk through the big wooden gate, there are stuck-together houses, a number of eight. The gatekeeper lives in the first one and the ninth one is for bathing, which is great. Across are three shops, and the inn with a mean lady who never grins."*

Banaya paused. "She is not the friendly part."

Smote nodded.

"The Groggery has drinks that make people silly, I think." She giggled. "I am not old enough to have grog. My pah says I am silly enough without it. Sometimes we help him make it. He always tells my brother, 'Don't spit in it, Baird!' I never do that."

Smote firmly nodded agreement.

"After the Groggery, if you are able, you can run out to the stable."

She stopped again. "I love animals! Nice ones. Not the Givens. They stay in the far fields. They have horns. You cannot ride on them. They are not friendly. Baird has a big scar."

Smote sympathetically shook his head.

Banaya took another deep breath. *"Sometimes the stable has stinky air, and behind that are the gardens fair. On the lane behind the inn are six stack houses and a Wise Woman cottage who hates louses."*

Banaya was annoyed. "That lady looks for bugs in my hair whenever she sees me. Sometimes I hide."

Smote had a sudden urge to scratch his scalp.

"Past the storehouse is the place of Adris, who looks at children like he hates us." "People who come to the Groggery think he is a poor leader. He started taxes. My pah hates taxes."

"Is the poem finished?"

"Here is the last part. *Next is some trees and a bench to sit on at your ease. The tower watcher can also spy on stack houses on New Side, and then there is a horrible school. Sending children there is cruel."* She rolled her eyes. "Schoolmaster Hill says I talk too much! Me?"

Smote copied her surprised expression. She appreciated his reaction.

"Back to Crim's front gate. It's not little, is it? Hope you had a lovely visit." Banaya smiled, broadly "Did you like it? I left out where they dump the squat pots. Is that best?"

"That is best," Smote agreed. "Wonderful poem!"

Banaya bowed. "Dah ye. Perhaps I will sing it next time."

Back at the window, she exclaimed, "Oh, I see the Wise Woman going to a Naming Ceremony at Molay's dwelling. They will have cake. I was not invited," she said, disappointed. "Woezy! There is another stranger by the well. Every day Gart chases men from Heb out of the village so they will not harm Taramae. Perhaps she will Pair with Gart. I wanted her to be my new mother. My pah says we live too poorly. But it would not be good for her to Pair with the old craggy leader. Taramae does not like him *at* all! She likes *you*."

Roused from confused thought, Smote asked, "What say?"

"I say, Taramae likes *you*."

"Truly?"

"Yes."

"How do you know this?"

"Because she does not want you to be hurt again, or for you to ever go away. That means she likes you *very* much. I should go now. Taramae might scold me for coming. But I thought wildflowers might cheer you. They are called stellaria. They are Taramae's favorite."

Smote briefly considered giving Owl to her but was not quite ready to part with it. Instead, he said, "The flowers have cheered me greatly, as has your visit and your poem. Dah ye, Banaya, daughter of Ori, sister of Baird, friend to Taramae."

Banaya skipped to the door. In passing, she said, "Do not forget, I am her most-friend. I have felt her baby move!"

"You win again," Smote conceded.

He could hear echoes of giggles all the way down the stairs as he sat confused, amused, and amazed. "Owl, I do not know what to ponder first? That a child has shown kindness with a gift of flowers? That there was no ship? Or, that Taramae likes me—*very* much?"

Chapter 21: Questions

S mote was contemplating Banaya's comments so much that he barely heard when another knock came at the door. "Enter," he called out, distractedly. He sat so still that Taramae was immediately concerned.

Tenderly, she placed a hand on his shoulder. "Are you well?"

He gazed at his beautiful, lopsided friend with her oddly curled hair and protruding middle and smiled. "A little girl brought wildflowers to me today. She claims to be your most-friend because you favor her above all others."

Taramae's eyes widened. "Banaya?"

Smote nodded. "She spoke of many things. She recited a poem and left me with many questions. I am hoping that you can help with the answers."

Taramae saw the stellaria. Tenderly she fingered the small white blooms, remembering times when she had worn them in her hair as she ran to play with friends. As a reminder of happier times, Taramae had worn stellaria blooms in her hair on the day of the PermaDevo ceremony.

Absentmindedly, she whispered, "He called me Stellaria—his wild blossom."

"What say?"

Taramae pulled off one of the blooms and held it up by the side of her hair trying one last time with something that might spark a memory within him.

"Those are your favorite," he said.

Her face brightened with hope, until he finished saying, "Banaya told me that those are your favorite flowers."

Banaya told him. It was not a recollection. Taramae dropped the flower back into the bunch. "Sorry, what was it you asked?"

"I said, Banaya left me with questions. Will you answer them?"

"If I can." She beckoned him to sit by the table so that she might begin the ointment treatment on his head.

As she placed her hand on his shoulder to steady his tremors, Smote reached up and placed his hand over hers. Surprised, she flinched but did not move it. "Who am I, truly?" he asked.

Temptation to burst with the truth flooded Taramae's soul. However, what was *true* and what was *best* in this instance was not the same thing. Memory distress had made him ill before. Pushing down selfish emotions, she took a deep breath before cheerfully replying, "You are Smote! Smote, the Watcher in the Tower. And how are you feeling today?"

He studied her expression thinking that perhaps she had no knowledge of his origin either. "I am better now, Dah ye. That little girl is a loyal friend, very brave for one so young."

"Her friendship is precious to me."

"Her mother is gone?"

"Yes, she died during childbirth when they lived in Heb."

Smote became solemn. "Such a terrible demise!"

Taramae made a sound of agreement, allaying her own fears, and worked quietly on the ointment application. When finished, she asked, "Should we continue the story? I may not be able to visit much longer." She placed a hand on her abdomen. "My child will come soon, and then ..."

"Then you must choose," Smote finished her sentence. "Mother Kess explained it to me."

Taramae frowned. "Let us speak of more pleasant things."

Shakily, Smote picked up the writing instrument.

Taramae touched his hand. "Just listen now and write it when you are feeling stronger."

Smote was relieved. "Dah ye. Go ahead."

Taramae began putting the ointment away, took a deep breath, and began. "Larus was a good leader, but not ambitious like his son, Adris.

The village of Crim was peaceful for many years. His second son, Narus, learned the ways of the land from his father, and the village prospered with much food from the gardens."

"The gardens fair behind the stable?" Smote asked, grinning.

"What say?"

"Never mind. Please go on."

"Adris had no patience for growing things. He became good at trading."

"And he has never married—I mean, Paired?"

"Yes, when his brother, Narus, Paired with a pretty girl of the Peaks People, Adris was jealous. It caused so much contention within Crim that Narus took his bride and returned to her village. Not to be outdone, Adris went to Heb for trading one day and brought back a wife named Shayza. They say she was tall, with dark hair and beautiful eyes. Adris made many promises before their Pairing so she would agree to come here. But because she was different and not well accepted, when a formidable illness came upon the village, some superstitious ones blamed Shayza, though it was not her fault.

"Leader Larus and many others died. Nadee became ill also and her heart weakened. The Wise Woman duties were given to her apprentice, Kess. Adris became leader and immediately moved Nadee to the smallest dwelling, next to the bath house."

"Was she not as a mother to him?"

"Yes, but Adris has always loved power more than people and soon was unkind to Shayza also. One day she left everything behind, including their young son. Adris claims she died. Others say she ran away."

"Did you know her?"

Taramae shook her head. "Adris says I may have her belongings if I choose him." Taramae shuddered. "It is believed that belongings of a sad heart will bring the same sadness to the next wearer. I would not accept such. Even if it was *not* an odious offer, she was tall. Would her clothing fit me? No! The man is shameless!"

Smote agreed, then asked, "Did Nadee help mother Adris's son?"

"Adris would not allow it. Neither would Leader Adris take in his brother's son—my Jeric—after his parents died—but that rejection was for the Great Good. Nadee taught Jeric many ways of wisdom and learning."

129

Taramae no longer expected recognition of story details from Smote. She finished her recitation by saying, "Nadee's heart fails. It is good that her story is told. She is a wondrous woman, very brave. She has helped many people and should be remembered. Dah ye for assisting, Smote."

Energy depleted, Taramae prepared to leave. The weight of her child was almost unbearable. She groaned as a kick from within rippled across her abdomen. "My son is impatient to be born."

Amazed by the movement he saw, Smote asked, "Does it hurt?"

"At times. He is strong." She lightly pushed on her stomach. The baby kicked back.

Smote appeared uneasy.

Taramae studied his reaction, and said, "It is a curious feeling."

"Banaya said that she has felt the baby move."

"Give me your hand."

Smote was astounded. Was this appropriate? He was not certain. However, he *did* want to feel it. So, with the reassurance of Taramae's smile, he held out his hand.

She placed it on her abdomen and pressed it lightly. The baby kicked back.

Smote's face lit up. He pressed again. The baby kicked again. "What a wonder!" he proclaimed, smiling broadly.

After a day of such tribulation, there was finally laughter. Taramae left the Tower feeling worn down yet elated. Jeric would never hold his child. However, for a moment the child had known his father's touch.

Taramae protested, "It is not fair!" as she sat at evening meal with the Wise Woman.

"You are correct. It is not fair. But fairness is not always possible. There have been complaints that your visits to the Tower appear unbefitting a young woman of your circumstances."

"Complaints? Who complains? Leader Adris, of course!"

"And others."

"Zaela? Rauma? And because of their prejudice, visits are canceled?"

"Not only for that reason. It is your rest-in time, even past the usual beginning. You should not be seen out until the child is born."

Taramae hit her fist on the table. "First, I must prove I am not a ghost. Then I must have a Pairing if I wish to stay. Now women of such condition are not to be seen? Must custom abolish freedom? I do not accept!"

The Wise Woman was firm. "You must accept. The people need to see that you are willing to abide by usual customs before you ask for the Tribunal decision to be reconsidered. Changing too much too fast will turn opinions against you."

"I *need* to see Smote, to say goodbye."

"The greater need is for your rest before the child is born, and to calm the village before next Tribunal."

"It is not fair!" Taramae whimpered. "Is there anywhere one can live and not be at the mercy of laws?"

"Yes, it is called Heb. But even in that chaos, others control more of their lives than the people choose to admit. You have seen how that transpires. The rulers are simply more calculating, ensnaring subjects around them with favors. Would you choose to go back to the prison of obligation over the annoyance of tradition?"

Taramae thought of the daily procession of villagers she had seen who sued for assistance from Heska, and the high price they paid for her patronage. "No," she conceded.

Wise Woman Kess patted her young friend on the shoulder. "We will go to the Tower one more time. There cannot be so many complaints if we are together. Afterwards, you must begin the rest-in."

Defeated, Taramae relented.

Chapter 22: The Message

One late afternoon, Gart was surprised to see his friend and former neighbor from Heb waiting outside the inn. "Pel!" he greeted the man with a slap on the back. "I was not expecting visitors. It is good to see you!"

Pel was relieved that his presence had received such a response. He had been warned that Gart easily dismissed outsiders with his imposing size and gruffness. Pel was nearly the same height as Gart, with slightly less stature. It now occurred to him that Heska had chosen him for this venture due to his size and existing friendship.

"You look well," Gart added, cheerfully. "Are you still building crates for Irv? With more ships coming in, his business should be flourishing."

"His business *was* flourishing until recently. He began gambling and lost so badly that he had to let all workers go and begin training his young son to help."

Gart shook his head. "That is too bad. Heb is not known for honest gaming. Fortunes can evaporate easily. But let us talk of happier times. It is great to see you, man! I see you still carry the scabbard I gave you."

"Yes, the scabbard is the same, but the knife …" Pel bragged, proudly displaying a newly forged masterpiece.

Gart was awed. "That is a fine weapon—very fine! Life must have improved. I am on my way to the Groggery. Come, let us have a drink, and you can tell me about your family. How is sweet Savah and the girls?"

"Savah is well."

"Do the girls grow as pretty as their mother?"

"Yes, thankfully they look more like her than me!"

Gart laughed. "That will make it easier to find husbands for them when the time comes."

Pel chuckled. "*They* will do the finding. They are quite headstrong."

"So, they *do* take after you," Gart joked.

Pel laughed. "I am feeling quite outnumbered. But that may change. We have other news. We are expecting another baby—hopefully, a boy this time!

"I will drink to that!"

"Me, too. But first I must deliver a dispatch to the innkeeper."

Gart stopped short. "A dispatch for Rauma?" he asked, suddenly realizing that his friend had not come to visit him. "*Please* tell me that you are *not* here from Heska! As I have told many others, *Leave Taramae alone!*" Gart demanded and reached out to grab Pel's tunic.

Pel dodged his grasp. "Wait, wait! It is not what you think. It is not about the girl—only a message for the innkeeper!"

Gart felt used. He was angry. "I would have thought better of you than to accept Heska's devious employ. You have a family! You have a life! Why did you do it?"

"Because you left!" Pel snarled back. "They came looking for you. They found me. They needed a replacement. I needed work. I had *no* choice! I have a growing family. Building crates was barely enough to support us, and no longer an available option. Heska provided an opportunity. She has made generous promises to improve life for my family. After this I will be the agent for all dwellings in the southern quarter and my family will receive better lodgings."

"Her promises mean nothing!"

"Heska told me *your* story. You left before fulfilling your bargain; therefore, you lost your claim for a favor. It does not mean she will treat me thus."

"You fool! You will be her slave henceforth and will be required to do her bidding—*whatever* the task—to maintain her goodwill. I know this better than anyone. I became one of her Enforcers to pay back the shaman's medicine that my sickly mother needed. You saw what happened. It *never* worked. She died anyway. After that, all I ever wanted was to be given the names of other family members so I might not continue to be alone. Heska never relented. There was always one more task to perform, each one becoming more horrendous, until I sickened of living in her stench, surrounded by her heart-darkness."

"It will not be so with me," Pel challenged and attempted to push past Gart again.

There was a scuffle until Gart pinned Pel against the wall of the inn.

"Enough!" Pel shouted. Pushing Gart away, he placed his hand upon the handle of his knife as a warning.

Gart stepped away and shook his head in disgust. "Oh, I see. Your allegiance has already been purchased. She gives a gift, and the trap is set."

"Why do you care what I do?" Pel yelled.

Gart yelled back, "Because evil cannot always win. Someone has to fight against it."

"No. It is best to be on the winning side. Whatever that might be," Pel countered. "My family's welfare is my prime obligation."

Frustrated, Gart shook his arms in the air. "It is for the sake of your family that I am trying to discourage your entrapment! But I see that my warning is useless. Your pride has earned your position. I will not argue further." Gart heaved a heavy sigh. "Some people must be trampled before they notice a stampede. Deliver the message and leave immediately!"

Pel objected. "It is nearly dark. The gate will close soon, and I have no lantern. Could I not stay the night? I am no threat to the girl."

"No one from Heska can be trusted. I said, deliver the message and go!"

"And if I do not?"

When Gart reached out to take ahold of him, Pel sprinted into the inn. He was out of breath as he handed the parchment missive to Rauma. "M—Mistress Hes—Heska bade me to a—await your re—response. She is at the Cr—Crossing."

Rauma considered the message. Her first thought was that it might not be genuine. Heska was not well liked at the Crossing. Many had moved to less desirable living circumstances just to avoid her control. However, since the man had not been immediately chased off by Gart, she considered his dispatch seriously. "I will meet with your mistress in two days."

"Dah ye. I will tell her," Pel said, and started to leave, then stopped. "Forgive me for bothering you, but I have a personal request."

"And that is?" Rauma tapped her foot impatiently.

Message delivered, answer received, Gart made certain that Pel left the village immediately with the lantern he had borrowed. No friendly words of farewell were exchanged.

Two days later, just about midday, Rauma arrived at the Crossing. Heska stood outside a long row of tents. She hailed Rauma enthusiastically and, with her usual foul breath, kissed Rauma on the cheek. "Greetings, old friend! It was good of you to come. Pel, do not stand there like an idjit. Take care of her beast and cart!" she commanded.

Pel placed the borrowed lantern in the back of the cart and obeyed.

"It is also good to see you," Rauma replied, then cautiously asked, "I was surprised that you have called for me after so many years."

Heska whispered, "We will discuss further details inside my tent."

Settling onto a wide, comfortable cushion, Rauma accepted a cup of steaming brewed chicory from a quiet servant. "Ooh, my favorite!" She appreciatively stirred a spoonful of honey into the dark, steaming swirl. "We rarely get luxuries such as this in Crim."

"I know. I control the chicory trade and your storekeeper refuses to meet my price."

Heska sat down so hard that the key on her necklace bounced up and hit her on the chin. "Stupid thing," she chuckled, pushing it down into her bosom. "It is the key to my treasury. I rarely remove it or Tarce would pilfer funds to gamble with."

Rauma was perplexed. "For this you urgently wished to see me?"

Heska laughed, then her casual demeanor faded. "No. I have called upon you for assistance with an important, personal matter."

"Heska of Heb needs *my* assistance? How can that be?" Rauma asked, flattered that her powerful former friend even remembered her.

Heska leaned forward, urgency in her tone. "There is a wayward girl in Crim with whom I must communicate. However, all my messengers keep getting waylaid by a young brute named Gart, quite the bully."

"Gart? A bully? No, but he is strong. He watches over Taramae—to protect her from ruffians. Is that of whom you speak?"

"Yes, that is she! Do you know her?"

"I do." Rauma held the urge to lash out as she waited to see if Heska would admit to any part of her daughter's abduction. "What would you have communicated to her?"

"It is a private concern."

"Old friend," Rauma spoke, with as much pretended sweetness as she could muster. "Do we need secrets now after so many we shared as children?"

Heska relaxed somewhat. There was a history of trust with Rauma, yet each woman knew of the other's shrewd reputation, so she proceeded with caution. "I have made a claim against Taramae, to obtain her child."

"Everyone knows this. That is why she has a protector."

Heska frowned. "Yes, and one day I will have much more to do with that so-called protector. Nevertheless, back to our discussion." Heska relaxed and leaned in once more. "You may have known that being the granddaughter of Hebarcet, it was not easy to find a suitable Pairing. Attractive men were not plentiful and some were intimidated, as you can imagine."

Rauma knew there was more than one reason no Pairing Proposals had been made for Heska but held her tongue. "Go on," she said.

"After years progressed, I accepted the less likable Tarce for the sake of having a child. When that did not happen, I grew frustrated seeing other mothers have continuous progeny and, you may find this hard to believe, I was not always pleasant to them."

Rauma could believe it but still held her tongue. She gave a phony smile. "You have my attention. How may I help?"

"You must convince Taramae to give me that child, for her future safety and for the safety of your village."

Rauma barely held her contempt. She stirred her drink to bide time. "Why do you want a baby? You have everything you could need or desire."

"True, but I will not live forever. I need someone to continue my legacy and since there is a fair likelihood that the idjit Tarce is the child's father, I have a right to claim it. Do you know her?"

Rauma could not contain her anger any longer. Her smile disappeared. "Yes, I know her *very* well. She is my daughter!"

"Splendid! The plan will work!"

Rauma's nostrils flared. "No! Your claim for her child will *not* hold. The entire village is behind her." Rauma was incensed. "You stole my daughter. You beat her. You starved her. And now you brazenly ask me to convince her to surrender her child? You ask *too* much!"

Defensively, Heska added, "I did not know that Taramae was *your* daughter!"

Rauma was aghast. "You knew that she was *someone's* daughter!"

"Yes, but *I* did not steal her. Tarce brought her to me! Fool that he is, he was persuaded by bribery to take part in the folly. He has since been corrected, and your girl has been returned."

"Returned? Taramae was *not* returned! She escaped!"

"Calm yourself," Heska warned. "As I admitted, it was folly. I hope we can move past the mishap and work together now. It would be so simple!"

"Simple? What under the heavens do you speak of?"

"Just listen!" Heska commanded, then changed to a more coaxing tone, as she unfolded her outrageous proposal. "The child of Tarce can be given to me openly at Tribunal. No one is hurt. Taramae starts her life anew with no more to fear from me, I recover the respect I lost from the embarrassment and you will have favors granted."

Rauma was outraged by the audacity of this woman. She sat silently until the wheels of greed began to roll through her mind. She could see how the proposal might work *and* be beneficial. "What if Taramae does not agree? She can be stubborn."

"Make her see reason! Beat her if necessary."

Rauma was horrified. "You already tried that, remember?"

Heska chuckled. "As I said, I did not know she was *your* daughter."

"And will you beat your own?"

Heska was indignant. "Of course not! I will teach her. My daughter will rule the world!"

"What if the child is a boy?"

Heska shrugged. "I will teach him too. It will merely take longer. His father is not of bright mind. Besides that, he may not be with us much longer."

"Oh? Is Tarce ill?"

"His welfare is of no importance in this matter. Let us move forward."

Rauma excused herself and walked out of the tent to ponder the proposition. If Heska did not get her way, it would mean continuous trouble for Taramae and for Crim. It would be difficult to convince Taramae to cooperate. She was tenderhearted and would not sacrifice a child to Heska's care, even to save herself.

Yet the thought that Heska of Heb would owe her favors was delightfully tempting to Rauma and would greatly suit her purposes. She returned to the tent, finished her drink and then clarified, "If I assist in this matter, do you swear that even if you later have regret, you will never again threaten Taramae? Will you so sign, and place your seal upon it?"

"I will so swear, sign, and seal it! And grant additional recompense. What do you want?""

"About that," Rauma grinned. "I request a cache of chicory and more at a bargain price. It would likely bring more customers to the inn."

"And …"

"Compiled records."

"Concerning yourself?"

"Your records concerning me cannot be completely accurate if you did not know that I have a daughter. No, I want the records of Leader Adris."

"Ooh, that is worth much!"

"The transaction of a child has a higher value."

"True. But why Adris?"

"The answer is of no consequence to you," Rauma said, smiling.

"Come now," "Heska insisted, "I must know. Is it to keep him from Pairing with Taramae, or to require him to pay more for the privilege?"

"How did you know of the Pairing Proposals?"

"There is an old saying, 'When served ale, secrets fail.' There is much revealed at your village Groggery."

Rauma made a mental note to be more careful what she spoke about at the Groggery in the future. "We do not ask payment for brides in Crim."

"We do! Adris wanted young, fair-haired, and tall. We do not have fair-haired in Heb, another reason your girl would have fetched a grand price."

Rauma riled again.

Heska raised her hands. "Let me finish. Adris agreed to take one of our dark-haired beauties. I almost took him for myself, but he preferred another and paid dearly for the privilege. Years later, when she returned, he tried to recoup some of his costs, but of course, it was not possible. For the way he treated Shayza, he was lucky to leave Heb with his hide! If your daughter and child were in Heb, he would pay thrice as much."

"Adris wants Taramae now for the sake of obtaining an heir."

"What of his son?"

"His son drowned."

"What say?" Now Heska was perplexed. "Both of them?"

"What say?"

"Oh, never mind about that. For now, we should complete our business."

"Yes, I must return to Crim before the gates close."

Heska agreed, gave Rauma copies of the requested documents. She glanced at them briefly, saying, "Oh my, this is not what I expected but this will do nicely."

"I thought you might think so," Heska said, and delivered another smelly kiss on the cheek, the bargain was struck.

Smote sat on the stool once more to watch the predictable actions of the gatekeeper at near dark. He spoke aloud in a dull tone. "The gatekeeper rolls each hefty rock out of the way and brings each heavy wooden side to the center. Suddenly, the gatekeeper stops."

"What say?" Smote snapped to attention. "The gatekeeper stops?"

Smote watched as the man looked about covertly and when it appeared that no one was watching, deliberately did not close one side of the gate all the way. The lock was also left off. Then the gatekeeper went home.

"Something is amiss, Owl. Watch closely!" Smote said. To avoid being silhouetted, he did not light his lantern, but stood in the dark peering out for any signs of additional movement. It was well past dark when the gate began to open once more.

Smote reached for the warning horn. The gatekeeper came running with a lantern and finished opening it. He did not seem alarmed at the sight of a wagon entering but hastily ushered it inside.

Smote squinted to see more clearly. The person handed the gatekeeper something. He promptly closed the gate, placed the lock, and ran home.

"A very odd night, Owl!" Smote whispered. "The gatekeeper is generally trusted so perhaps there is no concern," he said, and placed the horn back into its dusty corner. Yet the fact that something was vastly different felt foreboding. "What else do you suppose might be different, Owl, when the shadows give way to the light of day?"

Chapter 23: Rumblings

Reverberating thunder awoke Taramae the next morning. As a child, she usually cowered under the covers during a storm but felt a defiance rising within after being told that soon she could no longer visit Smote because she must begin the rest-in. Taramae feared she might run mad if she was cooped up for the last two weeks of her pregnancy. She had no talent for stitchery or sketching with which to while away the hours, only the companionship of regret.

Her visits to Smote had become as much a healing remedy for her as for him. When she felt relaxed, her words came clearly, with little stammering. He was many things that Jeric had been, yet he was not Jeric, and there would be no miraculous moment of remembering to bring back their loving times. Jeric was gone. Taramae no longer saw him in the man who had taken his place—the man called Smote.

The bond with Jeric had been of childhood recollections and struggling to achieve their dream of being together. He was strong and beautiful. There was little physical resemblance left of him in Smote. With Smote she felt a bond forged by their prevailing over the adversity that each of them had endured. There was understanding, admiration. Could she love him? Would she have the opportunity?

Smote seemed to enjoy her company, yet nothing had transpired to indicate that he felt more than friendship for her. She needed more time with him to determine if anything more was possible. That was the reason that the required rest-in was so irksome! She needed to know what course to take. If there could be nothing more between them, she would simply have to walk away and begin her life anew, fighting for herself and her child step by step.

Another succession of thundering rattled through the sky. It reminded her of the forceful pounding of Plateau Falls—so frightening! The memory of passing near it as she escaped shook Taramae from her ponderings.

"Good! You are awake," came the cheerful voice of the Wise Woman. "Perhaps we should visit Nadee and do other errands first and then go to Smote to explain to him why things have changed. Come now, First Meal is ready."

Taramae did not want to eat but knew her strength must be maintained for what was to come. Amid the tea and honey cakes there came a knock at the door. There were whisperings, and when Wise Woman Kess returned to the table, she said, "Someone at the inn must urgently speak with me. Enjoy your cakes. We will go on the errands upon my return."

Taramae hastened to dress as soon as Kess left. She must see Smote—alone.

As Taramae gently placed the ointment on Smote's head and neck, she quietly explained, "I will not be here again for this."

Smote's back stiffened. "What say?"

"It is nearly my time, and I must have rest-in to gather strength before my child is born."

Smote relaxed. "It is best. But after, you will come again."

Taramae placed her hand on his shoulder. "After the Naming Ceremony there will be another Tribunal, possibly a Pairing choice and a Pairing Ceremony. The man I choose might not understand my visits here."

"How is it done?" he asked, weakly.

"What say?"

"How is this Pairing Ceremony done?"

Taramae carefully began to explain. "First, the couple must have permission. They stand together at the Pavilion—not touching—and ask if anyone in the village denies their petition. No one speaks—at least not in any of the times I have witnessed. Then the couple walks out through the gates to the Sacred Stone."

Smote listened, intently.

"The man gives a necklace with his family token to the woman and says, 'Accept this token of my fidelity, if you will,' and places it around her neck. The woman says, 'Accept my hand as a token of my fidelity, if you will.' A kiss is shared, and they return through the gates holding hands to the Pavilion to celebrate with others."

"And what of this token?"

"It is a sphere of precious metal or fine wood engraved with his family symbol. It is hung on a thin leather strap or chain."

"It is always so?"

Taramae hesitated. If there was ever a time when a memory needed to be sparked within him, it was this moment. Carefully she proceeded. "If—for an honorable reason—the people cannot openly ask permission from the village, they may claim PermaDevo and obtain permission from a village elder, someone who would vouch for them later. They exchange vows at the Sacred Stone privately and announce to others later." Emotion welling in her voice, she finished by saying, "This is like the Pairing Ceremony I had with my Jeric."

Smote seemed moved. "And was your reason honorable?"

"If justice and love are honorable, then it truly was. Our devotion grew from childhood. My mother sought to thwart it. Therefore, we drew upon the law and hoped that the village would understand, even if she never would."

Smote rubbed the temple of his head to diminish a sudden pain. "Is this new Pairing one that you desire?"

"They say I must choose for the sake of my child's future and I will appeal that decision before Tribunal. But too many villagers are uneasy about my circumstances. A Pairing would calm concerns."

"Is it what you *desire*?" Smote insisted on knowing.

Taramae was irked. "You know it is not. But if I am to stay in ..."

Smote interrupted, "Are there any others in the village living unPaired?"

The thought dawned upon Taramae. "Yes, Old Soul Nadee, Wise Woman Kess, my mother, Adris, Brun, and the gatekeeper."

"Have they been asked to leave the village?"

"No."

Confidently, Smote smacked his fists together. "There—it is plain! They cannot require a Pairing when examples of otherwise exist. Harsh governance—this control of freedom—is not this why they left Heb? You *must* remind them!"

Taramae answered feistily, "It *is* so! I had not pieced it together thus. Dah ye, Smote. Your reasoning may help me appeal the judgment." She almost hugged him.

"And afterward, all will be well," Smote said jubilantly. "You will stay free and return as you desire to visit your decrepit Tower friend."

Taramae started to agree, then stopped, her countenance falling. "All will not simply be well. Heska of Heb has a claim against me—to obtain my child—and without the support of the village, we are not safe." She looked around Smote's sparse accommodations, and added, "Besides that, if Adris does not get his way, he might hurt others I care for."

Smote realized that she was referring to him. "Do not fear for me! I will be well soon and able to leave the village." He knew he could not bear to live there if she was Paired with another.

Taramae was alarmed. "Leave the village? Where would you go?"

Humorously, he declared, "I will live in a hut in the hills, with shuttered windows to keep prying eyes away, lest others be frightened by my appearance and blame me for malevolent dreams—calling me the Smote Menace."

"Do not say that!" Taramae began to place the ointments in her basket. "With your knowledge, ye should live openly and teach. They will accept when they better know you."

"And if they will *not* accept?"

"Then, we will run away and establish our own village!" Taramae announced, with a humorous protest.

"We? "Smote asked, curiously.

"Yes, of course!"

They laughed, each pondering what Taramae had just implied when Wise Woman Kess hurriedly, stepped inside. Breathlessly, she said, "There you are! Come. We must talk!"

Taramae protested. "I need to say farewell."

"There will be another time. Come now!" the Wise Woman insisted, grabbing the basket and pulling Taramae along with her. "Forgive me, Smote. Do not distress. We will return on the morrow."

Listening to hurried footsteps, Taramae's protests, and echoes of "Mizzafrizzaritz!" down the stairwell, Smote said, "Something is very wrong, Owl. Very wrong, indeed!"

Back at her dwelling, Kess explained Rauma's arrangement with Heska. Taramae was outraged. "She should have known that I would never agree!"

"She seeks only to free you from Heska's grasp that you might not live in continual fear of retribution."

Taramae was suspicious. "There must be other benefits. Rauma always sees all sides of the barrel."

Kess understood the distrust. "True, but her good intentions have at least provided us with more time to figure another course to take without Heska sending a constant barrage of threatening strangers. We just need not quash the rumor that you are considering it."

"No, no, no. I do not want that said of me, even for a temporary reprieve. It will damage my reputation further. We cannot let it happen."

Kess winced. "The tale was already told at the Groggery last night. It seems to have calmed things. Heska's men left this morning. It does not have to be true. Heska just needs to believe it might be."

Taramae wearily asked, "How is it that some wield such evil power?"

"Perhaps because the good build their lives upon love and future promise, and the bad spend their lives crafting ways to use those virtues as weapons against them. It seems always to have been so. Yet occasionally, evil will punish evil and leave the good alone."

"That would be nice. Should we pray for the Vast Vex to swoop down and carry Heska away—and Tarce with her?"

"It will not happen. It was the Vast Vex that dropped them here in the first place."

There was melancholy in the tone of their laughter.

After a few minutes, Taramae gasped. "And what of Smote? He will be upset about it."

"Then stay away."

"No! Please let me see him again to say farewell."

"In all of today's visit, there was no farewell? What did you speak of?"

"Of running away," Taramae mused, recalling the last conversation with him.

"You know such a venture is impossible," Kess reminded her, sympathetically. "One exhausting thought at a time, my dear, please!"

Taramae was upset. Already the rumor had caused askance glances from others at the storehouse and Nawhi seemed to avoid her. Rauma pulled Taramae aside as she walked back.

Taramae jerked her arm away, saying, "Know right now, I did not agree to your scheme."

"It will keep you safe."

Taramae scoffed. "You appeased Heska. How will you appease Adris?"

Thinking of the information that she had received from Heska, Rauma said, "There will be another way. You should move back to the inn until the child is born," Rauma insisted.

"I will stay with Kess."

"At least stop going to the Tower. It is causing great concern."

Taramae's eyes narrowed. "I will go where I please. You have shown little regard for me since I returned. Do not attempt to enforce parenting now. Your agreement has brought shame upon me. I should denounce you immediately as a fraud and end this."

Rauma was at once furious at being spoken to in such a way, yet proud that her daughter had shown such courage. She bowed pretentiously and stepped aside so Taramae might pass.

An hour later, Rauma walked directly to the Tower. She planned to confront the person who seemed to have such a hold on her daughter. If Taramae refused to end this embarrassment, she would! Retrieving the key, she stormed up the stairs, prepared for battle, to put an end to this ridiculousness.

A sharp knock at the door startled Smote as he sat at his post on the stool by the window. He jumped at the sound, not expecting other guests. It was too early for the Wise Woman. "Enter, and welcome," he called out.

A stern-faced woman strode in hastily. At first, due to the resemblance, he believed her to be Taramae. However, the countenance was rigid, and the hair much darker and pulled tight against the top of her head. Smote stood up so quickly that the stool fell over, crashing onto the floor. Embarrassed, he joked as he picked it up, saying, "This is a good day. Sometimes I am even clumsier." Then, dragging his foot as usual, he walked over to properly greet her. "My name is Smote. And you are?"

For a rare moment, Rauma was speechless. Was this twisted shell of a man really the person her daughter preferred to spend her time with? For this smelly creature, Taramae would risk losing a prosperous Pairing? Disgusted, Rauma prepared to unleash a tirade of displeasure.

Smote noticed her scrutiny of him, and asked again, "And you are?"

"My name is Rauma. I came to speak of my daughter, Taramae."

"Your daughter? You must be *so* proud! She is such a kind-hearted young woman." He motioned to the stack of written pages on the table. "We have been compiling the stories of Old Soul Nadee's life. What a remarkable woman! Do you know her? Of course, you know her. It is a small village. Then surely you already know how remarkable she is. Forgive my rambling."

Something about the way Smote spoke reverberated through Rauma's fuming brain. Suddenly she gasped.

"I am sorry! Forgive me for being rude. Please sit down," Smote said, retrieving the stool, he dragged it closer to her.

Stunned, Rauma sat down to gather her senses. A dead man—or one she had been told was dead—stood in front of her acting as though he had never met her. Memories of past callousness bestowed upon Jeric flashed uncomfortably through her mind. "Uh, I should leave."

Smote was puzzled. "I thought you came to speak of Taramae. I am glad. I am quite concerned for her."

Rauma's thoughts snapped back to the present. "What say?"

Smote repeated, tenderly. "I am quite concerned about Taramae and the Tribunal judgement. The strain of this Pairing decision weighs heavily upon her. It is not healthy for her in many ways, and there are grave concerns over other threats. I also see in her eyes that she is still grieving the loss of her beloved one."

Touched by the man's sincerity, Rauma smiled slightly. "I am trying to help her, but she has struggled to make decisions. Now I understand why."

"It seems unfair to force a decision. Do you not agree?"

Rauma replied, softly, "Yes, I agree that it is not the correct thing for her to do."

"Dah ye. My circumstances make it impossible for me to assist further. It is a relief to know that she can rely on you. Dah ye for the visit. Forgive me for not having proper refreshments to offer."

"Do not trouble yourself about refreshments," Rauma said. "I am glad that we met, Smote. It is good to know that Taramae has such a fine friend. Dah ye." With that, she left.

Rauma's mind was awhirl with all the complications Taramae had been swept up into. No wonder the girl seemed overwhelmed and irritable whenever they spoke! As if expecting a child was not enough, she was being pressured to Pair when her original Pairing was still in effect. No wonder she delayed the choosing! And what of the heartache? Rauma knew that Jeric had been in her daughter's heart for many years. Now Smote was in his place. How painful it must be for her daughter! For the first time in years, tears trickled down Rauma's cheeks. It was an uncomfortable, uncontrolled feeling, and she fought to contain it.

She mulled over the events of the past hour. She was usually privy to all secrets in Crim—had made it her business to be so. How had she missed this one? She was determined to learn how Smote had come to be in the Tower—and who else knew about him.

If Adris knew, he hid it well behind an insistent drive to Pair with Taramae. Such lack of compassion for an injured kinsman was disturbing, even by Rauma's liberal standards. Obviously, Adris did not know. The prospect of revealing it to him fit well into Rauma's plan. His taxes were becoming unbearable. Now she had two possible forms of leverage. Another rare smile crossed Rauma's face—until she remembered her promise to Heska.

Chapter 24: The Awakening

The next morning, Taramae slept in. Lying enfolded in the warmth of the furs made it easier to ignore, for a moment, the reality facing her. During her cozy reverie there was a soft knock on the door. Wise Woman Kess answered it, whispering. Not yet motivated to arise, Taramae listened. She could hear Kess clattering kettle and cups. There was more whispering, and then the smell of chicory. Mother? The reverie was dashed. What was Rauma up to now? Taramae lay still, eavesdropping.

"And, now that you know?" Kess asked.

"It changes everything. She must *not* accept a Pairing! It is against the law! And she has a blameless reason to keep the child."

Taramae was amazed. Her mother, who had been intent on forcing her into a Pairing with Adris and handing over her child to Heska, was now was decidedly against it. What had changed?

Rauma continued, "I cannot believe that he is there! It was told that he abandoned her, and then that he was dead, not that he was in the Tower and so injured that his mind is not intact? What has happened, and why was it kept a secret?"

"Not everyone needed to know, for Jeric's sake. Clearly someone had attacked him and left him to die. We did not know who that person was and could not take chances that it might have been someone with a desire to complete the task."

"You could have told *me*."

148

"Could we? There was concern that *you* might have cause to hurt him had you known of his plan to abscond with your daughter."

Rauma raised her voice in protest, "I *never* would have harmed him!"

"Shh!" Kess admonished. "We could not know that. You have always been angry about his attention to Taramae."

Rauma continued her protest, at a lower volume. "I *never* would have hurt Jeric! I just wanted him to go away."

The Wise Woman's voice broke. "He *did* go away, as far away as possible, and yet still be alive."

"And now there is this *creature*!" Rauma's voice betrayed her disgust.

Now Kess raised her voice, "Smote is *not* a creature!"

"Shh!" Rauma admonished. "I know, I know. But you must admit, he is a mangled mess of a man. What hope for a traditional life can he have now? He cannot even carry his own squat pot to the dump wagon!"

Kess was very defensive. "There is more to a person than the ability to carry a squat pot! Smote is kind, intelligent, humorous, and caring. Are those not substantial qualities?"

"Yes, but those alone will not feed a family. Does he still want her?"

"How can he want her? He has no recollections. It is tormenting her that cherished memories no longer exist. The first time was such a shock that she nearly lost the baby!"

"No!"

"Yes! In weeks since, I believe she has come to appreciate Smote as Smote, and I believe he genuinely cares for her. Perhaps in time …"

"Time, time, time!" Rauma groaned aloud. "There is *little* time now. No wonder the girl's head is spinning!"

"And her heart. Can you see how your recent imprudent venture has not helped her?"

"How could I have known? It sounded like a solution to the impending Heska problem."

"What a heartbreaking choice you have presented your daughter!"

"You agreed to it!"

"No, I agreed to tell her about it. The cart was already racing downhill when you announced it at the Groggery. I am merely trying to slow its descent."

Rauma stopped as she passed Kess's mirror. She stood, sadly looking at her reflection. "How did we come to such a disconnect?"

"Ask that of your reflection another time. Go now. I must prepare for my rounds."

Rauma did not move. In a faraway tone, she said, "When Ven died, all I could think of was how to survive. Panic made me driven to succeed, terrified that we would end up starving."

Kess shattered her moment of illusion with the truth. "This village has never let anyone starve. Your children needed your love and you were not there for them."

Rauma began to justify her choices. "I know, but Aven clung to Taramae so it seemed as though his needs were taken care of while I sought work."

"She was a child too! What of *her* needs? Even then she carried the burden of responsibility."

"But she was her father's favorite. I did not think she needed me as much as Aven did. How I dread that I often missed times of holding him and telling of my love. I always thought there would be time another day— and then he was gone." Rauma turned away, sniffling.

"Taramae did not take that time away from you and yet you agreed to her punishment."

"I know, it was wrong. But the Vast Vex fed off the grief and anger in the village and permeated my heart. All I could think of was to stay busy. As soon as I obtained funds to purchase the inn, we at least had security. But we stayed together the whole time. I did not turn her away."

Kess shook her head. She wanted to say, that's because she was your best servant, but knew it was a waste of breath. Everything was about the inn to Rauma. It gave her status.

Rauma continued her justifications "I was trying to help Taramae. Heska insisted that she be given the baby or else. She was convinced that Tarce was the father and I thought that giving the child would keep Taramae and the village safe and end the constant reminder of Tarce's likely unwanted advances."

"Do you believe now that Jeric is the father?"

"If Jeric was alive, I have no doubt that he is the father. They thought to hide their affection and eagerness but I was not unaware, nor really surprised. I was, however, offended because of their sneakiness, and upset that their departure came at a very inconvenient time."

Kess pretended to do a nit check when she really wanted to jerk Rauma by the bun. She listened, grinding her teeth. How much easier it would have been if she had given Taramae permission to Pair with Jeric in the first place. So much tragedy could have been prevented!

"There is a problem now about Heska," Rauma rambled on. "But the meeting was not without benefit. I obtained important information that Heska was privy to. She would have thought it odd if I did not ask for something."

"Hoping to find a new way to gain Adris' affection?"

"Once I was interested, but now I need a way to get him to back off on tax collection!"

Wise Woman Kess had had enough and knew that Taramae had likely heard the discussion. She patted Rauma on the back as she gently pushed her toward the door.

"So. what are we going to do?" Rauma worried, trying to slow the departure.

"We? You should consider that answer but do *no* more intervening! I will tend to Taramae. Do not distress her further!"

Rauma opened the door to find Banaya standing there. "Go away!" she barked.

Kess rushed up. "No, no, let her enter. Taramae enjoys her visits."

Rauma leaned down to Banaya's level, saying, "Do not be a bother, girl!"

Banaya circled her face with her finger and touched the tip of her nose.

"What does that mean?" Rauma asked, suspiciously.

The Wise Woman pulled Banaya inside and closed the door, she said, "Come, dear. We have a new drink for you to try. It is called chicory."

It was evident that Taramae had heard the previous conversation by the redness around her eyes. However, she did not mention it, merely asked, "Where have you been, my little friend?" as she held out her arms for a welcoming hug.

The Wise Woman answered. "She was ill with a fever but was a good girl and took her medicine. Now she only has a slight cough."

As further proof, Banaya coughed slightly then sat at the table.

"I am glad you are better. I have missed you."

"Woezy! You got big!"

Taramae's face reddened. "It is true."

"You got *really* big! Are you having a bear?"

Taramae laughed. "No, silly girl. Sometimes babies need more room to stretch."

Kess intervened. "After the braiding, we are going on rounds. Would you like to walk with us?"

Banaya's eyes brightened. "Will you go to the Tower?"

Kess was alarmed until Taramae explained. "Banaya has already met Smote. She took flowers to him."

Still concerned, Kess said, "Taramae will visit him briefly this morning," Kess accentuated the word *briefly*. "You may go with me to care for others."

"Smote likes her," the girl mumbled with a mouthful of toasted bread.

"What say?" Taramae and Kess asked at the same time.

"The Tower man likes Taramae," the child mumbled again.

"Did he tell you?"

Banaya was annoyed. "He never *said* it. He *looked* it. Whenever he speaks of her, he looks of very much liking. But I am still your most-friend, right?"

"Of course. Finish your food and we will deal with this unruly mop you call hair," Taramae tickled her on the side of the neck.

Banaya giggled, wiped her mouth on her sleeve, and quickly pulled the chair farther away from the table so Taramae could walk around.

Taramae's belly bumped into her as she sat there. "Woezy! They will need a bigger wager," Banaya exclaimed.

"What say?" the Wise Woman asked.

"The men at the Groggery placed a wager on Taramae. I heard them say thus while I was ill. They are using storehouse coins. They will need many to cover her!"

"What wager? Is it about the Pairing?"

"Yes, and if she will give her baby to the mean woman." Tears filled Banaya's eyes. She took Taramae's hand, asking. "Why would you do that?"

Taramae put her arms around the girl's shoulders, "No matter what you hear, do not worry, little one. It's just the talk of idle minds. Crim could not breathe without a gust of rumor for fresh air."

Rauma sank down onto her bed trying not to let her emotions get the better of her but recent conversations with her daughter had stung her to the core. Taramae was right about some accusations, but Rauma was not guilty of selling everything nor dismissing their former life recklessly. From a dark shelf in the closet, Rauma unpacked the box of little carved animals that Ven had made his daughter. She touched each one gently. Taramae had kindheartedly begun giving them to others and Rauma feared she would regret it one day, so had hidden them away.

Rauma had not forgotten the times of blessed happiness—the Great Good as her husband called it—when their family was whole and love enfolded them. But even now, dwelling upon those memories brought absolute madness, so she pushed them back into the corner of her mind where they could not torture her daily lest she run screaming with grief, pulling her hair out.

She had planned to give the cherished keepsakes back when Taramae married but then all this craziness had transpired and there had been no tender moment between them. Now she was not sure what to do. She packed the box away on the shelf, along with the sorrowful memories that came with them.

Chapter 25: Conflicted

As usual, Gart was waiting for her—and so was Zaela. Immediately confronting her, Zaela demanded, "Taramae, you must release Gart from his Pairing Proposal!"

Gart shook his head. "It will go forth if it needs to, Zaela."

"But—but ..." Zaela sputtered, pointing at Taramae in disgust.

Before Gart could scold her, Taramae asked, "Why should he be released?"

Zaela continued to sputter, "Because ... because he is too young to be saddled with such responsibility—and another man's child!"

"I am not!" Gart scoffed. "I am older than Taramae by a year."

Taramae agreed. "If he feels ready to move forward in life in such a manner, why should he not move forward with me?"

"Because he might have other opportunities—within a year or two. Other opportunities worth waiting for."

"What opportunities?" Taramae and Gart asked, simultaneously.

As Zaela walked away, she spouted, "I ... I ... do not know, but he may have opportunities that even he has not yet thought of. You *must* release him!"

Taramae hid her mischievous grin until Zaela was gone. Then, turning to Gart, she shook her head. "Do you truly desire to be tangled with that whirlwind for the rest of your days?"

Gart grinned. "More than ever. She is even lovelier with a flash of fire upon her cheeks."

"You are the bravest of men, friend Gart."

He laughed briefly, then became serious. "No braver than you, friend Taramae. What is this you are tangled in?"

"My mother has made Heska an impossible promise. I do not plan to honor it. But the rumor is supposed to keep me safe." Taramae shook her head, doubtfully. "What can be done to appease Heska?"

"Nothing!" Gart whispered firmly. "I have witnessed her despicable dealings many times. I worked for her until eight months ago. I was desperate to discover the identity of my family, information only she knew. I finally had to threaten her life and all she would say is, 'Go to Crim.' I am still no closer to the answer. Heska always uses others for her benefit. She is *not* to be trusted!" Gart put his hand on her shoulder, "You will live longer than any of your advisors. It is your life. Take the reins!"

Taramae was annoyed. "It sounds good. But it is not easy for a woman."

Gart pointed down at her expanded frame, "If you can create new life, can you not create the living of your own?"

Taramae took a deep breath. "I have an idea of what can be done. but it will take much support from friends in order to be accomplished."

"You will have it," he pledged, with a grin and a short bow. Then with complete seriousness said, "Taramae, my proposal was sincere and will still be honored if need be."

She touched his arm, saying, "Dah ye, Gart. You are the kindest man here. But what would become of lovely Zaela, without you to champion her?"

Gart shook his head. "I fear she would become as withdrawn as her sister."

"We cannot have that! It would spoil that face you so admire," Taramae teased. "How long will you keep her dangling?"

"Until she turns of age and her father sees that I am worthy."

"You are more than worthy!" she said, as she walked toward the Tower. Calling back over her shoulder, she gave familiar advice. "It is your life. Take the reins!"

As Taramae entered his chamber, Smote could not help staring at her appearance. "As your most-friend, Banaya would say, 'Woezy!'"

Embarrassed by his comment, she turned to the table, unloading the basket as usual. "Lower weight happens to all mothers at this point in pregnancy. Would you like to take a turn carrying it?"

"No, no. You are doing well enough."

Taramae laughed. "I am not so sure. Please sit so we can begin the treatment. I need to tell you something. Because of my mother, others think I will give my child to Heska, for the safety of the village. It is not true but I must not openly deny it. It is a temporary remedy."

Smote was appalled. "How could you agree to such a stratagem?"

"I did not agree! But the word was spread."

"I met your mother. She did not appear crazy. But to think that you would surrender your child to a horrible person does not seem of sound mind."

"Very true, and I will not do as she says, though others will believe I might."

"If empathy is needed from the villagers for your appeal of no Pairing, they might think you are coldhearted and opinion turn against you. To have them question your character is not advantageous and from what I hear of that woman, it is a dangerous course to take."

"I know, I know. I wish I could stand in the square and scream, 'It is all a lie!' But Kess says to leave it for now, that she will think of a better solution."

Smote shook his head, disapproving of the whole situation.

This was not the reaction she had expected from him. Some sympathy, perhaps. Concern, hopefully. But not such intense disapproval. It bothered her that he would presume to lecture her on a difficult social situation when he himself was far removed from community realities.

Taramae's mind was awhirl. She could see his point. She could see her mother's point. She could see Kess's point, and even Heska's. Then there was Gart's, Adris's, and even Zaela's. There were so many points she feared a mortal wound. So much advice from every quarter. How she longed for someone to simply hold her, reassuringly. But alas, no one had offered. Her brain hurt, her back hurt, and now her heart ached with disappointment that this visit had unraveled in such a way. "I should leave," she said, tears trickling down her cheeks as she closed the basket.

Smote stepped close to her. "I do not want you to leave. I want you to be better advised—to find another way to be safe. I wish there was another way."

"As do I," she answered, weakly, and sought to change the subject. She leafed through the scribed pages of Nadee's story that lay neatly piled on the table.

"You are an able storyteller. Nadee is a remarkable woman—like you. Is she kindred?"

She looked at him, yearning. "No, not to me." A moment of silence lingered before she added, "Dah ye, Smote. It will mean much. Her heart fails more each day."

"It would be amazing to meet her."

Taramae smiled. She wondered if such a meeting might actually aid in healing Nadee, give her some joy in her final days. But the Wise Woman had forbidden it, reasoning that since Smote had no memory of her as his grandmother nor have the same devotion as Jeric, it might be harder to tolerate than the grief. However, Taramae believed that if Nadee was prepared, it might not be so bad. "Nadee will enjoy knowing that her story has been written at last. May I take a few pages to her?" Taramae asked.

"Will you bring them back? There is more to add."

"I will see that no harm comes to them."

"*And* bring them back?" Smote asked again.

"They will be returned by someone trustworthy. Dah ye, Smote. This endeavor has brought me great happiness during troubled times. I must go. Farewell."

He caught her arm, gently. "Farewell? Will you not come again?"

"Not until all is resolved."

"I ... I feel ..." he faltered.

"*What* do you feel, Smote?" She looked longingly into the eyes that had once belonged to her loving Jeric but he was no longer in them. She could see the compassion of a friend, perhaps even affection. But if he could not lay claim to what he was feeling, she could not do it for him.

Smote groaned with frustration. "I feel as though I should help, but do not know how?"

Taramae smiled. "Do you mean to rescue me?"

"If it is possible."

"It is *not* possible. No one can save me. The last person who tried ...." Taramae turned away. "It will unfold as it must. I know not when I will return or if. It would be unfair to cause you further concern. So, please, let us say farewell."

"But ..."

She shook her head no, touched him on the cheek and left.

Chapter 26: Traces

Taramae slept for most of the first day of her rest-in time. By the second day, with so much on her mind, she found it impossible to laze about. Yet the exuberance of her eight-year-old daily guest was more than she could sustain energy for. Therefore, after the braiding was accomplished, she immediately sent Banaya out to play and went to visit Old Soul Nadee. She placed the first of the story pages that she had borrowed from Smote safely into a pouch and carried two slices of honey cake.

On the way, she noticed Zaela speaking with Gart by the well. She nodded slightly in their direction.

"See what I mean?" Zaela accused. "She is odd and unsociable—a blight on the village! I heard that she is going to give her child away."

Gart became upset. "A nasty rumor! She is *not* a blight on the village. She is brave! People would benefit from being more like her."

Zaela huffed indignantly. "Why do you say such things?"

"Because she is my friend, a *true* friend. She has never asked for my help, but has been grateful for all given. She is always kind, brings honey cakes to share, and does not consider me lowborn or without merit."

"You have other friends."

"Who? The villagers are polite, but most are afraid of me, and few have done as much as Taramae to welcome me."

"You are in love with her!" Zaela scoffed.

"Not in the ways of a husband and wife. But if she needs me for the Pairing, to spare her from unkindness of others, I will do so."

Zaela shook her head. "You are a fool!"

Gart gazed upon Zaela forlornly. "In more ways than one," he said.

Nadee was thrilled for the surprise visit.

"Kess has gone to a Naming Ceremony on New Side. I hope you do not mind."

"Of course not! Come in, come in."

"How are you?" Taramae asked, as she set out the cake and helped serve tea.

"The more apt question is, how are *you*?"

Taramae half laughed, half groaned. "It is a misery. This wild one prods and jabs to get out. It will not be long now."

Nadee chuckled., saying, "They do not understand that it is safer inside, away from worldly cares. They fight to face it and yet cry when they see the light."

"I believe there is a reason for fierceness within this child. I feel a resolve regarding him, as though he understands his destiny."

"And what if it is not a he?"

"I have often thought it is a boy and have been addressing him as such. If it is not a boy, we will both be surprised," Taramae giggled.

When they had finished the cake, Taramae handed Nadee the pouch, explaining that it was the beginning of the promised writing.

Happily, Nadee opened it. "Another lovely surprise," she said, then suddenly turned and very seriously asked, "*Where* is *he*?"

"What say?" Taramae stalled, slowly lowering onto a chair.

"Where is Jeric?" she demanded. "I know this writing. I raised him. I taught him the letters. They told me that he is dead, but here is my story in his hand. Where IS he?"

Taramae wondered how to answer that would cause the least harm. She settled on the truth. She beckoned Nadee near, and then, holding her hand, said, "Jeric—the Jeric we know and love, *is* dead. When I was stolen, he tried to save me, was terribly injured and left for dead. Somehow, he was found and placed secretly in the Tower. He calls himself *Smote*. Kess has been nursing him back to health."

"You should have told me! Kess should have told me! He is my grandson! Was there no thought of *my* grief?"

"Kess feared it would be too much for your heart to bear, concerned what the shock would do to you. He is barely recognizable! I only found out by accident and I was devastated. He did not know me. Jeric had great love for you. Smote would not know you."

Nadee pondered the information. "He remembers *nothing*?"

"He has *no* memory of his former self nor of others in his life. He calls himself Smote because his body is marred and twisted. They have kept him hidden, not knowing who hurt him, and fearing that the sight of him might spark calls of Dark Menaces and demands for his banishment. It would be a disaster! Smote is helpless in many ways. He *must* not be cast out!"

"Still, Kess should have told me!" she said, placing a hand on her chest and breathing deeply for a moment. "I want to see him! While I yet abide on this earth I should be allowed to choose the fate of my heart. Besides that, my *brain* still works. There might be something I could do to help him."

Taramae stood to stretch her aching back. "I wish something could be done. But it would take the touch of SkyFa himself to change the course of this. Kess and I had hoped the telling of your story would spark memories. It did not. When he tries to gather thoughts of the past, it causes horrible head pain."

"Does he know your child is his?"

Tears filled Taramae's eyes. "There is no recollection of our love nor Pairing."

Nadee took her hand, "How awful for you, my dear. I know how long you waited to be together. This is tragic in *so* many ways."

"Adris has declared I must accept a Pairing to stay in Crim. Yet my husband lives, though he is no longer my husband."

After a moment's pause, Nadee asked, "This man—this Smote—has he become someone you care for?"

Taramae smiled. "It has been difficult to reconcile. Smote is not the same as Jeric. But Smote is good. He is his own self. Funny. Kind. Stubborn! It is hard not to like him. However, I doubt that Smote considers me more than a friend in trouble."

Nadee could see that more than friendship existed in Taramae's heart. Yet for her own sake, she said, "I still want to see him. You could say it is to thank him for his writings."

"He could not come here safely. He walks poorly, tires easily and someone might be tempted to hurt him again should his location be revealed."

Nadee gazed out her window at the Tower. "It is harder than a death to be near him, yet know he is beyond my reach!"

"Kess will scold, but if you promise not to depart from us soon, I will find a way for you to see Smote after my baby is born."

Old Soul Nadee patted Taramae's hand. "With such renewed hope, I will not allow my heart to fail soon. That is a promise!"

As they embraced, Taramae groaned loudly.

Old Soul Nadee felt her abdomen. "Was your water colored this morning?"

"A little."

"You best be finding that Wise Woman, my dear!"

As Taramae was leaving, back spasms hit so intensely that she nearly fell down. Gart and Zaela noticed her struggling to walk. Taramae cried out in pain as Gart ran to assist her.

"Find Kess," she pleaded. "Run to New Side."

"There she goes again!" Zaela chided him. "Can you not see how she uses you?"

Gart lost his temper. "Go away, brat! How could I have been so blinded by your beauty that I did not see your ugly heart? You are *worse* than a spoiled child lacking in compassion! I will have no further regard for you!"

Zaela stood, stunned. Gart picked Taramae up in his arms and carried her the rest of the way home, then ran for the Wise Woman.

Chapter 27: A Deeper Connection

S mote paced the floor, his anxiety growing with each additional hour. He had not slept, concerned about what he had seen the evening before—Taramae in distress and Gart carrying her toward Kess's dwelling. Greatly troubled, he tried to focus on his usual duties.

"Here comes the gatekeeper," he began. "He stands and looks at the gate. Why? How could its appearance have changed overnight? The gatekeeper checks to see if the latch is---is ...

Smote could not remember the usual wording. He could not concentrate.

"Mizzafrizzaritz, Owl! Do we care what happens next to the gatekeeper? No! If he wants to live a life of predictable monotony, let him. We want to know what is happening to Taramae!

"She must be delivering her baby, Owl. That is a good thing, right? If so, why do I have such a bad feeling?" he asked and began pacing once more.

"Not knowing is maddening! Why? You know why. Because I truly care for her. I more than care for her. There, I admit it! But I have no right to expect any affection from her. How could she fancy a—hideous man?"

Smote was relieved to hear footsteps ascending the stairs and to hear the key. But it was only Nawhi bringing his First Meal basket. How could he eat? His stomach was in knots. Still, he was glad for the company, however briefly.

"Dah ye for the food. Please tell me," he pleaded. "What word of Taramae?"

Nawhi finally spoke to him, "What say?"

"I saw Taramae in distress near dark. She was taken to the Wise Woman's dwelling. How fares she? Have you heard?"

Nawhi's eyes narrowed. "Why do you want to know?"

"She is my friend. I am worried about her!"

Nawhi carefully considered whether to give any details. After a moment she said, "I have heard that she struggles with the birthing. They fear—"

"Take me to her!" Smote interrupted.

"What say?"

"You must take me to Taramae. I will encourage her."

"You cannot leave here."

"I can if you will assist."

"You do not understand. You are not *supposed* to leave here—ever! People may see you. It is not good."

Smote retorted, "I do not care for the opinions of others. I must help my friend!"

"I *cannot* take you. It is *not* permitted," Nawhi insisted.

"Permitted?" Smote grew angry. "If you will not take me, find someone who will! Find that young man from the Groggery. Send him to me."

Nawhi did not appreciate the command. She left, deliberately locking the door loudly behind her. She would *not* be the one to let him out. She had enough to worry about. Nearing the storehouse, she saw Gart taking extra blankets out. She chose not to tell him of Smote's request.

"Mizzafrizzaritz!" Kess exclaimed as she sat down, exhausted.

Taramae was having an unusually complicated labor and had weakened to the point of giving up. The hours of groaning with each contraction had diminished to whimpering moans.

The Wise Woman was exhausted as well. She did not know what else to do. Of all the births she had attended to, no one else had presented this way."

"Do something!" Rauma insisted. "Can you open her to take the child?"

Kess was horrified. "It would *kill* her!"

There was only one other option, though it would put another at risk. She called for Gart. "Go quickly and ask Old Soul Nadee to come."

When Nadee saw Taramae in such decline, she was extremely upset. "How could you let it go this far?" she demanded to know.

"I did all I knew to do," Kess apologized. "I had her change positions, drink the tea, and do the breathing."

Nadee saw the bloody discharge on the bedding. Taramae cried out as Nadee felt her abdomen. "This baby is distressed and likely breech. It must be turned immediately!" She shook Taramae softly. "Child, you must wake up and help us with this."

Taramae's eyes flickered, but she did not respond.

Rauma whined, "I have tried talking to her, but she does not answer."

"Rauma, your voice would not help. Her soul perceives you as an adversary. There must be someone else. Think!"

"I have tried over and over!" Kess answered, choking emotion in her voice. "She is not responding to me either."

"Stop! Your resolve must not fail now. We must work together." Nadee pondered, then suddenly declared, "Bring that man from the Tower!"

"Smote?" Kess and Rauma exclaimed at the same time.

"Yes, him!"

"No, no, no!" Rauma protested.

"Yes, yes, yes!" Nadee insisted. "She has a deeper connection to him than you realize." Turning to Gart, she demanded, "Bring that man here at once!"

Smote's pacing was making him dizzy. He tried to eat some of the bread and fruit Nawhi had brought, but each swallowed mouthful churned in his stomach. He washed his face and changed his tunic just to fill the time. He was not expecting company. He had seen Nawhi walk past the man from the Groggery without speaking to him, so there was little hope there. What a relief it was to hear the key again in the lock.

Gart stood before him, wincing in distaste at what he saw and smelled. "Taramae labors with difficulty. The old Wise Woman calls for you. I do *not* understand why. Do you know?"

Smote ignored the query and moved forward with his quest. "Dah ye for coming! I am Smote. I am Taramae's friend. I have seen how you care for her. I heard she is suffering. I must go to her! Please assist me."

Gart grumbled. "I have seen Taramae leave this Tower upset *many* times and believe that you should stay away. She does *not* need more trouble. Yet I am told to bring you."

164

Smote shoved Owl into his pocket and moved to the Tower door. He was afraid of what lay beyond. He had been told never to leave, that the stress would be too much to bear, possibly causing his demise, but he did not care. "I will go, with your assistance or without!"

Gart looked over this determined man. He was not convinced that his presence would help Taramae but finally agreed. "We must go now before more villagers awaken."

Smote agreed, and for the first time opened the Tower door.

Looking at the stairs below, Smote was wary. "I fear your strong arm will be needed for the descent."

Gart was not thrilled but soon realized Smote's walking limitations. "Put your hand on my shoulder. I will walk down step by step. When we get outside, you are on your own. But I warn you ..." Gart said man to man, "When we get there, do *not* cause greater distress, or I *will* remove you!"

Smote understood.

When Smote arrived, Rauma was flabbergasted. "Again, I ask, *why* was this *person* brought here? It makes absolutely *no* sense."

"There is no time to explain," Nadee replied. "Taramae is beyond reason now. She must be brought back by any means necessary to get this baby delivered, or both will be lost."

Smote bowed respectfully to Nadee. "I am Smote. You sent for me? How may I help?"

Nadee's emotions began to swell. She wanted to wrap her arms around her missing loved one but patted his shoulder instead. As she did, she could feel how thin and weak-muscled he had become. How could her ruggedly built, handsome grandson have come to such a pitiful state? She would deal with that later. Now was not the time.

Pushing harsh feelings down for the sake of the task at hand, she said, "Taramae is weak. Her child is also. Both must fight. She needs all possible friends to support her. We have tried. Now it is your turn. Help me revive her, and *whatever* she says to you, no matter *how* strange it sounds, *agree* with it! Do you understand?"

Smote nodded and sat on a stool next to the bed. Taking her by the hand, he said softly, "Dearest Taramae, what is this you are up to—worrying us so?"

Taramae's eyes fluttered as she groaned.

"You must wake up and finish this," he said, stroking her hand.

"It is not helping!" Rauma protested, jerking Taramae's hand from Smote's grasp.

Calling Gart from the doorway, she commanded, "Take him out of here! He is not helping, and he smells!"

Taramae whimpered.

Nadee stomped her foot. "One more word and I will have Gart take *you* out of here. See how your voice distresses the girl? You may wait outside, young man." Then turning to Smote, Nadee encouraged, "Go on. I know she has visited you. Has she said *anything* during her visits that might rouse her?"

Smote rubbed his temples. The head pain was returning in sharp jabs. Something she said … something she … Suddenly he perked up, and taking her by the hand once more, Smote called softly, "Stellaria—Stellaria. Wake up, my wild blossom, it is time to deliver your child."

"This is ridiculous!" Rauma griped.

Nadee raised a finger, warning her to shush.

"Stellaria—Stellaria," Smote called again.

Taramae's eyes opened. "Jeric? My Jeric?" she whispered. "Is that you? Have you come for me at last?"

Smote turned to Nadee, questioning. She nodded emphatically, so he took a deep breath and answered. "Yes, I am here."

"I hoped you would come," she feebly squeezed his hand.

"I am sorry to be delayed, but I am here now."

Taramae winced and shifted on the bed. "I am tired. I cannot do this. I want to go away. *Please* take me away."

Smote panicked. "No, no, you must *not* go away!"

"Calm your voice," Nadee said, softly.

Smote took a deep breath. "You *can* do this, my girl." The familiarity in his tone even surprised him but he felt inclined to continue it.

"My baby will not come. He does *not* want me. He is *ashamed* of me."

"No, no, he is *not* ashamed of you. You are brave, wonderful, and kind. He merely waits for you to gather strength. Then he will join us here, and you may rest."

Taramae cried out, "I cannot do this alone!"

"You are *not* alone. Wise Woman Kess is here, and Nadee, of whom you told the stories. And your moth—" When he started to say *mother*, Kess waved her hand to stop him.

"Nadee?"

"I am here, my dear," Nadee assured.

Taramae opened her eyes. "Why does it hurt so badly?"

"Your baby is breech. We need to turn him. Kess will help me. It *will* hurt, but then your baby can come out. Breathe now. Hold on to Jeric." With that, Nadee and Kess placed their hands upon her abdomen and with several strategic movements adjusted the baby's position. Taramae groaned louder and louder. With the last maneuver, she screamed and fainted.

When Smote roused her again. Taramae cried, "Jeric, I have tried to be brave. I have tried to live without you. I *cannot*! Why did you go away? I want to go where you are!"

A tear trickled down his cheek as Smote comforted. "I am back now for whatever it takes. Hold my hand tightly. Pull from my strength."

Taramae looked directly at Smote's face. Others in the room feared that she would reject him upon sight and sink back into unconsciousness. But instead, she tenderly touched his face, saying, "Oh, my love. No one loves me like you do."

Rauma whispered to Kess, "How can she see him thus?"

Kess whispered back, "At such a time, people see what they *need* to see, even otherworldly. It is a blessing when what they need appears."

When the next round of contractions hit, Taramae seemed to find a reserve of energy.

"No one speaks but him and me," Nadee ordered, as she signaled Kess to help raise Taramae into a more upright position.

"You can do this! You can do this!" Smote cried out.

Taramae began to cry, then stopped, and began to push.

"You are doing it! Keep going!" Smote coaxed, louder.

"I will. I will! Do not leave me!"

"I will always be here, my love." Smote had moved past wondering where his words came from and focused on the anticipation surrounding him.

Several pushes later, Taramae's child was born. His cries, though weak, brought shouts of joy from all in the room.

"You did it, Taramae! You did it!" Smote called out, joyfully. "It is a son! Indeed, a *beautiful* son!"

Taramae smiled and fainted once again.

Nadee wrapped the baby in a blanket and handed him to Smote. "You must warm him while we clean her up."

Rauma stepped forward to take the child, but Kess warned her away.

Smote gazed down at the baby bundle. "What a marvel—a *precious* marvel!" he proclaimed. As he touched the tiny hand, the little one grasped his finger. His heart melted.

After Taramae was attended to and Kess had received further care instructions, Nadee sat down, depleted. "This is too much excitement for this old frame," she chuckled.

"I am *truly* grateful that you were able to help," Kess said, humbly. "It was a blessing you could attend! I fear what might have happened if—"

Nadee waved her hand. "Tush, tush. This was a challenging circumstance."

Kess knew the truth. This had been the most life-threatening delivery of all in her Wise Woman experience. That it had happened with her sweet near-daughter Taramae made it even more heartrending.

As Rauma handed the ladies some tea, Taramae's baby made a noise. "He will need to eat soon. We will have to rouse her," she said, the sound of regret in her tone.

"Not yet," Nadee advised. "We can give him drops for a day. Let her rest. She will need proper nourishment for many days to rebuild her blood and strength."

Overhearing this, Gart left his post.

"Of course. We will give her the best available," Kess agreed.

Rauma chatted nervously. "Now, we just need to discern what to do about Heska."

"What about Heska?" Nadee asked.

"Well, you may not have heard, she believes that her husband, Tarce, is the father of this baby and claimed PairCompe at Tribunal."

"Preposterous! I have been assured that my grandson is the father and I do not doubt it."

Rauma was even more nervous. "Yes, but Heska may have been given the impression that Taramae would be willing to surrender the child to bring peace to herself and to Crim."

"What halfwit gave her that impression?"

Rauma winced and explained.

Upon hearing all the details, Nadee swirled the last of her tea in the bottom of her cup. "Hmmm. So, am I hearing correctly, you agreed to Heska's plan that she might obtain a child and all she has to do is leave Taramae alone?"

"Yes," Rauma said, softly, as a child might when expecting a scolding. "It sounded like a good idea at the time."

"And you *all* agreed to this? Even Taramae?"

"I agreed on behalf of Taramae—and for Crim's sake. The rumor unfolded before she could voice disapproval."

Nadee looked at Kess and with a piercing, hawk-eyed glance, chided, "This is *not* wise! You should have known better! How would you dare consider such a thing?"

Kess looked sad. "The word was spread before consultation."

Rauma interrupted, "It was for Taramae's future safety that the bargain was discussed."

Nadee turned sharply, "For someone who loves to barter, you have surely made a poor bargain here!"

Rauma protested, "We had to do *something*. Heska is a monster!"

Nadee answered firmly. "A monster is created from the imagination of frightened children and superstitious adults. They do *not* exist. Evil exists, and where it is allowed to take root, freedom is dashed. Heska has taken over Heb in the same way her grandfather did. We fought *a war* to maintain independence from the usurper of Heb."

Rauma shrugged. "I thought the war was about Heb wanting some of the Givens herd."

"Fool! You were not here. The war was about freedom! The Givens were only an excuse. Hebarcet intended to enslave the people of Crim as he had in the past. We fought to stay free. Now, your agreement gives Heska a foothold in Crim once more."

"She pledged that she would never harass Taramae again," Rauma insisted. "I have her seal on it."

"Evil *always* lies! With this success, what is to keep her from asking for the ransom of someone else who lives here? Nothing! She has no honor. You have no bargain. You have only strengthened Heska's position! For Taramae to be seen as willing to give her child away to such a creature— even if only in rumor— will make her an outcast."

Smote responded. "I told her as much."

Rauma glared at him.

Head bowed, Kess asked, "What are we to do? The plan is in play."

"You change the plan before Heska does."

"You might persuade her to stand on the Sacred Stone as Hebarcet did and hope for lightning," Smote smirked.

Nadee smiled.

"Be quiet!" Rauma snarled yet was slightly amused that he had some mercenary sense.

Kess repeated the question, "What are we to do?"

Nadee pondered briefly, then said, "Keep Heska away from here! Rauma, you will write to Heska—exactly as I tell you—informing her that the child is not of Tarce. Therefore, she has no claim and is forbidden to enter the village ever again! Her trade will be denied for one year."

Rauma was frightened. "She will be furious and will send endless spies. With a snap of her fingers, she can give an order and make people disappear. Tarce has a particular knack for making that happen."

"Good! When people are furious, they make irrational choices. Anger is one of her weaknesses. We can use that to our advantage."

"How?" Smote asked.

Nadee answered. "You are not aware the woman's gift for gluttony. We will remind her that we have spies too and that it would be extremely easy to poison someone like her. Each bite she chews, every sip she takes could bring her demise. She has made many enemies within Heb. She will be too busy watching out for herself to worry about Taramae."

Rauma was still skeptical. "Will it be enough, I wonder."

Nadee nodded confidently. "It will work. You will be surprised how well. Besides that, no trade for a year will hurt her treasury."

"Why a year?" Rauma asked.

"It will take her that long to find a trustworthy tradesman in Heb," Nadee chuckled, then became serious. "Come to my home on the morrow and I will instruct the letter writing."

Gart returned bringing Molay to the doorway.

"May I help nurse the baby until she can?" Molay offered.

"Dah ye," Kess said. There was a moment of light tugging with Smote, who was not keen to let go of the child. "It is for the best," Kess assured him.

Reluctantly he let go.

"Back to our discussion," Kess said, "It is good to try this plan for Heska but what of the rumor? It has likely hurt Taramae's good name already."

Disgusted, Nadee turned to Rauma. "Go to the river. Throw a handful of pebbles as far as you can and then gather each one at a time."

"An impossible task!" Rauma protested.

"So is retrieving a rumor. But *you* started it. *You* find a way to repair the damage!" Then turning to them all, she said, "Regardless of what it takes, Heska cannot have this baby!

Taramae stirred. "Baby?" she asked, weakly.

Kess stepped closer to comfort her. "All is well, dear. Rest a little longer. He is being cared for."

Smote arose. "I should return to the Tower."

Nadee reached out to him. "No. There are too many villagers up and about now. My dwelling is a shorter distance. We will discuss the history you have been compiling."

"It would be my honor," he said, with a bow.

"Dah ye, Smote, for assisting with the delivery," Kess said.

Smote looked at Taramae. "Will she remember that it was me?"

Kess patted him on the shoulder. "We will see."

Rauma did not thank him as he passed. She merely said, "Take a bath!"

Chapter 28: The Bonds of Friendship

As Taramae rested to regain her strength and give her full attention to the care of her newborn son, she sang the Hope Song.

"What a lovely vision this makes," Kess said, one afternoon, as she wiped a tear away. "And what would you name this boy of yours?"

"By Crim tradition, the Wise Woman has the final say at the Naming Ceremony. However," Taramae grinned. "I may have some influence with that person."

"It is so," Kess chuckled. "But if you alone could choose, what name would it be?"

"I have considered naming him after my father, or brother, as an honor. Or, naming him after his father, Jeric. It would be a noble choice, yet it brings such sadness to mind."

"Truly it does. What about Smote?" Kess kidded, to lighten the mood.

Taramae winced. "It is not my favorite name but would be no disgrace. Smote has many challenges, but there is much to recommend him."

"Smote was here at the birthing. Do you remember? Our dear Nadee had him brought from the Tower."

"What say? I thought I was dreaming."

"Yes, Nadee knew what to do when your strength failed. It was the two of them who truly helped you through it and saved you."

Taramae was astonished. "It is hard to recall. There were many voices. In my delirium, I even believed Jeric was amongst them."

"It was Smote! He was your supporter. And after your son was delivered, Nadee handed him to Smote to keep warm."

"Did he seem pleased?"

"He was so protective that I had to pull twice to take the baby for feeding. Blessings to Molay! When she heard of your distress, she nursed your child as well as her own for two days."

"I need to thank her!"

"You will have time to do that when you are feeling well."

"It is curious that Smote was allowed from the Tower. You said that to leave would ruin his health."

"Thankfully, there were no ill effects, though he needed a good cleansing. It was more obvious away from the Tower."

Taramae had to agree. "The odor has been a challenge. Of course, he had little control over it. I cannot believe that my mother allowed his presence at all."

"Your mother had *no* choice. Nadee took charge. She had him brought from the Tower. She was the one who knew how to complete the birth. Afterward, Smote went with her to her dwelling."

"He went *with* Nadee?"

"Yes and seemed pleased to do so. It looks to be a permanent arrangement. She had his cot brought from the tower."

Taramae arose quickly. "I must thank them!"

"It is too soon to take your child outside!" Kess warned.

Taramae winked. "If he can withstand such a harsh entry into the world, a little fresh air will not harm him."

At near dark, Taramae went to the dwelling of Old Soul Nadee with her son warmly wrapped and secreted within Kess's long, heavy cloak. She paused by the inn to give Gart a peek at the wee one who had caused so much tribulation. He pretended to be upset that she was out, but knew better than to detain her.

"You had best hurry before Rauma catches you," he whispered.

"Walk with me?" she requested.

He was more than happy to oblige.

"Dah ye for watching over us so well," she said, quietly. "It has been days since we have spoken. How are you?"

"I am well, though some are angry with me."

"Who is angry with you?"

"Banaya circled her face and touched her nose. I think that means I am in trouble, and Zaela is not speaking to me."

Taramae laughed. "What have you done?"

"I would not allow Banaya to visit you yet, so she brings flowers every day."

"Oh, that is why there are so many wilted flowers on the doorstep. Tell Banaya that she may visit tomorrow. Why is Zaela upset?"

"I told her to grow up."

Taramae was amused. "A needful thing. Perhaps, it is best to let Zaela forget you."

Gart groaned. "If it is for the best, why does it feel so bad? It is hard to live with denied love. You know this well."

"Too well." Taramae sighed.

When Taramae knocked on the door of Nadee's dwelling, she expected to hear a feeble voice beckoning her to enter as had happened many times before. But instead, a rejuvenated Nadee answered the door in person.

Nadee threw her arms up in delight. "Oh, my dear, what a lovely surprise! Come in. Come in. Oh my, yes, come in!"

Once inside, Taramae grinned. "I have another surprise for you," she said, and withdrew the baby from under her cape.

"Oh! Oh! I should scold you for bringing him out so soon, yet I am delighted to see him."

"What is all this clamor?" Smote called out from the back room.

Taramae caught her breath as he entered. He wore clean clothes—Jeric's old clothes—his scraggly beard was shaved. His previously shaggy, matted hair was trimmed evenly to the collar of his tunic and shone from recent washing. With these improvements, he naturally smelled better and even appeared more upright than before as he walked slowly towards her.

Nadee invited, "Come, dear boy, and see our special guests!"

"Special indeed!" Smote reached out to take the baby, but Nadee denied him the pleasure. "It is still my turn," she said, and took the baby to her rocking chair by the fireplace.

"Woezy! Being out of the Tower has brought great improvements, I see," Taramae noted.

Smote bowed. "It is not difficult when the surroundings are more favorable, *and* so close to the bath house. I did not comprehend how much a tower can feel like a dungeon until this kind lady took me in."

Taramae and Nadee exchanged glances with a hint of sadness that he still did not recognize her as his grandmother.

"Yes. This *kind lady* has always been amazing," Taramae said. "I am told it was she who aided in the delivery of this little prince. Dah ye, dear Nadee!"

"It was an honor to assist. He looks wonderful. Already the tiny cheeks are filling out."

Taramae laughed. "They should be. He is a great eater!"

"As he should be," Nadee chuckled. "He had a difficult journey and is no doubt making up for lost time. You appear to be well. How are you faring these days?" Nadee asked.

Taramae stepped next to her and answered in a confidential tone "Still very sore, but improving by the day,"

"Keep taking the healing teas and eat meat when you can. It will build the blood back up faster," Nadee quietly advised.

Taramae nodded, then turned to Smote. "Dah ye for being there as well. It was quite a risk for both of you."

"Did you know it was me?" Smote asked, eagerly.

Taramae winced apologetically. "I do not remember much of who was there or of what happened beyond the pain. But I was told of your generous encouragement. Again, dah ye."

Smote seemed disappointed, but his expression brightened immediately as soon as Nadee handed him the child. It was a lovely scene to see Smote gazing upon the tiny face. It made Taramae's heart swell. Tears filled her eyes.

"And what will this child be named? Perhaps after his father?" Nadee asked, as she prepared the kettle for tea.

Taramae sniffled. "It is hard to choose. I have considered *Jeric*."

Smote scowled. Then, realizing how obvious his disapproval had been, he humorously added, "If so, he will be called Little Jeric his entire life, and look at these hands. He will never be little beyond this point." He lifted the baby's arm up in a bold motion. "No, he will be strong—a warrior."

The baby made a squawk.

"See, how he roars!" Smote added.

Taramae laughed, but warned, "Shh! If you awaken him, you will have to feed him."

Knowing that would be impossible, Smote whispered, "Sleep, baby, sleep."

Taramae giggled once more. "I would like him to have a noble name. Perhaps after my pah or brother, who were cherished."

"Why not after the one who assisted you most? Call him Nadell?" Smote suggested.

"Do not!" Nadee protested. "It is not an honor I desire."

"*Smote* is a noble name," he said, in obvious jest. "A smaller version could be Little Smit. Whenever need be, you could call out, 'Come here, Little Smit!'"

"NO!" Taramae and Nadee protested at the same time, laughing.

Taramae settled it by saying, "We will see what the Wise Woman suggests at the Naming Ceremony."

Suddenly serious, Smote asked, "How soon will that be?" He remembered that Taramae would then be pressured into making her choice of a Pairing.

"In two days," she sighed.

"A Naming Ceremony is a joyful time," Nadee said, placing the tea on the table.

Taramae shook her head. "Not when it is attached to Tribunal."

"Do not dwell on unpleasantness now," Nadee advised softly, and picked up the child for another snuggle. "All will come aright in the days ahead. Fear not, it sours the milk, and this little one must always have the sweetest."

Taramae took another sip of tea. "It is late. We should go," she said, wrapping herself and the child securely up. "Again, dah ye both, and good eve!"

Once Taramae and the baby had gone, Smote was forlorn. "What will happen to them?"

"What say?"

"How will their future be if she Pairs with someone she does not love?"

"Bleak in many ways. Nevertheless, she will persevere for the sake of the child. She has lived with unhappiness before."

"It is not right."

Nadee stated the obvious. "You care for her."

"Truly. As little Banaya would say, she has become my most-friend. And that baby boy stirs tender feelings that I do not understand. Alas, I am only Smote. I am nothing. I have nothing. I am powerless to aid them."

Old Soul Nadee popped him on the shoulder with her fist. "You are a grown man, not an invalid! There are ways you could assist. Think on it!"

"I *have* thought upon it. But I keep coming to the same conclusion. I am a disfigured man, with naught to offer, and alarming to look at."

"Does Taramae avoid looking at you? No! So quit saying you are nothing! You have always had a sharp mind, and much potential. Such are wasted on endless hours as the Watcher in the Tower."

Smote looked at her, curiously, "It is amazing how you know me so well."

Nadee growled in frustration and walked away.

Gart appeared again to walk with Taramae across the courtyard to the inn.

"When will you finally tell Smote who he is?"

Taramae stopped walking. "When did you know?"

"The night of the child's birth. Even delirious, you knew to call him Jeric."

Sadly, Taramae said, "But he has no memory of our Pairing. Now you can see how complicated Tribunal will be."

"Truly! But I stand by my word to help you, if necessary."

"Oh, Gart. You are a treasure! It is unfortunate that Zaela does not see it yet."

"Perhaps she—" Gart started to say, then stopped. "Wait! Someone blocks the doorway."

They approached cautiously until they could see clearly that it was Leader Adris grumpily gazing at them.

"Where have you been with my son?" he challenged.

"He is *not* your son!"

"Not yet, but soon. Come inside this instant, and stay put until Tribunal," he commanded, reaching for Taramae's arm.

When Gart pushed him aside so Taramae could continue inside unimpeded, Adris glared at Gart. He vehemently distrusted this young man. Something about his defiant demeanor raised suspicion yet had a sense of familiarity. Where had he seen that before? Adris shook his head to recenter his concentration, determined to obtain some respect from this nobody, he threatened, "Do not interfere! I have the power to make you leave in the morning!"

Gart raised his large fist close to Adris's face and returned the intimidation, "I have the power to make you *disappear* before morning."

Adris made several sputtering noises and stomped away.

Chapter 29: Choosing Sides

On the day of the proposed infant exchange, Gart delivered the letter to the Crossing for Pel to give to Heska. As predicted, she was furious—so furious that those in nearby tents ran to the far side of the encampment.

"How dare they defy *me*! How DARE they!" She spat out the words. "There was an agreement! There was a plan! No matter what they say, I am not intimidated by a piece of parchment! I will go before their Tribunal and force Taramae to comply or they will *all* pay! Poison my food? Hah!"

"It sounds as though they are serious. You will not be allowed into the village. I am certain they will be prepared," Pel hesitated to mention. "You may need more guards than me."

"I know that, idjit! Take me home! I will return with a force so brutal that any defense they muster will be quickly vanquished!"

She swore and paced while Pel took her tent down. When he attempted to help her up into the wagon, she grabbed the whip from its hook and hit him several times with the hard, wooden handle. "I cannot believe you accepted that letter!" She filled the air with another foul tirade regarding his lack of value as a human being.

His cheek bleeding, Pel slapped the reins. The wagon jolted forward.

"You idjit! Are you trying to kill me? Why I picked you, I will never know. You are incompetent—worse than Tarce! Get going before I hit you again. Go. Go!"

Once they had traveled a distance from the Crossing, Heska relaxed a little. She was formulating the most heinous vengeance that her warped mind could conjure up.

Without realizing the reason for her calm, Pel humbly said, "I am terribly sorry that your plan did not succeed. I hope this unfortunate event does not mean an end to our bargain."

Heska chortled until a deep-throated cackle erupted from her hellacious-smelling tooth prison. She loved it when people groveled. She laughed until her sides hurt, then said, "We have *no* bargain! What a fool you are to think so. What nerve you have to ask! I have been threatened and humiliated. I did not get what *I* wanted, therefore, you certainly will not get what *you* want! In fact, I have been devising a special punishment for you. However, there is one way you can avoid it and regain my favor."

Nervously, Pel asked, "What way is that, Mistress?"

"Retrieve Taramae's child immediately!"

"What say?"

"Yes, the more I dwell upon the notion, the more it appeals to me. Go, get her child."

"If you still want a child, there are many orphans at the Crossing who could use a home."

The wagon went over a bump.

"Owww! Heska yelled, "Hit another bump and it will be your last. Get an orphan? No, I do not want *another* child. I want Taramae's child! Leader Adris will pay handsomely for its return. Perhaps Rauma will feel responsible and pay even more," Heska laughed. "Rauma should have known better than to swindle me! I have a fancy to own an establishment in Crim, and her inn would suit me just fine. The mere thought gives me enormous pleasure. Those who think they have cleverly thwarted me, must pay!. You may prove your remorse for previous failures by snatching Taramae's child."

Pel sat silently, not knowing how to respond.

Suddenly sounding inspired, Heska cackled again. "I am brilliant! I just came upon an even better idea. After the baby is retrieved, you will simply tie a rock around it and throw it off Plateau Falls. That would be perfect! It is deep, rocky, and the falls would keep it from ever resurfacing. We will ask for a ransom and when it is delivered, *surprise,* no baby! It would serve to punish them all!"

Pel was appalled. "I could not do such a thing! The very thought strikes horror within me. Besides that, it would start a war!"

"A war? Hmm—that might prove useful. We have more people by far. We could reunite the territory under one leader—me. My grandfather, Hebarcet, had the original idea, but my father was too cowardly to fight, and made a truce. Why should we fear war? It is decided. You *will* take Taramae's child and do as I have instructed. A war would be grand! Yes, yes, great idea, Pel! I may turn you into a mercenary yet."

"Taking that baby will be an impossible task. Surely there are others— more experienced—who could better accomplish such a task," he pleaded.

Heska's foul-smelling face pressed within a hair's breadth of his ear. "*You* will do the task. If not, I will command one of the others to throw a child of *yours* off the falls. Or better yet, since the crate builder owes me much in gambling debt, I will have *all* of your children sealed into a crate and taken to a faraway island to slowly starve to death. Is that your preference?"

"Of course not." Hate-filled panic brewed inside Pel.

"And one more thing ..." Heska added. "Tonight, when it is dark, I want Tarce to stay outside. There is a message to be delivered." She touched the handle of the knife in the scabbard on Pel's hip. "This was given for just such an occasion. He apparently did *not* father Taramae's child and since he will never again be allowed back into Crim for trading, he has outlived his usefulness. Get rid of him! It should appear to be an accident." Moments later Heska added, smugly, "It does not have to appear as an accident after all. It is not as if anyone would care enough to ask questions. After that, you will go to the other guards and tell them to prepare for a journey and bring weapons. We will meet at Plateau Falls at dawn. If they hesitate, re-mind them of the oaths they have taken and what horrors I will do to their loved ones if they defy me."

Pel tried not to vomit. This depraved beast was without any feelings. Doing as she demanded would make him evil too, and she would forever have extortion power over him—never to be satisfied. The bargain he had struck in order to care for his family, would never be realized. He had un-wittingly brought a ravenous wolf to his own door. Gart's warning words echoed through his mind.

181

Tarce was not good at waiting. It made him anxious one minute and angry the next. The skin on the back of his neck tightened. This frantic feeling had only occurred a few times in his life, and it had always been accompanied by a hazardous event. The first time was on his wedding day and look where that had gotten him, Paired to a treacherous female, more a slave than a husband. She was the Vast Vex of his existence. He had tolerated her control and abuse for the sake of good food, comfortable lodgings, and having the merchants of Heb indulge his every whim. But it was not worth all he had endured.

When Heska arrived from the Crossing, she did not look at Tarce, speak to him, nor offer to show him the baby. There was no baby! Not only that, but she took the dagger from his belt and pointed it at his chest when he tried to enter their establishment and then she locked him out. Even Pel, who had previously been cordial, would not make eye contact. The skin on the back of Tarce's neck was so tight that it nearly strangled him. He grabbed the tent from the back of the wagon and set it up by the back door. He pretended to sleep, leaving the lantern lit, until he could hear Heska's heavy, drunken snoring inside. He planned to sneak back into the house through the window later. He knew where to step to avoid any squeaking floorboards.

Suddenly, Pel pushed the tent flap open and, knife in hand, yelled, "This was not my idea!" He lunged forward.

Scrambling beyond arm's length, Tarce screamed, "No—no! Wait! You are not a killer! You are not a killer! I can fix this! WAIT!"

Tarce's screams woke Heska up. She listened briefly. When she was satisfied that there were no other noises, she placed her treasury key necklace on the bed table. With Tarce gone, there was no more risk of embezzlement. She belched and went back to sleep.

Heska awoke the next morning in a gleeful mood, her exhilarating plan of vengeance was foremost in her mind. She hurriedly dressed. Her key necklace was not on the table. She looked behind it briefly but did not have the patience to look further. Her heart quivered with excitement. As she ate a hearty breakfast, she said to Pel, "I do not see Tarce mewling about. It appears that you have followed orders. That effort will go toward consideration of safety for your family."

He stood stoically by the door. He barely nodded.

She did not offer him any food, but issued her next command, "Bring my wagon around front. I will be out as soon as I finish here. The men had better be there!"

"They want to be paid," Pel said, plainly.

"Money!? They should not be thinking of money! They need to focus on the task at hand. We are going to storm Crim. I have a list of the people who should especially suffer. Gart must be first or he will impede the implementation, Taramae and her child, of course, Adris just for good measure, and then before it Crim is completely destroyed, I will make Rauma *eat* the letter they sent to me! She will choke on it. Betray a bargain without consequences? Threaten to poison my food? Ha!"

She was so amused with her own cleverness as Pel struggled to hoist her to the seat, that she barely noticed the blanket-wound human shape in the wagon box. When she did, she merely said, "Dump it into the falls before we leave for Crim."

She complained all the way about every bump in the road, yet giggled as she imagined, "I will do what my grandfather failed to do and every survivor in Crim will bow to acknowledge my power."

Pel did not respond.

Thirty rough men were gathered as instructed. They were not happy.

Heska was oblivious. "I am glad that you all had the good sense to show up. We are going to ransack Crim and get rid of a few troublemakers while we are at it! Pel, turn the wagon around."

Pel did as he was told.

"Get to your mounts!" she yelled in a rallying cry. "It is time to go, men!"

Each man withdrew a sword or dagger, but none moved toward their animals.

"You promised to pay us," one yelled.

"There is no time for this! We need to go!" Heska protested, then encouraged, "There will be plenty of valuables to claim in Crim!"

"We have friends in Crim!"

Heska rebuffed them. "Then kill the strangers. I do not care! We need to go!"

"Our homes are in shambles," another man called out.

She stomped her foot, impatiently. "We will deal with that when we return. Stop wasting time!"

"Our families are starving. You take all the good food!"

Heska puffed up her shoulders, threatening, "Are you insane? Have you forgotten to whom you are speaking? I will call the Vast Vex upon you! Your families will die in agony or disappear if you do not obey me *this* instant!"

The tallest man laughed. "Who will do that?" He pointed to men around him, saying," He will not hurt my family and I will not hurt his."

As the men began to close in around her, Heska finally sensed her doom. All of the men she normally used for defense were about to dispatch her. Surrounded by advancing blades, she panicked, "I will fix your homes, I promise!"

"You have broken too many promises!" someone called out and many agreed.

The armed men began backing Heska toward the cliff. In vain she tried to scream over the noise of the waterfall. Failing at that, she forcefully stepped forward shaking her head, and snarled loudly, "You cannot do this! I have your signed contracts! I own you!"

The men were not intimidated. The blades came closer. Finally, Heska began to grovel for her life. "Fine, fine," she cried out. "I will cancel all contracts and pay triple the money owed!"

At that moment, Tarce came out of the blankets in the wagon, yelling, "I have already paid them, idjit!" He held up her treasury key. "You heard what she said, men. Stop wasting time!"

Heska shrieked, "I call the Vast Vex to rain down upon you—all of you! I command the Vast Vex to—to obey!"

Suddenly the waterfall seemed to roar even louder, spewing a surge of turbulence. The ground of the cliff began to shake so much that the advancing men fell back, some falling over others in an attempt to get away. Several horses bolted. Pel had difficulty controlling the animals pulling the wagon. Heska laughed wildly at the scene in front of her as though her Vast Vex demands had created it. And then, the cliff edge suddenly collapsed beneath her feet. "No! No!" she screamed and fell cursing into the savage swells below.

Pel drove away as soon as the long, descending screams ceased.

Chapter 30: The Unveiling

The Naming Ceremony was held in Nadee's dwelling. She and Wise Woman Kess would pronounce the blessing. Taramae, her hair perfectly curled, appeared radiant in a new dress—a gift from Molay. Rauma was invited, as were Banaya, Baird, and their father, Ori. Storekeeper Brun brought Nawhi and Zaela. Gart followed. Molay's reluctant husband, Asa, held the door open as if ready to bolt. He only came for the cake but the fresh air was appreciated. The table and chair had been moved to the farthest wall to make extra space. Still, there was standing room only. Despite being tightly corralled, the guests cordially chatted.

Annoyingly, Leader Adris had insisted on being invited. He moped around the table, snitching nibbles of the cake when he thought no one was looking. Since someone had attempted to kill Jeric, and Adris was not above suspicion, Smote stayed in the back sleeping room.

Banaya sidled up to Taramae before the event began. Handing her a round, gold object, Banaya said, "My brother snagged this in the river. He thought you might like it."

Taramae gazed at the token that Jeric had bestowed upon her at their Pairing. It must have fallen out of Tarce's pocket when they dumped Jeric into the river. No wonder she had never found it in Tarce's belongings. Poor thing! Much had changed since the first time she received it. Of such significance before, it was now scratched and bent. Like her, the token had been through turbulent times in the past few months. Looking through the crowd, she caught Baird's watchful eye and mouthed, "Dah ye, Baird."

The boy blushed and ran outside.

With a sigh, Taramae placed the token into her pocket, and listened again as Banaya rambled on. "I know you have a son. He is a sweet one, and it is fitting that you should like him, but may I still be your most-friend?" she asked.

"Truly," Taramae reassured her. "If you would like, you may resume morning visits for help with braids."

"Woezy!" Banaya hugged her, and whispered, "You should know that the nasty leader man is tasting the edge of the cake."

Taramae whispered back, "As part of your most-friend duties, tell him to stop."

"I will!"

Soon everyone heard Adris loudly complaining, "Quit pestering me!" "Quit snitching cake!" Banaya said, as she circled her face and touched her nose.

"Go away, girl. Go away!"

"Quit snitching cake!"

"Ori, control this child!"

Ori nodded for Banaya to come stand by him. When she reached his side, he patted her on the shoulder.

After the ritual nit check, Wise Woman Kess announced, "It is time to begin."

As her only family member, Rauma proudly stood next to Taramae. Each of the Wise Women touched her forehead as if in deep thought, then suddenly looked surprised. Nadee leaned closely toward Taramae and whispered, "This is a Child of Promise. He will bring your family great joy."

Kess stepped forward whispering, "Love him dearly. Teach him kindly, and above all, keep these words to yourself, lest they provoke the jealousy of others," she said with a wink.

With that, both women stood upright and announced, "His name will be VenAven, for the honor of family members no longer with us."

There was congratulatory clapping, except from Adris.

Pronouncement made, Nadee was exhausted and gladly sat down by the fireplace to hold the baby. A concerned Kess watched over her.

Taramae was pleased with the name VenAven. It would suit him well.

Deeply touched, Rauma wiped tears from her eyes. "He is such a beautiful boy! He reminds me so much of ..." She cleared her throat, then quietly extended an offer. "After much consideration, I believe there *is* a place at the inn where you might have customers for the caring of hair, and I will serve chicory—all for pay, of course. We should not be afraid to try new ideas. After all, I became Crim's first woman innkeeper! I also brought a little gift." With that, Rauma brought forth the wooden box containing the remaining carved animals that Taramae's father had made. "I did not give everything away," Rauma said, her voice trembling.

"Dah ye, dah ye!" Taramae exclaimed and kissed her mother on the cheek for the first time in years.

Ruining the moment, Adris scoffed to Brun, "She will *not* touch other people's hair and I will choose a better name once the Pairing ceremony takes place at Tribunal tomorrow."

A pained expression crossed Brun's face. "It might be best to wait longer."

Adris snarled, "No! Tribunal *will* take place and the issue settled immediately. We all know the logical outcome, and I have waited long enough!"

His booming voice made VenAven cry. Taramae excused herself to remove the baby to the back room where Smote sat waiting. As she passed through the group, Zaela stopped her to admire the squealing infant. "He *is* a lovely child. Dah ye for inviting us," she said, then nodded at Gart to make sure he noticed of her improved behavior.

He noticed.

As she passed Gart, Taramae whispered, "Take the reins."

"You too," he mumbled.

Taramae pondered Gart's words, as well as those from the Wise Women, *"for the honor of family."* She did have an honorable family. Her mother, though questionable at times, was a determined worker, and her father had always been admired by others and was a hero in her eyes. Taramae no longer wondered what he would have advised her to do. She must stand up for herself and do it now. Kess might not approve but there was no time to ask for permission.

In the back room, Smote gladly took the baby from her and began comforting him. "Come here, my poor little friend. Too much noise out there and not enough cake? I agree!"

With tears in her eyes, and hand pressed against the token in her pocket, Taramae quietly asked, "Do you care for this child?" Her voice soft but steadier than it had ever been.

"You know I do."

Taramae took a deep breath. "Do you care for his mother?"

Smote teased, "Perhaps a little."

Taramae smiled slightly and then became serious. "There is something I *must* do, for the sake of my child, and you are part of it. Soon you will hear a strange tale that may cause you pain. I *hate* for that to happen. I *never* want to hurt you! But I do not know what else to do."

"It sounds ominous."

"It is, and it may be very confusing, but there is no time to explain further. Just know that you will *never* be required to do *anything* against your will. Do you trust me?"

Smote had never seen her so forthright nor heard such urgency in her words.

She earnestly asked again, emphasizing each word, "*Do you trust me?*"

He looked down at the baby and back at her. "I trust you. Do *whatever* is needed."

"Dah ye, dear Smote," she said, touching him on the cheek, a tear running down hers. "I will return presently." With that, Taramae rejoined the gathering.

Adris was still griping to Brun when Taramae spoke loudly, "Do you still insist on having Tribunal tomorrow?"

The group became quiet.

She repeated, "Do you *still* insist upon having Tribunal tomorrow?"

"I do! Unless you will be reasonable and accept my Pairing offer this very moment."

"Do you insist upon it, *even* if by doing so we will be violating the fourth Rule of Honor? An action which will cause you to lose your leadership, and result in banishment for us both?"

"Girl, you are demented! There is not *one* thing that could cause such."

"No, not one *thing could*, but one *person* could." Taramae whispered to her mother, who followed her to the back room.

Kess firmly shook her head, no.

Regardless, Taramae went to Smote, held out her hand, and said, "I *am* sorry for this. But, please come with me."

Smote hesitated only briefly and handed the baby to Rauma.

Protectively, Taramae walked him through the astonished group to stand before Adris.

Embarrassed by the reaction of the gathering, Smote braced himself for what might come. Whatever was happening, he and Taramae were apparently in it together.

With emboldened confidence, Taramae declared, "Sir, I would like to introduce Smote—the man who was once before—my husband, Jeric, your brother's son, and the father of my child."

Gasps filled the room.

"Woezy! I knew she liked him! I knew it!" Banaya verified to the astonished adults.

Smote's eyes widened. He looked at Taramae to see if she was exaggerating. Getting no sense of a prank, he felt his balance waver.

Taramae steadied him with a side hug, saying, "Smote, meet Leader Adris."

Smote stood upright in a dignified manner and nodded. "We meet at last, Adris. I have heard much about you."

Adris was astonished. This person sounded like Jeric, but his appearance was so damaged that it was not immediately clear. "Is this a joke?" he roared.

Taramae answered firmly, "It is *no* joke."

There were many amazed looks in the room as she explained. "As I was being abducted, Jeric tried to save me. He was terribly injured and left for dead. Somehow, he was found and returned to Crim to be cared for in the Tower."

"The Tower man? *This* is who has been in the Tower?"

"Yes. It is he. But sadly, while his health improved, his memory of me, of our Pairing, or of his life beforehand has *not* returned. Even now, he has no recollection of being anyone other than Smote, the Watcher."

Taramae felt a shudder go through Smote. She hugged him tighter. Kess moved to the other side of him for additional support.

Adris objected, "This is ridiculous! I would have known about it. I know everything that happens in Crim!"

Brun stepped forward. "Only Kess, Nawhi, and I knew—and the gatekeeper. Taramae discovered it only recently. You had displayed such animosity towards Jeric that we feared you might interfere with his care, so we placed him in the Tower in hopes he could be healed."

"This cannot be! Brun, you are too smart to have fallen into a scheme with this impostor! It is merely some mischief invented by this so-called Wise Woman," Adris charged.

Smote looked to Kess for confirmation.

The Wise Woman placed her hand on Smote's shoulder, "It is *all* true. Though this is *not* how I preferred it to be revealed!" She glared at Taramae.

As Smote tried to remember, a tremendous pain shook his head. He touched his forehead.

Alarmed, Wise Woman Kess took him by the arm, "This is *too* much, as I feared it would be. Come, you must rest."

Smote walked a few steps with her then turned to Adris, and firmly asserted, "As you can see, you have *no* claim here, on *neither* the woman *nor* the child. The issue is settled!" With that, they left the room.

Adris paced back and forth, then turned to Taramae. "You have no proof! If this *Smote* does not remember, he may have been duped into thinking that he is Jeric. You have *no* proof that he was not coerced. You have always been deceitful!"

Taramae brought the Token from her pocket and held it up for all to see.

Agitated further, Adris bellowed, "Even so, this incident could *not* have taken place. That some scheming villain paid Tarce to steal Taramae, and that Jeric was killed as a consequence? Someone from *my* village? Preposterous!"

Nawhi stepped forward. "I must speak."

"Shush, Nawhi!" Zaela scolded. "It is not your place."

"No, *you* must shush, little sister," Nawhi spoke, sharply. "You have *no* voice in this matter. You were *never* included in the secret. I alone must confirm the tale." Nawhi's shoulders slumped, her voice trembled. "I am the scheming villain."

A tidal wave of disbelief washed through the room. Confused as all, Banaya asked, "So, the nice girl is the bad one? Woezy!" She whispered reminders about promised cake as her father quickly shuttled her outside. Molay's husband stepped inside and closed the door.

Chapter 31: The Revelation

"Well? Well? What do you have to say?" Adris asked, impatiently.

Nawhi began to cry.

"Just let her speak!" Nadee scolded.

"I am *trying* to let her speak, but she is not getting on with it. We have more important things to discuss. Get on with it, girl! We do not have all night."

Several people shushed him. Glowering, he looked about as if taking names of all who had disrespected him, then moved to the farthest corner of the room.

Nawhi looked around at her confused friends and family waiting for the explanation, then humbly began, "As a young girl, I was greatly enamored of Drayis, son of Leader Adris, and grieved tremendously when he drowned. For years there was no comfort from his loss. In the meantime, I had to work ridiculously hard because my little sister spent her time beguiling every man who gazed upon her instead of helping. My frustration grew. Dark Menaces tormented me.

"Later, whenever Jeric returned from the Givens watch, he would converse with me in a friendly manner, and to my unbearably lonely thinking it showed fondness. I endlessly dwelt upon the possibility of his love." She turned to her father. "I merely wanted a little happiness."

Brun's face turned bright red.

Looking down at her feet, Nawhi continued. "The last time I spoke with Jeric was at the Groggery the night before he ran away. He was excited, as though he would burst if he did not tell someone his secret. The drinkers were so noisy that, when he whispered something about meeting at the Sacred Stone at first light, I mistakenly believed it was directed to me.

"The next morning from my window, I saw Jeric speaking with the gatekeeper and quickly dressed to join him there. However, before I reached the gate, Taramae had joined him, and they left together. I followed, and from a distance witnessed their Pairing Ceremony at the Sacred Stone. His love had been meant for *her*, not for *me*!" Tears tumbled down her face.

"Suddenly the Vast Vex cast a plague upon my mind and incensed me to fury! It was an overpowering anger, like no other evil I had ever felt before. My thoughts were irrational. I wanted to lash out! I was crazed with jealousy, believing that if Taramae was gone, Jeric would need comfort, and might turn to me."

Taramae gasped.

Rauma handed the baby to Molay and walked to Taramae's side, glaring at Nawhi.

"Two days later when Tarce entered the storehouse, I offered him money to find Taramae and take her away. He eagerly agreed." She turned to Taramae. "But I came to my senses and changed my mind. *I changed my mind!* I ran after him as he left Crim to tell him not to do it, but it was *too* late. He found you alone by the river. Then Jeric came. I never wanted anyone to be hurt! But Jeric fought with Tarce and was struck hard with a rock. We believed he was dead when he was rolled into the river."

"We?" Rauma raged. "You were there and did not stop it?"

"I did not get there in time. I had no idea that she and Jeric were in love. It was well hidden!"

Taramae was stunned. "How could you do this? You are—you were—my FRIEND!"

"I know! I am SO sorry! I ran, crying all the way home, and could not rest for two days. Then I told my father that I had seen something strange while out walking, I thought we would find a body, but instead we found Jeric lying on the riverbank—unconscious. He was hurt very badly, unrecognizably. Since no one knew how he came to be injured, it was decided it to keep him hidden in the Tower while the Wise Woman began his care."

Taramae was incredulous. "Why didn't you tell who had taken me? Why let them believe I drowned?"

Shamefully, Nawhi admitted, "I was afraid of becoming an outcast. I am not brave like you. Tarce planned to sell you immediately to a merchant vessel, and I believed it was too late to be undone. I have rarely rested one night since."

"Brun and Kess conspired too? Why was this not mentioned before?" Rauma demanded.

Nawhi defended them, "Do *not* blame them! Neither my father nor the Wise Woman has known the full account until now. Jeric—I mean, Smote's condition was kept secret because they feared for his safety. They have provided well. My penance for the reprehensible deed has been to assist Smote daily by bringing food, washing clothing, and replacing the squat pot. I was prepared to continue doing it for the remainder of my days. Then Taramae returned and there was hope that at least part of the disaster could be made right."

With a murderous look, Rauma declared, "So, the mouse is a monster!"

Zaela howled, "Nawhi, what have you done? We are a fallen family! No one will have me now!" Nawhi looked up at Gart, whimpering.

"Do not fear, sister. Your disgrace will be short-lived. I will leave the village." She turned to Taramae once more. "I am sorry beyond imagining! I dare not even ask forgiveness for such betrayal." She stepped forward as though ready to fall at Taramae's feet.

Rauma blocked her. "Forgiveness? FORGIVENESS!? For such suffering?" she spat out the words. "How dare you come here tonight, feigning friendship. GET OUT!"

Asa opened the door.

Weeping, Nawhi ran out without looking back. Zaela followed, sobbing.

Taramae stood as though frozen, truly drowning in disbelief.

Humbly, Brun approached Taramae. "Please come to the storehouse *whenever* you need provisions. It will *always* be a gift." Then he followed his daughters, choking back tears.

Banaya suddenly appeared in the doorway. "Woezy! What is happening? Why are people crying?" She tugged on Taramae's sleeve. "Did someone hurt you? Tell me who hurt you and I will hit them!"

Ori snatched her away, accepting a plateful of hurriedly sliced cake from Rauma, and took his children home.

Molay handed the baby to Nadee and touched Taramae's arm, "I must go to my baby, but we will speak again soon."

Asa looked upon Taramae sympathetically, took two pieces of cake, and they left.

Taramae nodded slightly. "Dah ye for coming," she said, her words barely audible.

Adris looked around the near-empty room in disgust. "This cannot be all. Hand out the cake and it is over? The girl gave a sufficient explanation. I do not condone her actions and we will settle with her during Tribunal, but even worse was the secrecy that occurred! It undermines the legitimacy of order in the village. Mark my word, there will be a *serious* discussion about that. However, a more important issue tonight was not resolved."

"What say?" Rauma was incredulous. "More important?"

"Yes. I *need* a son! That is more important to me."

Old Nadee snapped, "You great bully! You do not *need* a son. Crim was never meant to become your kingdom! You were allowed the position only because no one else wanted it, not due to exceptional competence on your part!"

Adris ignored her. His mind was already conjuring up his next move. "Perhaps this man, this Smote, if he does not recognize Taramae as his wife, perhaps he will give up his rights to her and my Pairing offer may still be accepted. I will go and discuss it with him."

Rauma grabbed his arm, and stood face to face with him saying, "Did you *not* hear Smote, you foolish twit? He *retains* his rights. You have no hope of a claim. Besides that, you *have* a son!"

"Yes, I did once. But what use is a drowned son to me now?"

"None, but you had another son by Shayza, your missing wife. You told everyone that she drowned too, but she did not die at that time. She ran away from your tyranny and had another child in Heb. I have seen documents held in Heska's possession to prove it."

194

Adris scoffed, "Where is this so-called son?"

"He is here! Without your corrupting influence, he has become a fine young man. It should have been obvious. Who in this room resembles Shayza?"

Gart was the only man left. He and Adris stared at each other, dumbfounded. How could they possibly be father and son? They detested each other! The incredulous stares became a battle of contemptuous glares. Adris could see Shayza in Gart's defiant stance. He was strong, capable. Everything Adris had hoped for in a son, yet Gart looked upon him with disgust.

Adris backed down first. "We will see about this!" he argued.

Rauma continued. "I *dare* you not to believe me. Go ask Heska yourself. She will be glad to show you proof—for a price."

"It is all nonsense! There will still be Tribunal tomorrow." Adris declared. "We will discuss what is best for the child."

Suddenly alert, Taramae became enraged. *"Do not go near my son— ever!"* She spat out each word.

Gart stepped to her side. *"Ever!"* he accentuated much louder.

Adris stomped out of the dwelling.

Gart watched as Adris walked away cursing. He stood, hand against the doorframe as if needing support, saying, "I have so longed to know who my father is. Now I understand why my mother refused to tell me. He is *despicable!*"

Taramae came to his side, consoling, "But *you* are a *good* man, the *best* kind of man. It is not a fair comparison. Do not despair, dear friend," she said, lightly squeezing his arm once before going into the back room to face the other consequences of the evening.

Gart helped Rauma move the table back to the center of the room. Then they walked back to the inn together.

Smote lay on his bed in Nadee's back room, one arm bent over his eyes. The noise from conversations in the other room faded slowly as the powerful pain draught took effect. Smote wanted to hear what they were saying but needed to fade away—to run away from the intense misery in his head. He thought he heard Taramae saying *so sorry.* Kess was angry with her and he wanted to defend her but could not. Her voice floated away and so did he.

He barely moved when Taramae touched him. "I should have prepared him better for such an unveiling."

Wise Woman Kess stopped Taramae from rousing him further. "Enough has been disclosed for one night. Let him sleep."

Taramae lamented. "I never meant to harm him! I could not see another way to end Adris's Tribunal travesty."

Kess was indignant. "All these months of healing care and he is once more reduced to this. Mizzafrizzaritz, girl! You could *not* have revealed it more clumsily!"

"Will he forgive me?"

"It is not for me to guess, nor for you to request. It is up to him now."

Taramae gathered up her baby from Nadee and left in tears. The solving of one problem had created another, and there was still Heska to worry about.

Adris sat by his fireplace stewing in self-pity juice. Nothing of his plan had come to fruition. Gart, his son? How could it be? Preposterous! They were not alike in any way. But he did rather look like Shayza. No, no!, Adris pushed that picture from his mind. It had to be a lie that Rauma told in order to dismiss his demands. Adris was about to take a drink from his secret stash of high-quality spirits when a memory came to him.

He dropped his cup and ran for the wrinkled, faded letter from Shayza that he had saved. He reread the phrase, *'I am leaving before two lives are ruined.'*

He had always thought she meant Drayis' life and hers. He had not imagined that she might be pregnant with another child when she left. But there it was. Gart was born in Heb and Adris had never been told. He did have a son, but what could he do now when there was so much animosity between them?

CHAPTER 32: Life Goes On

Nawhi left Crim as soon as the gates were opened the next day. She took few possessions. She would not need them where she was going. She had a long walk ahead. She stopped briefly at the Sacred Stone where she left a scrolled note for her father and one for Taramae. Then she continued her journey. It was hours before anyone realized that she was missing.

After Wise Woman Kess, Storekeeper Brun, and Leader Adris had taken their usual places for Tribunal, Adris rose to address the crowd. "Dear people of Crim," he greeted, with his usual air of stern superiority. "We are grateful to see that so many of you have come to witness the helms of justice once more. It is an important day for Crim. Let us think back upon our great fortune for living here at this time."

Wise Woman Kess interrupted. "Let us keep to the purpose."

Though obviously irritated, Adris smiled. "Of course, Wise Woman," he agreed, and turned once more to the crowd. "This Tribunal was to hear of the Pairing decision made by the young woman, Taramae, who thankfully is not a ghost. She desired to live amongst us, and it was determined by judgment that it would be more appropriate if she had a Pairing so as not to risk Dark Menaces coming amongst us. She had respectable offers to choose from, one especially fine offer that would have included …"

A loud coughing sound came from the side of the pavilion where Gart stood, arms folded. Disapprovingly, he shook his head.

Adris finished quickly. "However, Taramae has decided to move forward with another choice. Feel free to wish them well. Now, let us deal with more relevant village concerns.

"The squat pot minder has once more complained that lids are not being secured on the pots prior to pick up. Please be more considerate of those working for the good of us all. No one wants squat pots sloshing in the square!

"As you can tell, Crim is getting crowded. There are more requests for occupancy than we have room to build dwellings. Therefore, in months to come we will be opening a new section nearby. The tax monies collected will go toward that. If you are interested in the venture, speak with Storekeeper Brun.

"Parents, a collection of high-spirited children are racing and chasing around the village. Apparently, they are referred to as The Wildlings and the young girl, Banaya, is their rowdy leader. Please discuss proper respect and village decorum with your offspring! I cannot watch them all the time and fear that if control is not obtained, someone may get hurt."

Gart waited to see whether Adris would speak of their newly discovered kinship. When he did not mention it, Gart felt no obligation to listen further. He stood with new confidence. He had not yet decided what to do about any claims he might make but relished the thought of how it might make the blustering Adris squirm. The man was more irritating than a thorn in one's sandal. His aggravating voice echoed across the square.

"The gatekeeper would like a few days respite from his duties to heal from splinters. If anyone would like to assist, please speak with him. Positions are still available with the Givens keeper. If you crave time away from the clamor of Crim, this may be the occupation for you."

The clamor of Crim? Gart shook his head as he walked away, enjoying the fact that Adris's droning grew fainter and fainter the farther away he got. However, as he passed by the gate, the gatekeeper urgently summoned him.

"There is a man outside who claims that he dare not enter and asks that you meet with him. He looks as though he might collapse if he gets down from his wagon."

Gart hesitated. In the past, he might have gone headlong into the situation, but now that he had a new future, there was more to risk. However, he had never known any previous deception by the gatekeeper so he stepped through the gate. The man waiting was Pel.

"I told you never to come back here!" Gart warned.

Pel raised both hands to show that the impressive new knife was missing. "I have a better message this time," he said, appearing unsteady.

"Are you ill?" Gart asked.

"No, very tired. I came to tell you that Taramae has no further fear of Heska."

"You mean, until Heska sends a small army or Tarce with more malicious antics."

"Heska will send no one."

"Until when? Until her mood changes?"

"That will *never* happen, you can rest assured."

"But Heska will—will …," Gart began to dispute further.

Pel shook his head, no. "She was on her way to destroy Crim when she and her men came to a pointed disagreement near the cliff at Plateau Falls. The men won the argument."

Still doubtful, Gart asked, "And Tarce? He did not defend her?"

"Tarce set the whole thing up. Any loyalty he had to her ended when she ordered him killed the night before." Pel then explained the details of Heska's vicious planned rampage.

Gart was horrified to hear how he and many others were to suffer in the attack. "Will Tarce renew the incursion?"

Pel laughed. "Tarce? He is likely buying grog for everyone in Heb as we speak. No one knows who will be in charge when the town sobers up. Just wanted to let you know."

Gart was still stunned but truly appreciated the exhausting sacrifice Pel had made in order to inform them. "Will you come and rest the night?" he offered.

"No. I have been away from home too long. I need to go meet my new son," he said, grinning. But before he drove away, Pel asked, "Might the petition to move my family to Crim be reconsidered? We will need a change of residence soon."

Gart smiled. "I have some influence that could get it granted. Congratulations on the boy! I owe you a drink. Give my best to Savah too. Safe travels, my friend. Dah ye!"

As Pel's wagon disappeared into the distance, Gart stood motionless, processing what he had been told. Heska of Heb was no more? He found it hard to believe. He tried to find some empathy for the terrible, plunging death she had experienced until he considered the terrible, plaguing life she had led and the suffering that she had caused so many others.

Anger and humiliation swelled within him as he recalled the first time he had gone to Heska to plead that her shaman be allowed to treat his dying mother. Heska had leered at him as she walked around him, seeming to appreciate his imposing fifteen-year-old frame. She agreed to help but said she might need a small favor afterwards. Though uncomfortable with her lustful looks, he had readily agreed. He was desperate. That was how she got her hooks into him.

The day after his mother died, he was summoned to Heska and given what was to become the first of many dreadful assignments—to beat up a sailor who had won against her while gambling—and bring the money back. Doing so made him sick inside and he had hoped it would satisfy the bargain. But Heska was *never* satisfied. There was always another assignment. When he became one of her Enforcers, people who had once been friends began to avoid him—everyone except Pel. Gart was ashamed for the way he had treated his long-time friend but he hated to see Pel be ensnared in a trap as he had been.

In order to do Heska's bidding and avoid her advances he had guarded all emotions until he felt hollow inside. Yet he yearned for a sense of belonging. She knew it and used it against him. Whenever he asked about other relatives he might have, Heska stalled with excuses or could never quite recollect. He knew that was a lie. For years, her family had compiled records on everyone for blackmail purposes.

Then one day, Gart had snapped. Heska wanted him to break the arm of a widow with young children, crippling her for choosing not to become a cook at Heska's beck and call. 'If she does not cook for me, she does not cook for anyone!' Heska declared. That was it! Gart warned the woman, who fled Heb immediately. He then pinned Heska against the wall and threatened her life if she did not divulge the family information he needed. Even then, she simply spat in his face and said, "Go to Crim."

Gart still felt conflicted about how the Crim part of his journey had resolved. But he did not miss Heb and the poison that had permeated it for the three generations Heska's family had ruled. At least now, no one else would be contracted to evil obligations in order to survive. All debts and cruel bargains owed to Heska had been swallowed up with her over the cliff at Plateau Falls—the one place louder than her and one thing she could never control.

Heska of Heb was dead! The Vast Vex that she had so frequently commanded to curse others had taken command over her in the end. Crim had been spared a bloody battle, Taramae was free to build her life, and Gart could begin to let go of the haunting guilt brought by Dark Menaces of his past.

Taramae waited all morning for word to come that she would be allowed to visit Smote. No word came. She rocked her son and did her best to keep busy. The villagers peacefully went on with their lives as the hours of her waiting dripped by—until there came a knock on the door.

It was Gart, saying, "I have something to tell you."

When Taramae heard that her nemesis was no longer a threat, she hugged Gart and cried with relief. After a while, Taramae said, "We should let Mother know. She grew up with Heska. She may be somewhat sad."

Gart shook his head, saying, "When she hears that she was high on the list for Heska's torturous revenge, she may find more reason to rejoice than to mourn."

Smote awoke very groggy late in the day. Had it all been a dream? If so, why was he not in the Tower? Oh, now he remembered. He was Jeric, the missing man, the dead—but not dead man. His thoughts assailed him. He suddenly felt uncomfortable in the clothes he wore. They had been Jeric's but they did not fit. Unfortunately, he could not go back to his familiar tunic and breeches. They had been burned. "Not washable!" Old Soul Nadee had declared.

Nadee hovered over him, peppering him with questions. "How are you feeling? Are you hungry? Do you need medicine?" She had so easily welcomed him into her home. Was she just being hospitable or did she expect that her caring would burst the ugly Smote cocoon and he would become her loving grandson once again—Jeric the beloved, the brave, the longed-for. No wonder she seemed to know me so well, he thought.

He felt for Owl in his pocket. It was still there. "Are you *my* friend, Owl? Or another sad leftover from Jeric?" he asked and looked it over. "You are mine now. That is what matters." In the moment, it was all he was certain of.

An odd wondering occurred. Were his thoughts even truly his own? He had been told that Jeric was quite intelligent. That part of Jeric he liked. Sometimes odd knowledge popped into his head—like the word *cocoon*. He had never thought of it before and yet knew what it meant, and several times as he scribed the Nadee story he knew how to spell words he could not remember using before. Why did words for things come back and not people or events in time? Might other memories come back in that way as well?

His stomach had a memory. It grumbled. "Oh, yes. There was cake last night. I wonder what happened to it? Did Jeric like cake, Owl? Mizzafrizzaritz, I do not care! I like cake! And I like …" Smote stopped before he said her name. Was that his own thought or was he being pushed? "You have seen her, Owl. Can we trust the feelings that Taramae seems to have? Or am I just a poor substitute for Jeric. Kess had said that Taramae would never love another. Did that include or exclude me?"

When he had held her to comfort her—even briefly—were those merely the feelings of desire by a lonely man or did his body as Jeric recognize hers? He had truly enjoyed that part so decided to ponder it a while longer before dismissing it. Pain suddenly pounced upon him. It was too much to bear. Another draught was given and again he floated away. His last thought was, I have a son!

On the second day, Smote overheard Nadee telling Wise Woman Kess, "He seems to talk to himself a lot. Perhaps you should give him less medicine?"

Kess made him get up to eat and walk around to see how steady he was. Mother Kess he had called her at times. But that day when he looked at her, instead of someone who had been so caring, so dependable, he saw someone who had lied about who he was and about the consequences of leaving the Tower. He barely spoke to her. He was not incapable. He was angry. Why didn't she tell him sooner? Was she keeping him dependent on purpose? No, he would not let himself believe that. It would destroy his entire Smote foundation. He had to have something to hang on to.

"Would you like to speak with Taramae?" she asked.

He shook his head, no. "Not ready yet."

Taramae—the beautiful, strong yet frail, uncertain yet determined. How could he face her when he was still unsure of her, of himself? What would he say to her? She had lied to him too. Not exactly, but she had certainly delayed telling the truth. When she looked into his eyes, was she merely trying to unlock the prison of his mind where Jeric was held?

Her friendship seemed sincere and their heart-to-heart moments felt genuine. In his eyes, she was a precious person. What was so important for Jeric to get from Crim that he would leave Taramae vulnerable? "I would never have left her alone, Owl," he whispered.

When the head pain hit again, Wise Woman Kess motioned to Nadee, "Yes, less medicine tonight."

As he faded slower, Smote lay searching for Jeric in his mind. There was no voice crying out for rescue. Good! That would have been markedly more disturbing than talking to an owl.

Smote decided not to dwell upon the man he had been. More importantly, there was a son for him to wrap his thoughts around, already a cherished child. It felt like a miracle that he had survived the harrowing birth. Miracle—another one of those words that just came to him. Did he believe in those—in the SkyFa being? Taramae said Jeric did. Smote tried not to be rude about it but he was skeptical. Still, there was this baby boy who seemed Heaven-sent. No wonder he had felt an instant connection when he first held the child. But what kind of father could he be when he was such an embarrassment?

CHAPTER 33: Regret

Nawhi looked over the edge of the long stone span into the treacherous Wild River below. For three days she had walked to get to this point, seldom resting. She stood, dirty, disheveled, shaking from exhaustion and hunger. One fifty-foot drop and the feelings of humiliating, tormenting remorse for the pain and chaos she had caused would be over. She thought she deserved to be crushed and tossed on the boulders below until the unrelenting surge suffocated her last breath. Six more inches and it would be over. Her knees were beginning to buckle. She closed her eyes.

"Do not jump, please!" a low, gentle voice entreated.

Startled, she looked up into the dark, pleading eyes of the compassionate man whose large hand firmly gripped her arm. Feet sliding forward, she barely had time to choose.

Zaela cried in frustration as she once again failed to get her long braid wrapped on the top of her head properly. Nawhi had effortlessly done it for her. Perhaps it was the years of practice she had had. Zaela regretted their last conversation. She had complained about Gart watching over Taramae. "Why does he follow after her?"

Nawhi said, "He is being helpful, being her friend when she needs one most."

Zaela had said, "But she is not pretty anymore."

Nawhi had defended, "Neither would you be if you had suffered tribulations as she has. But she is still as good and kind as she always has been."

"I am good! I am kind!" Zaela had declared.

Nawhi had almost laughed, then asked, "Why the comparison? Do you desire Gart's affections?"

Zaela had lied. "Of course not! It just does not look appropriate."

Nawhi could not hold laughter in. "This opinion from the girl who has been punished in the past for flirting with Paired men."

"It was a misunderstanding," Zaela had insisted, "I was just being friendly." She swatted Nawhi on the leg. "Ouch, quit pulling my hair!"

"Pardon me," Nawhi said, but added. "You are sixteen years-old. You should learn to braid it yourself."

Zaela had retorted, "Why? You are not going anywhere!"

Nawhi sighed. "And what if I do?"

Zaela had scoffed. "I will not fret about it. You are almost twenty. It is unlikely someone will whisk you away to everlasting bliss."

Nawhi had flinched, then dropped the brush in her lap, saying, "And this remark comes from someone good and kind?" she asked, and walked away.

Wait! It is not finished," Zaela had protested.

"I am finished!" Nawhi said, disgusted.

As usual, Zaela had called for their father to intervene, "Pah! Nawhi will not help with my hair!"

As he left for the storehouse, Brun had said, "Nawhi, *please!* I have enough to deal with today."

Dutiful Nawhi had finished the hair work, then remarked, "As I said, not good, not kind. Quit wondering about Gart. You do not have a chance!"

Zaela had thrown the brush at her. How she regretted doing so now! Nawhi was gone. She had not even said goodbye. "You should have gone after her!" Zaela scolded herself, aloud. But at the time, she was too angry and ashamed. Now there was nothing but remorse. Her obliging sister—who had become like a mother to her when theirs died, who held her during fearful night storms, who helped with reading struggles, and often tolerated her laziness and vanity—had simply vanished. Now there was no way to thank her.

Zaela pinned her hair the best she could and dejectedly went to help in the storehouse.

Chapter 34: Waiting

For four days Kess barely spoke to Taramae. She was upset about the untimely unveiling of Smote's identity and the confusion it had caused him. "Speaking with him must be done according to *his* time and willingness," was all Kess would say after her visit to him each day.

Taramae knew it must be so. Nevertheless, the delay did not diminish her concerns. What did Smote think of her? Her mind raced with possible answers almost to the point of Dark Menaces ascending, but she pushed those aside. She had to stay strong and ready to sincerely speak with him. She had promised that he would *never* be required to take on any responsibility against his will. She wanted him to know there was a choice. Jeric had a family obligation. Smote might not accept it. Who could blame him? He already had many challenges.

Her feelings for Smote had grown but if he did not feel the same way, what then? Speculation pummeled her tired mind. She fought it by staying busy. She prepared the meals and the food baskets for the Wise Woman rounds each day and had Last Meal waiting for Kess when she arrived home.

One afternoon, after VenAven had been gathered up for snuggling time with Grandmother Rauma, Taramae walked to the Sacred Stone to calmly meditate. Sunbeams burst through a cloud, bathing her head with warmth and cascading down her back in much the same way as they had on her Pairing day. Those memories were precious to her. How handsome Jeric had looked! How excited they were that the longed-for day had finally arrived! Taramae's heart beat faster remembering the moment that he had placed his Pairing Token necklace around her neck. A tear trickled down her cheek. She allowed a few more memories of their tender togetherness and then shook her head. It was time to go.

Leaning down to place a flower, she saw the scroll that Nawhi had pressed into the stones for her to find. She shoved it into her pocket. She could not bear to read it. Nawhi's betrayal was like a knife to her heart. Bad memories threatened to crowd out the tender ones. She fought her thoughts to not let that happen. She looked up, pleading aloud, "SkyFa, please help us!"

Turning to leave, she saw a smooth rock about the length of her hand and cleaned it off the best she could. Regardless of Smote's decision, she had one more task to do. She kicked around in the dirt looking for a smaller, sharp stone to engrave it with.

When she arrived at the Last Rest, she scratched the name *Jeric* in large letters as deeply as she could onto the flat rock and placed the *Jeric* stone next to the stone marked *Taramae*. She was tempted to remove her name rock because it was placed there erroneously, but as she reached for it she realized that *that* Taramae *was* a ghost. She was not the same person. The life she had known was over. She left the two stones side by side and solemnly started for home.

At the gate, Gart was waiting to walk the rest of the way with her. "This looks slightly familiar," she chuckled. "Are we trying to make Zaela jealous again?"

He grinned, "No, that effort has been discontinued. We have not spoken for a while. Have you been able to speak with Smote yet?"

"Not yet. Soon, I hope"

"May I ask, so Jeric—I mean, Smote, is my cousin, right?"

"So it would appear. Do you mind?"

"No, I have always desired more family."

"Some relatives might avoid him."

"No. He has more good qualities than I first thought. I hope that he can forgive my gruffness. I would like to get better acquainted."

"He would enjoy that too, I am sure. Dare I ask, how are things with Adris?"

Gart shook his head. "Truly an odd man! He stopped to speak with me outside the Groggery the other day. When I asked him why he has not acknowledged me at Tribunal yet, he said, "I am not popular with the people. You are. I do not want to jeopardize that for you by my association until I think they will better accept it.""

Taramae chuckled, "Word travels fast in this village. Everyone already knows."

"True. And then strangely, he asked if I wanted to throw a ball back and forth out by the gardens sometime."

"That *is* strange! Does he know how old you are? What did you say?"

"I told him, no. But if he had offered to buy me a drink, I would have considered it. Speaking of drinks, did you hear what Rauma did?"

Taramae looked worried. "What now?"

"She stood on a table and announced that you had *never* agreed to give your child to Heska. That it was merely a ploy to save the village."

"Do you think they believed her?"

"Yes, after she bought a few rounds."

Taramae shook her head and groaned.

Once Gart and Taramae reached the well, Zaela approached. Her clothing was wrinkled and her braid was wound off-centered on the top of her head. She handed Taramae a baby gift of a blanket and knitted footlets. "I hope you can use these. I do not know how to make such things but they were the nicest ones in the storehouse," she said, then continued, her cheeks blushing dark red. "I would like to apologize for my unkind behavior since your return. It was meanly done and I am ashamed. I hope that you can forgive me. If I can help in some way, you need only let me know. I am not good at many things but I could rock your baby while you rest."

Taramae could have been as harsh as she had been treated but she had compassion on the struggling, penitent girl. "Dah ye, Zaela. Your words are greatly appreciated," she said, then after a moment of thought, she added, "I could use more practice braiding as I do with Banaya. Would you like to help me with that?"

"Oh yes! I would be glad to assist in that way. I am available almost immediately," Zaela answered, smiling. She handed Gart a small honey cake and ran to the storehouse.

"That was a very kind offer, Taramae," Gart said, "Clearly *she* will benefit the most from helping you."

"I used to blame her for Nawhi not visiting me. But I know the real reason now." There was sadness behind Taramae's smile. She was still struggling with Nawhi's betrayal, but as for Zaela, a burden of bad feelings was beginning to lift. It was a personal moment so she did not explain it to Gart, instead she redirected the conversation. "Is her cake as good as mine?"

Gart took a big bite, then winced and looked around to see if anyone would notice if he spat it out. Instead, he swallowed, then cleared his throat. "She forgot the honey and some other ingredient, but at least she is trying. Perhaps you could discuss recipes while braiding."

Taramae giggled.

"She also seems to be helping her father more than before," he noted.

"Does that change your opinion of her?"

Gart chuckled. "It helps. I just hope that the change is genuine."

Taramae shrugged. "You might ask her father. He knows her best."

"He does not like me," Gart grumbled.

"Brun likes everyone, especially those who keep Zaela happy and occupied."

"That is good to know," he said, and started to walk away.

"Where are you going? Forget something at the storehouse?" Taramae teased.

"I am going to thank her for the cake," he answered, with a short bow. "It is the polite thing to do."

"Of course," Taramae replied, innocently, then she mumbled, "So, my friend, the beautiful whirlwind begins pulling you in once more."

After Last Meal of the fourth day as Kess settled into her favorite chair by the fireplace, she said, "Dah ye for being so helpful. I am sorry that my frustration delayed forgiveness. I know you meant well and felt pressured."

"In the moment, I did not know what else to do. Adris had to be stopped. Still, I am sorry to have caused such pain," Taramae apologized once again. "Will Smote *ever* forgive me?" She bit her lip to hold back tears. "The waiting is so hard!"

"I know about *waiting*," Kess recalled, longingly. "But save your tears for …

"… for the joy that is to come," Taramae finished the sentence.

Kess was startled. "Where did you hear this?"

"From my second rescuer. He was an unusual man, yet truly kind."

Kess brought a thin book from far end of the shelf and took out a loose drawing. Handing it to Taramae, she asked, "Did he look like this? "

"Oh my, yes!" Taramae exclaimed. "Who is he?"

Kess looked at the drawing then held it to her chest. "He is my husband," she sighed.

"What say?! Husband? Why is he not here with you? I need more of this story!" Taramae insisted and sat on a nearby stool.

Kess pondered how much to tell. But as Taramae was so dear to her, perhaps it was time.

"His name is Eled," she said, then appeared as though she wandered down her own trail of memories. "Eled came to the village when I was nearly your age. We were about to give up on Crim and return to Heb, defeated. You know the tale. One morning Eled came to the village leading a herd of animals and Crim survived."

Taramae turned to a page in the book showing the first rectangle sketch of the village.

Kess nodded. "Eled helped Larus organize the village. Yes, this is it. He drew it all. Everyone collaborated with him, and it came together faster than we imagined possible.

"Eled was a great fascination to me. Working alongside him and learning as much as possible was exhilarating. He had never sought my affection but seemed to care deeply for me. When I told him of my love, he said, 'You do not want to Pair with me. I cannot stay nor give you a family. I must leave to help others. Pairing would be bittersweet.'

"But a young heart is not often wise, nor do their ears listen to the wisdom of others."

Taramae blushed.

"I would not hear reason and pestered him for a year before he relented. Our time together was amazing, but when the war was over and Crim fully established, it was time for Eled to leave. I wept and begged him to stay, but he had warned me of this time. He held my hand saying, 'Save your tears for the joy that is to come. You will yet have a family.' He left the next morning before I awakened."

Taramae was astonished, "He disappeared quickly after he helped me also. Is he a Holy man? A wanderer? A mystic?"

"He is who he is."

"Did he bring the lightning upon Hebarcet?"

Kess raised her hands as though questioning, but there was a wry smile. She continued the tale. "After he left, there was little sympathy for me from others, mostly curiosity and gossip. I despaired for a while and then focused my frustrated energy into learning how to become a Wise Woman from Nadee. You might say I have mothered many children over time. Perhaps that is what he meant. I could have married someone else. I have had offers. But for some, one Pairing in a lifetime is all they desire."

Taramae certainly understood that feeling.

"Dear Taramae, you have struggled with waiting for days. I have waited for years, yearning for a surprise knock on my door, yet knowing it will never come."

"He will never return?"

Kess shook her head, no. "Eled brings the Great Good in visits to others as he did to you. It is enough to know that he is well." For a moment, it was her turn to weep.

"Calm ye. Calm ye," Taramae said, hugging her friend. "Kess, you were so brave to love such a man. Your poor heart! You have done much to help others. Many appreciate you—especially me. Dah ye!"

Kess wiped away tears. "It is enough," Kess said, and dreamily smiled as she put the pictures away.

Days and questions flowed and swirled in the Wild River of Smote's mind. On the fourth night, Smote refused the pain draught. He must think clearly even if it hurt! He ate a little. He paced a lot. When Kess had gently applied the ointment earlier, it reminded him of how Taramae used to apply it, almost caressing. Thoughts of her continually crept into his mind.

He kept going back to, does she love me for me? Didn't she say they could run away and start their own village if not accepted in Crim? Didn't she ask more than once in that night of hard decisions at the Naming Ceremony, *do you trust me?* In that moment, he had trusted her implicitly. Could he trust her again?

She had other Pairing Offers. What was she waiting for? If he was not Jeric, was she even still legally bound? She could certainly do better than to be Paired with him and she deserved better. "But what if I let her go, Owl, and then one day I remember—everything?"

On the fifth morning, Taramae enjoyed the aroma of baking honey cakes as she lazily lay enfolded in the warmth of the bed covers nursing her baby. During her cozy reverie there came a knock on the door. Wise Woman Kess answered it. There was whispering, and a few minutes later, Kess asked if she could take the child. Taramae assumed that her mother had come to visit. She handed the baby over, then snuggled down to rest a little longer. She had just gotten comfortable when she heard, "Burrppp!"

"Impressive belch, my boy!" a man laughed.

Taramae hurried to dress.

Smote sat near the fireplace holding VenAven upright, patting his back. Another burp rocked the baby's entire body.

Smote laughed again. "How does he keep his head attached?"

"It is a wonder," Taramae giggled, and knelt beside them.

Without looking at her, Smote asked, "Did I ever go to sea on a ship?"

She took a deep breath. "No, but you talked about it many times. You have always longed for adventure."

"Coming to Crim has certainly been an adventure, and not always a favorable one!"

"True. I am sorry for the pain and anguish you have received here."

"It was not your fault."

"Some of it has been, and I am so sorry."

There was awkward silence until Smote commented, "There have been a few pleasant moments. The Naming Ceremony itself was mostly enjoyable."

"What part did you enjoy most?"

Smote chuckled. "That it was brief. I was hoping to have some of that cake."

"I will make you another one," Taramae giggled. "Did you think the name was fitting?"

"Rather unique, but good enough."

Taramae stroked the baby's hair. "He is a unique child. I can sense it."

"VenAven is lengthy. It will do in times of mischief like 'VenAven, stop throwing mud on your sister!' or for special occasions such as 'Father, I would like you to meet VenAven.'"

Taramae laughed, "Oh my, so young and he already has a sister and a possible Pairing? I was hoping he could stay a babe for a while longer. If not VenAven, what will he be called?"

Smote smiled. "I could see him as *Vave*, the wonder child or *Vave*, the warrior. Unless his mother has objections."

"She does not."

"Did I know those whose names were honored?"

"You only knew my little brother, Aven. He greatly admired you. He was such a sweet boy. You and Adris's son Drayis tried to save him."

"It appears that I have failed more than once with that river."

"No! It proves that no matter how hard the Wild River tries, it cannot defeat you."

"Nevertheless, I will not risk the ire of the Vast Vex by challenging the river further."

"That is best."

Wise Woman Kess stepped forward to take the child. Wrapping him snugly she said, "I have promised Nadee a visit. We will return shortly."

Taramae stood and retrieved honey cakes for Smote and herself. She cleared her throat before saying, "I have been awaiting your visit so I could apologize. At the ceremony, the manner of my revelation caused you great distress, even pain. But I saw no other way to end the threat of Tribunal and insistent Pairing from Adris. Again, I *am* sorry."

After another bite, Smote said, "The pain *was* miserable, but I understand why the method was necessary. That man needed to be stopped. But you could have told me about being Jeric that day in the Tower when I asked who I was."

"You were recovering from *another* dreadful day and I feared to distress you further. Now you see, when you were told, it *did* distress you further. I feel terrible about that, but I needed your help to halt the harassment by Adris."

"Has he ceased his prowl?"

"Yes."

"Then at least there was some gain for it."

"You also gained a grandmother," Taramae said, cheerfully.

Smote smiled, "She has been wonderful. She is a feisty one, puts up with no nonsense and has washed my hair repeatedly."

Taramae laughed. "It does look very clean."

After another bite of cake, Smote changed the subject. "Will you ever forgive Nawhi?"

Taramae fought back tears. "Will *you*?"

"It will be easier for me. I have no memory of what was lost."

Taramae's shoulders drooped. "I do not know how to feel. It was such a betrayal by my dearest friend! Jeric also considered her a friend. Did he speak to her only as a friend, or of more to hide our plans? I do not know. Nevertheless, her actions caused *such* suffering …" Tears trickled from Taramae's eyes. "We lost everything!"

"Now *she* has lost everything. They say she has disappeared," he said, sympathetically.

Taramae nodded, sadly. "I do not wish bad things on her. How do you suddenly hate someone that you have loved? She wrote a letter to me, but I cannot read it yet."

"Perhaps in time we can read it together."

"Yes, In time." Taramae sniffled and felt in her pocket for something to wipe her nose. Jeric's bent clan token was still there. She held it out for Smote to view. When he did not look upon it with any sense of recognition, she said, "It was a gift."

"I was not told that gifts were customary upon such a visit," Smote said, embarrassed. "I do not have—" he stopped short. From a tunic pocket he withdrew something especially important to him. "Would this be acceptable? I would like you to meet, Owl. He does not speak, but he is a good listener." With a tug to his heart, Smote handed the little wood carving to her.

Taramae lovingly touched the owl that she had so long ago given to Jeric, saying, "Yes. It is *more* than acceptable!" The urge to embrace Smote was nearly unbearable. Instead, she said, "I will save it for VenAven—I mean, Vave. Dah ye!"

Smote chuckled. "A unique gift for a unique child?"

She laughed, "As I said! But perhaps you might keep it safe until he is a little older?"

Smote readily agreed, but when he stood to place Owl back in his pocket, he lost his balance and swayed.

Taramae grabbed his arm. "Do you need to go rest again?"

"Yes, but before I do, a few more questions."

"Of course."

He looked into her eyes with deep seriousness. "I have tried to remember who I was as Jeric. No memories are found in my muddled mind. What if they never return? Truly *never*? How can you accept that? How can you take into your life such a broken man?"

Taramae took his hands in hers. "We are both broken. I am not the girl I once was. I hoped we might mend together."

The feeling of their hands pressing together felt strangely familiar, and amazingly powerful, yet he said, "I do not remember our Pairing Ceremony."

"We can have another one, if you would like. And have more cake."

Smote smiled, then seemed troubled. "I do not know if I believe in SkyFa."

"It is not a problem. He is a patient sort," she said, winking. "There are many things we will discover anew, if you desire."

Smote wanted to say, desire is not my problem. But instead added, "Taramae, you have much to offer—much to live for. If you are free, you could choose *any* man, rather than an ugly, poor one who may be a burden more than a help with raising your son. Someone your child will grow to be ashamed of."

Taramae frowned. "Are you sending us away?"

Smote shook his head. "It is not my desire, but perhaps it would be best."

"No! It would be best for *our* son to see his father's daily courage, to feel your constant love. The love I can see from you every time you hold him. None of the other concerns will matter if you are with us."

"But how will we live?"

"My mother has agreed that I can establish a small hair care enterprise at the inn. It could work." Taramae thought of Jeric's dream to become the schoolmaster but knew that it may not be what Smote wants. "Someday, you will discover something you enjoy doing," she said.

Smote choked with emotion. "I want to believe that it will work but …" He turned his head away to hide tears.

She squeezed his hands. "Believe!"

He cleared his throat. "It will take time getting used to being called by a different name."

Taramae reached up to move a lock of hair that had fallen across his forehead. "No. The days of Jeric are gone. Henceforth, you will be my Smote," she declared.

He gazed upon her beautiful, hopeful face, and asked, "*Am* I your Smote?"

In a flirtatious tone, Taramae asked, "Do you desire to be?"

Smote pulled her close for a long-yearned-for embrace.

As she heard his beating heart, Taramae wept with relief.

Alarmed, Smote pulled back. "Have I done something wrong?"

"No, nothing is wrong. These are *the tears for the joy that is to come,* that he spoke of."

"That *who* spoke of?"

"An explanation for another time," she said, and gently pulled on his tunic until his head was lowered enough that they could kiss—and kiss—and kiss.

As she walked Smote back to Nadee's dwelling, Taramae felt the overwhelming peace of the Great Good returning to her heart. Their life in Crim would not be perfect, but enough of the tangles were becoming untangled. There was hope.

On her way home, she looked up at the sky and whispered, "Dah ye!